MY SINFUL DESIRE

BOOK TWO IN THE SINFUL MEN SERIES

LAUREN BLAKELY

ABOUT

A passionate, emotional, sexy-as-sin romance novel from #1 New York Times Bestselling author Lauren Blakely...

I live my life by a few simple rules — let no one in, trust only my family, and don't ever spend more than three nights with a woman.

Those are easy enough to abide by when I meet gorgeous, captivating and absolutely brilliant Sophie Winston. Who wants nothing more than to explore all her sinful desires with me after dark. Desires that put me firmly in control in the bedroom.

That works for me — as long as I can keep the secrets I need to protect. Not only the ones about my family, but the ones about how she's interwoven into my dangerous past.

But the night she learns the truth, I'm faced with a stark new choice — let her go or give up control of my heart for the first time ever.

Trouble is, the past is chasing both of us right now and it just caught up.

MY SINFUL DESIRE

By Lauren Blakely

To be the first to find out when all of my upcoming books go live click here!

PRO TIP: Add lauren@laurenblakely.com to your contacts before signing up to make sure the emails go to your inbox!

Did you know this book is also available in audio and paperback on all major retailers? Go to my website for links!

This is an emotional, suspenseful series, with high-stakes action and consequences. For content warnings go to my web site.

1

───────

RYAN

The light was playing tricks on me.

The golden haze of the late-afternoon sun, and its halo glow around her, was some kind of illusion. No way, no how was it possible for anyone to be so gorgeous that she actually shimmered.

Mirage was the more plausible explanation for the platinum blonde stepping out of the Aston Martin at three o'clock in the afternoon on a Thursday in July, looking as if she belonged in a gangster movie. She was the woman they all fought over. The woman who brought the men to their knees.

From the pinup dress, to the pouty lips, to the gleaming car that stretched a city block—or so it seemed—she was . .

.

Glamorous. Sultry. Voluptuous.

My fantasy woman.

No question about it.

I stared shamelessly over the top of my aviator shades as I walked along the palm-tree-lined sidewalk that framed police headquarters, cycling through the right icebreaker for a woman like that. A woman who wore a black dress with a cherry pattern and bright white sunglasses—busty and bold enough to roll up to the Las Vegas Municipal Court building at midday looking like sin come to life.

With one hand on the car door, she glanced to the left, away from me, and pushed her sunglasses on top of her head. In her other hand, she held a phone, a notepad, and a pen. She bumped her rear against the car door, shutting it with her ass.

What a lucky car door.

I half wished she'd drop the pen, so I could swoop in and pick it up. Bend down, grab it before it rattled to the street, and gallantly present it.

Then I'd get her number with that pen. She'd be the type to push up the cuff of my shirtsleeve and write it on my arm.

Checking my watch, I saw I had two minutes to spare before I met with the detective. I could do this. I could meet her in 120 seconds.

The sun pelted its hot desert rays at me, radiating off the sidewalks, as I ran a hand along my green tie and cleared my throat. I looked up from my phone, and instantly we locked eyes. Hers were blue like the sea. As she caught my gaze, she arched an eyebrow.

This was it. No time for lines. Just talk to the woman. "Seems I've been caught staring," I said as I reached her.

"I'm afraid I'm guilty on that count too," she fired back, her voice laced with a torch-singer sultriness, her words telling me to keep going.

She twirled the pen in her hand absently.

I tipped my forehead toward it, figuring this was indeed the best entrée. "Incidentally, I'm astonishingly good at picking up pens that beautiful women drop outside our fine city's government buildings."

Her lips twitched. *Red.* Cherry red and full. I wanted to know what they tasted like.

She brought the pen to her lips, danced it between them, raised her eyebrows in an invitation, and then let it fall. It clattered to the sidewalk. "Is that so?"

The pen was like a promise. Of something more. Of flirting, and then flirting back. Of phone numbers to follow. And then some.

"That is so," I said in a firm voice, bending down to pick up the writing implement, just as Sinatra's "Fly Me to the Moon" crooned from her phone. I rose, and she was tapping her screen, sliding her thumb across it.

"Must answer this. But thank you so much for rescuing my pen. By the way, I like your tie." She reached out to trail a finger down the silky fabric, her hand terribly close to my chest. Then she held up that finger, asking me to wait.

"So good to hear from you," she said into the phone, keeping her eyes on me the whole time. "I can't wait to see you tonight at the gala at Aria," she said, arching an eyebrow at me as she emphasized that last word. "It's going to be a fabulous event, and we'll raise so much money. My only hope is there will be some gorgeous man there in a green tie who can afford a last-minute ticket."

I shot her a grin—a lopsided smile that said yes, the man in the green tie could absolutely afford a ticket.

I nodded my RSVP to the gala. She waved goodbye and walked down the street.

Suddenly, I had plans that night.

* * *

Was everyone I encountered today hired from central casting? If there was a dress code for police detectives, rule number one must be "Thou shalt not tightly knot a tie."

John Winston had taken that to heart and was sporting the slightly-loosened look, as if he'd been tugging on his navy tie all day, frustration increasing as he questioned belligerent suspects. The other hallmarks of the job were straight out of Hollywood too, from the striped button-down with the cuffs rolled up to the paper cup of deli coffee on the desk in his office. Even the stubble seemed to have been custom ordered to fit the part of a homicide detective.

Funny how people could look like their jobs. Briefly, I wondered if the blonde was a movie star. I wouldn't be surprised.

"Thanks for coming in," Winston said, shutting the door behind him. Glass windows looked out over the rest of the department and a sea of half-empty desks. I wasn't sure if that meant business was good or bad in homicide. "Have a seat." The man gestured to a frayed brown office chair. "Ordinarily, I'd chat with you in a witness room, but they're all full right now."

So it was a busy day here.

"This works fine for me. What can I do for you?" I asked as I sat down, eager to glean any details I could about the reopened investigation into my father's murder eighteen years ago.

Winston had called earlier in the week and asked me to come in to help shed any light on the case that I could, as the victim's son and all. I was flying solo here today. There was no need to bring a lawyer along just for routine questioning—that would make it look as if I had something to hide. I *did* have something to hide, but not the sort of thing that would help solve the mystery of my father's death, and the vault in my brain was going to stay locked tight. That had been sealed for eighteen years, and no crowbar would get it open, so I wasn't worried.

I was, however, damn curious. I wanted to know what Winston knew about my family. About my mother in prison. About my father, six feet under. I quickly scanned the detective's desk for any clue as to who John Winston was—a family photo, pictures of the detective with his kid, maybe even some sports memorabilia. But there were no telltale signs, save for an autographed baseball in a plastic case amid a neat desk covered only with newspapers and a stack of manila folders.

The detective grabbed the chair opposite me. "I appreciate you coming in," Winston said, as he held up a digital recorder. "I'm going to record this. Standard procedure whenever we talk to someone." I nodded as Winston set the recorder on his desk. "I'm hoping you might be able to answer a few questions that could help us with the investigation. We're going to be talking to a lot of people, and I want you to feel free to speak about what you know of your parents. And I'd like to keep what's said just between us."

"I'll see what I can do," I said, shooting him a smile. *See? Nothing to hide.* "You've got us all curious. Not gonna lie— we were pretty damn surprised when you showed up at my grandma's house and told us the case was being reopened. Last thing I expected to hear. What have you got?"

My mother was doing hard time for the shooting. She'd gone to trial quickly for murder for hire, along with the gunman, and both were behind bars for life. After eighteen years, why had a closed case gotten hot again?

Winston revealed little when he said, "Some new evidence has come to light, and we're trying to determine the validity of it."

"New evidence about my mother's guilt, or innocence?"

Dora Prince had steadfastly maintained her innocence. Of course, there was hardly an inmate in any prison anywhere who didn't. Still, she was *my* mother, and I wanted to know if there was truth to her claim. I'd love to believe her. Hell, I'd be beside myself to learn my mother wasn't a killer. I'd held on to the possibility for as long as she'd been locked away, grasping it tenaciously, never letting it go, waiting for a moment like this. For the chance that she might not have done it. That I wasn't raised by a murderer. I dug my fingers into my palms in anticipation.

But the expression on Winston's face was stony, his eyes hard. "New evidence about the crime," he said, giving nothing away. "I know you were fourteen at the time, but do you remember at all any of the people your mother was associating with then?"

A muscle in my jaw twitched. The answer was yes, and the answer was no. I knew more than I should, but not enough to make sense of what my mother had given me, and I sure as hell didn't want to say the wrong thing. I bought myself some time. "Can you be a little more specific?"

"We want to know who she spent time with. Beyond Stefano," he said, dropping the name of the shooter, a former hitman with The Royal Sinners, a Vegas gang.

"I'd just finished eighth grade." Keenly aware of my own body language, I tried to strike a mix of casual and interested. Even though I was innocent, even though I didn't have firsthand knowledge of the murder, I had intel about my mother I didn't intend to share, and that made me hypervigilant. I could hear the words she'd said to me, crystal clear. *Never say a word. No matter what, no matter who asks, don't say anything. Promise me.* I'd taken that directive from her to heart when I was younger, and as the years went on too. Besides, what I knew would have no bearing on my mother or her freedom. But rather than focus on the classified documents in my head, I narrowed in on the truth as I answered, "I didn't have a great sense of the conversations she was having with that guy or any others—beyond the customers who came to our house to pick up clothes and costumes."

Winston nodded and rubbed a hand over his chin, slowing as he seemed to consider. "We just want to get a better understanding of everything that happened. Something that might seem innocuous to you could actually wind up being a key piece of information for us. Were there new people in her life? Did she have any new friends?"

My senses tingled as my analytical mind played connect-the-dots. "Does this mean you think there were others involved?"

Winston leaned forward, resting his elbows on his thighs, the classic pose for trying to get somebody to open up. "Listen, I'm really just trying to get a better picture of what her life looked like at the time of your father's murder. Trying to understand who she was involved with. It could be relevant to the investigation." Winston made an encouraging gesture with his hands. "The customers you said would come over to pick up clothes—was there anyone new in the months or weeks prior?"

I scrunched up my forehead, rewinding time. "Around that time, she was sewing leotards for a local gymnastics team. She tailored dresses for some of the girls in the neighborhood going to prom. She joked once that she had so much leftover fabric that she was going to start making dog jackets," I said, and Winston's lips quirked up in the barest grin.

"Big fan of dogs myself," Winston said.

We had that in common. "Man's best friend for a damn good reason."

The dog talk ceased when he asked, "Any idea who her clients were? Beyond the gymnastics folks? Her friends?"

"Sorry. I honestly didn't keep track of who her friends were," I said, speaking the truth, the whole truth, and nothing but the truth.

"Listen, if anything comes to you, I'd greatly appreciate it if you could share it with me," Winston said, turning off the recorder then pushing back from his seat and standing up.

I tilted my head, pressing, wanting to know what he was on the hunt for. "What is it you're looking for, detective? It would help me if I knew what sort of info you think would be useful."

"Honestly, *anything*," he said, emphasizing the last word with a touch of desperation. "Even if it seems like nothing —even if it seems like the smallest piece of evidence," he said as he opened the door and escorted me through the main office, where weary cops and detectives finished phone calls, shuffled papers, and glanced at the clock.

I couldn't blame them. I was eager to end this workday and get on the phone to sort out my new evening plans at Aria. I said goodbye to the detective and returned to the blanket of heat outside, scanning for the Aston Martin. The car was still there, but the blonde was gone.

Damn. I wouldn't have minded another chance to drink her in. She would be a balm after that conversation with the detective, which had stirred up too many memories and far too many buried emotions. The past was such a thorny son of a bitch. Diving back into my younger years was not a favorite hobby of mine. Those days were messy and dangerous, and I wished I could leave them behind.

I'd never been able to though. They had dug claws into me. Grown knotty roots inside my head and my heart.

All the more reason to focus on the things that would take my mind off my obsession with the past.

Like tonight, and the chance to see that woman again. As I walked down the steps, I wondered briefly what kind of business she had at the municipal offices. One thing I was fairly certain about—she probably wasn't talking to homicide detectives about an eighteen-year-old case.

A case I'd love to know more about. What I wouldn't give to know what was inside John Winston's head.

2

———

SOPHIE

After I finished chatting with two of my favorite people—
my friend Jenna, then my ex-husband Holden—I headed
inside the building, knocking twice on the glass window of
my brother's office. John looked up and flashed a brief
smile. I wasn't surprised to find him bent over his desk,
one hand pushed through his dark-blond hair, the other
flipping through some papers. Probably some case he was
hell-bent on solving, since that pretty much described his
single-minded mission in life. Always a hard worker, he'd
be burning the midnight oil tonight, either here at the
station or at home.

"Hey you," John said, after he opened the door and
dropped a quick kiss on my cheek.

"Hey you to you," I said, my voice bright and bubbly to
my own ears because I was still in a fantastic mood thanks
to Mr. Green Tie. I was hoping that handsome man—wait,
make that *devilishly* handsome, because he'd had a wicked
glint in those dark-blue eyes—would pick up the trail of
breadcrumbs I'd left behind. The way he'd looked at me on
the street . . . I'd never felt so deliciously naked while

wearing clothes. A man like that, bold enough to walk right up and talk to a woman . . . he was exactly the kind of man who would show up tonight at Aria.

Anticipation knitted a path up my spine. I barely knew the guy, had uttered all of ten words to him, but I had a feeling about him. A good feeling. A sexy feeling.

And it wasn't as if I'd invited him to a deserted house at the end of an isolated road. I'd invited him to an event that cost a pretty penny for a ticket, where security would be top-notch.

I crossed my fingers that he'd show.

"You're in a good mood," John said, then grabbed my arm protectively. He tipped his head toward the chatter and hum of the men at the desks behind me. "And get in here. Everyone is staring at you. Don't you own a jacket?"

I laughed with my red-lipsticked mouth wide open, and shook my head. "It's July. It's close to a hundred degrees outside. Why on earth would I wear a jacket?"

"Why on earth do you insist on wearing a dress everywhere you go? It doesn't even have sleeves," he countered as he tugged me into his office and shut the door.

"Thank heavens for the lack of sleeves." I raised my chin up high. "And you never know who you might meet. I certainly don't want to be wearing a sweatsuit when I meet the future love of my life."

"Perish the thought," he muttered.

My eyes widened. "I might bump into Mr. Right anywhere."

He scoffed and waved broadly at the offices and desks behind me. "You better hope you're not meeting the love of your life here."

But really, you never knew. My mother had met my father at a fruit stand in a farmers' market on the outskirts of town when she was buying a pineapple from him.

They'd locked eyes across the citrus, and the rest was history—thirty-five years of insanely happy marriage and two kids. I could recall many nights when I'd snuck out of bed as a kid and found them slow dancing in the living room to Ella Fitzgerald, looking so in love.

A love launched by a pineapple.

"In any case, Captain John Buzzkill Winston," I said, fishing around in my cherry-red purse to find what I'd come here for, "here is the transponder to get into my building." I pressed the flat white object into his palm. "Just wave it at the gate, and you can get into the garage. I have two spots. Use one twenty-one or one twenty-two."

"Thank you," he said, tapping the device. "Fucking termites. I really appreciate you letting me stay with you. I'd stay with one of the guys, but . . ."

I cut him off. "You'll do no such thing. Men who live alone live like pigs. Think of it as a vacation at the Ritz. Or really, the Veer," I said, since I lived in a penthouse condo at that luxurious building on the Strip, and it was as close to the Ritz as one could get. "I'll be leaving at six thirty sharp for the benefit. You sure you can't come?"

"No time for a benefit."

I pouted. "But you look so cute when you clean up," I said, then squeezed his cheek.

He hissed.

"Oh, you don't scare me with your hisses. You might scare all those poor little suspects you question, but I know you're just a hush puppy underneath."

He rolled his eyes. "You're killing me."

"I know. It's so much fun to embarrass you."

He held up a finger warning me not to.

Oh, but it was too fun to needle him like this. "Don't try on my shoes tonight while I'm out. Just promise me that," I said as I opened the door, then pressed my fingers to my mouth in an *oops* gesture. He huffed, and I walked out, winking at the mustached man at the desk a few feet away. "Hi, Gavin. Don't you work too hard."

"I promise I won't, Sophie," he said, then followed me with his puppy-dog eyes. "That is, if you'll finally go out with me."

I clasped my hand on my heart. "Oh, Gavin. You know I want to. But John just won't let his little sister date one of the guys he works with."

Gavin frowned, as he always did when I playfully said no, since he always asked.

I said hello to another guy I knew. "Hey there, Jason. You look handsome today. Say hello to Evie and the boys for me."

Jason gave a quick salute. "I will. She said to tell you she loved your peach pie recipe."

"I am so pleased to hear that. My sweet mother left that one for me. It's divine," I said, then blew a big communal kiss off my palm to the whole lot of them. As I pictured the red lips floating through the air, I caught one last look at my brother. He scowled from behind the glass in his office.

I winked, then walked out.

I, Sophie Winston, was a certified flirt. I hadn't always been one. Growing up, I was 100 percent geek. But those days were gone, and now I could be *this* woman. Flirting was like champagne to me—it gave me a rush, and I loved it. Besides, it let me bide my time. Until it could be more than flirting. Until it could become the real thing.

Maybe someday I'd meet someone I'd want to do more than flirt with, who'd want me in the same way. I wasn't entirely sure what that would feel like, but I craved that kind of connection.

I'd had a mere two lovers in my life, but I knew what I wanted.

I knew what turned me on.

As I returned to my car and started the engine, an image of the man in the green tie slipped into my mind. Of the way I'd felt when he'd stared at me—as if I were being hunted. How I loved that kind of hungry gaze. How I longed to be the prey.

A man who stared at me that way was enough to make me get down on my knees, and that was exactly where I wanted to be.

3

___

RYAN

As Johnny Cash leaped to catch the Frisbee in midair in my backyard, I scrolled through the search results. The sun inched closer to the horizon, still pelting bolts of pure summer swelter from the sky. I'd already taken a dip in my pool to cool off when I'd arrived home a few minutes ago, and the water had done the trick . . . momentarily.

After quickly tracking down the gala details on my phone in the parking lot, and snagging a pricy ticket for a benefit to raise money for a new children's wing at a local hospital, I had headed to the gym for a quick workout. Now, after five miles on the treadmill as I answered emails from clients and several rounds of weights, I had some time to dig deeper into my possible date tonight.

To learn more than simply the name of the event.

My black-and-white border collie mix raced to my side, nudging my bare leg with the purple Frisbee, etched with teeth marks around the rim. Johnny Cash was addicted to this Frisbee. I understood deeply the dog's single-minded focus.

"Ready for another?"

The dog thumped his tail on the emerald-green grass. From under the big yellow umbrella on the deck of the pool, I cocked my arm and Johnny Cash took off racing, barreling to the far corner of the yard, around the water, and past a cluster of palm trees that shaded the edge of my property. I tossed the Frisbee then glanced down at the iPad again, hunting for any clue that might yield a name for the bombshell.

She'd said something on the phone about raising money, so perhaps she worked for the hospital, heading up its fundraising maybe. I scanned the event page more closely. Tonight's fete was a silent auction with drinks and hors d'oeuvres, as well as a performance by a well-known Vegas torch singer. All the town's glitterati would be there. Probably even some of my clients, since the security firm my brother Michael and I ran had contracts with many of the city's top spenders.

Those were the only details I found.

As I neared the bottom of the page, I came up empty-handed in the information department. But I didn't need her name to know I wanted to see her again.

Wait.

There it was. In small print.

The gala had been organized by . . . *noted Las Vegas phil-anthropist Sophie Winston.*

Johnny Cash deposited the Frisbee at my feet, but I couldn't pull my eyes off that name.

Could she really be related?

Nah.

I was getting ahead of myself.

"It's just a common last name, right?" I asked the dog. He panted, then eyed the Frisbee. A reminder. Didn't matter to the dog what the woman's name was. *Throw the damn Frisbee.*

I picked up the purple disc, chucked it across the yard once more, and peered again at the screen through my shades. My fingers tingled, itching with possibility.

Winston.

Sophie Winston.

Showing up at the same building where John Winston worked.

The same John Winston who knew why my father's murder investigation had been reopened but wouldn't pony up the details.

Winston. Winston. Winston.

I took a deep breath. Maybe the detective just happened to have the same last name as the woman I wanted to see.

I popped open another browser window, plugged in her name and John's together, and soon the all-knowing Google revealed that the woman who'd invited me to the fete was indeed the detective's sister.

"Huh," I said, staring at the screen in a sort of awed silence. As my dog scurried back to me, I kneeled down and patted his head. "What kind of lucky son of a bitch am I?"

Johnny Cash panted, and I imagined he was saying, *The luckiest.*

I scratched his chin. "It doesn't make me too much of an asshole to hope she might know something, does it?"

The dog had no answers. Instead, he nosed the Frisbee.

Not wanting to deny my best friend and confidant, I pointed to the pool, then threw the Frisbee into the glistening crystal-blue oval in my yard. The dog splashed in loudly and paddled to the shallow end.

As I returned my focus to the screen, I told myself to slow down. Just because Sophie-come-hither-to-my-party-tonight-Winston was the detective's sister didn't mean she was going to serve up details of the case to me.

Hell, she probably didn't know anything. I didn't share the details of my job with *my* sister, so it was foolish to think John had told her the things I was desperate to know.

Besides, I was interested in the woman because there'd been some kind of fuse lit between the two of us this afternoon, and far be it from me to deny that kind of heat. I wasn't some fool who believed in love at first sight. I had no interest in love, nor any faith that it existed. I did, however, believe in the almighty power of lust.

I'd been invited to spin into Sophie's orbit, and that was precisely where I intended to be tonight. But I didn't like to be unprepared. I vastly preferred arming myself with data and details, so I spent a little more time with Google and Sophie, learning she possessed a hell of a lot more than a beautiful body.

Apparently, she had quite a large brain too.

She wasn't simply "noted Las Vegas philanthropist Sophie Winston."

Several business news articles told me what else she was, and it shocked the hell out of me.

Never ever would I have pegged her as a goddamn tech millionaire.

I zeroed in on a well-known tech blog and read its coverage of the sale of an internet start-up to an online search giant several years ago.

Stanford graduate Sophie Winston sold the encoding compression start-up InCode in a deal rumored to be valued at $100 million. She launched the company while finishing her computer science degree at Stanford, and oversaw two rounds of venture capital funding for the technology, which has been used by networks and broadcasters and in enterprise applications. Her brother was the original investor, having provided the initial seed funding from his savings, she has said. Winston tells us she is "delighted" with the acquisition, and plans to step down as CEO, *return to her hometown of Las Vegas, and begin charitable work. "I'm thrilled that InCode will be in good hands and am eager to return home to be with my family."*

I whistled in admiration. The sound caught the attention of my sopping wet dog, who cocked his ears as he trotted to me.

"Guess what, Johnny Cash?" I asked, as the dog shook the chlorinated water from his fur at Mach speed. I stepped away, making sure the tablet screen wasn't in the line of fire. "Seems I was wrong when I thought she was a movie star. The woman's a retired Mark Zuckerberg."

I chucked the disc into the pool again, and my dog raced after it, launching into the deep end.

But maybe that wasn't the best comparison, because there was nothing unfeminine about Sophie. She was all woman, and all sex appeal, and I intended to find out tonight what made her tick.

Because my desire for the beautiful—and evidently brainy—blonde had nothing to do with the fact that she might be privy to things I wanted to know. Nothing at all. It had everything to do with how she looked in that dress, and how insatiably curious I was to learn how she looked out of it.

I was living for that moment, and that moment only.

4

—————

SOPHIE

I was late.

I was often late.

Being on time was so hard when there was makeup to do and hair to blow-dry and stockings to pull on just so, inch by delicate inch, because you didn't want them to rip.

Stockings took time to do right, with the garter attached at the thigh.

I'd be wearing them even if I didn't have that fluttery little hope of a hot man in my near future. I wore them because I loved stockings. Stockings were sexy and fun, and after years of donning jeans and hoodies and knit caps —because as a woman in the tech field, I'd desperately wanted to look the part—I'd shed the old Sophie when I left the land of bits and bytes behind me.

Now, with my new focus on philanthropy, dressing up was not only embraced, it was essential.

The panties though . . . those were just for me.

Tonight's panties were black like my dress and sheer, with a slim crisscross tie up the side.

I smoothed a hand over my dress, gave myself one

more quick once-over in my full-length bedroom mirror, then snagged my purse from my bed. I headed down the hall, pausing in the living room, one hand on the back of the soft chocolate-brown couch, wondering if I'd remembered to put fresh pillowcases in the guest room at the other end of the condo for my brother.

A flicker of tension skimmed through my veins.

I knew I had. This was just a momentary bout of OCD making me doubt myself.

I stood stock-still, tapping my fingers against my forehead. I could recall perfectly having placed new linens on the bed just this morning. The gray-and-white striped ones.

I headed for the front door. But it *was* always better to be safe than sorry, right? Checking and double-checking, and then checking one more time in that final quality assurance test—well, that was what had gotten me far in life. I race-walked down the opposite hall, turned the doorknob, and breathed a sigh of relief as I took in the sight of the bed, as crisply made as a hotel room in the Bellagio.

Okay, I could go now.

I made my way to the front door and gripped the handle, when I was nearly knocked on the floor by the unexpected force of the door opening.

"Oh!"

"Shit. Sorry, Soph. I thought you'd be gone by now."

I waved off John's worry. "I should be. Running late."

He narrowed his eyes. "Were you checking everything three times?"

"Only your room," I admitted in a low voice.

He clasped a big hand on my shoulder. "Don't worry about that stuff. Besides, I'll happily sleep on the floor, or in an unmade bed. You don't have to check to make sure everything is perfect for me," he said softly, then gestured to my right ear. "But you might want to check on your earring. Looks like one is about to pop out."

Lifting my hand to my ear, I felt the edge of the earring slipping from my earlobe. I peered into a small mirror by the door, catching the reflection of a framed photograph of my parents from across the room, my heart lurching briefly at the image, and how much I loved and missed them. "I thought you were working late," I said as I repositioned the jewelry.

He shrugged. "Yeah, but I figured it'd be nice and quiet at your place, and you'll be out, so I can work on the case here."

"Close to solving it?"

He scoffed. "Not even remotely. Talked to some guy today who I'm sure knows something, but he won't let on what it is."

"What do you think he knows?" I asked, turning away from the mirror to face my brother, who was unknotting his tie and tugging it off.

"Something that would help me find the other guys I think were involved."

"What kind of case is it?"

He laughed. "You're not getting that out of me."

"I know. I just like asking, because it's funny to see how many ways you can say *no comment*." John never gave up details. He always spoke vaguely about his work so I could never connect the dots. Not that I wanted to. I vastly preferred operating on my side of the world, entertaining the wealthy and privileged and encouraging them to dig deep into their pockets to help those who needed it most: the children, the ill, the underprivileged, the animals who needed a voice. I'd helped raise money for all those causes, and I intended to do just that tonight for the hospital.

* * *

Sometime later, after the silent auction of a painting by Miller Valentina, I walked to the podium in the ballroom and thanked the sea of glittering guests in shimmery dresses and crisp suits.

"I am so unbelievably thrilled to share the news that, thanks to your generosity, we've raised well over our funding goal for the new children's wing, which will provide state-of-the-art care," I said, surveying the tables in the ballroom as the crowd clapped in recognition of the good news.

The man in the green tie hadn't made it. *C'est la vie.* I didn't know anything about him, and it had been silly to want a stranger so badly. Better to move on, and besides, I had a busy agenda for the rest of the evening. "We would not have been able to do this without your generosity," I said, beaming at the guests. My heart was full, bursting with joy over their willingness to give. "But don't think I'm going to let any of you gorgeous people—and for the record, you are all my favorite people—slip away this evening. We have Heaven Leigh here with us, and if her voice doesn't make you want to snuggle up to your date, then I don't know what will. She'll be on in five minutes."

My assistant, Kelley Jeffers, caught up with me as I walked through a small section of the wings backstage. Ever efficient and always prepared, Kelley tapped her clipboard. "You have forty-five minutes until we need you on again to close out the event with the awards."

"Perfect. I'll grab a drink and mingle."

"Be sure to be backstage at nine forty-five so we can stay on time."

"Absolutely," I said, then headed to the steps, ready to

chitchat and socialize. As I reached the ballroom floor, though, I nearly froze.

I wasn't sure if I saw him first or merely sensed him. I turned my head, and goosebumps rose on my bare arms as I drank him in.

In the distance, he leaned against the doorway to the ballroom, looking cool, sexy, and debonair, wearing a dark-gray suit that fit him like a glove—tailored and snug where it needed to be, revealing strength and tone. His light-brown hair was messy, but not sloppy. It was the type of hair that was too thick to be contained, that couldn't be combed into submission, but instead simply invited fingers to run through it.

But then, if I was doing things right, my hands wouldn't be free.

Across all the tables and chairs, past the dazzling chandelier lights, beyond the sea of designer dresses, he locked eyes with me.

His seemed to say, *I'm here for you. I'm coming to get you.*

I flashed a smile, aware that it was a high-wattage one, but then that was how I felt—bubbly, buoyant, and powered by the thrill of possibility. I hadn't misread the moment outside the municipal building. The chemistry had been electric and instant—and intense enough for him to come calling.

As I walked around the dance floor to find my way to him, a flash of gray hair appeared in the corner of my vision. Next came a phlegmy clearing of the throat.

Oh, dear.

Not now.

One of my regular donors placed a clammy hand on my bare arm—Clyde Graser, pushing eighty, sweet as could be, and more generous than virtually anyone.

He was also terribly out of touch with women.

"Sophie, how are you, my dear?"

He received one of my brightest smiles. "I'm very well, Mr. Graser. So good to see you."

After a minute of small talk, he cleared his throat once more, a sign he had *Something Important to Say.* "My grandson Taylor is coming back to town. He graduated from Harvard Law earlier this year and has been hired into a corporate practice here. I have a hunch the two of you would get along swimmingly, and I would love to introduce you to him."

A newly minted law school graduate was probably all of twenty-five. Divorced and thirty-one, I had a clear cutoff. You had to be over thirty to ride this ride. I simply wasn't into cradle-robbing.

"I'm sure he's lovely," I said, doing my best to be kind but evasive.

Clyde's matchmaking effort wasn't the first I'd had to deflect. These sorts of offers had been happening with increasing frequency since Holden and I had divorced two years ago. With the money I'd socked away from the sale of my company—even after Holden's cut of the profits—and the work I did now, many of the city's old wealth wanted me for their sons.

I wanted no such thing.

"Wonderful. Then I'll bring him to the Beethoven concert," Clyde said. The law firm Clyde had founded was a lead sponsor of that upcoming charity event, and I hoped to convince him to pour even more of his corporate cash into a community center that was being refurbished in a section of town that had been a hotbed for a local gang many years ago—a street gang that had been rising up again, which made it all the more important to revitalize the neighborhood.

"I can't wait," I said as Clyde walked away.

Then my pulse suddenly quickened.

I knew.

Knew the sexy man had to be mere feet from me. The little hairs on my arms stood on end. This man and I were two elements smashing into each other and setting off sparks. There was no other explanation, because I'd never felt this kind of intense desire for someone I'd just met.

It was a riot inside my body.

He placed a hand on the small of my back—gentle, terribly gentle, and it unleashed an electric charge in me. "Can't wait for what?" he asked.

Oh God, his voice. His deep, sexy voice was an aphrodisiac. It was the opening act in the seduction of me.

"For the evening to turn more exciting," I said as I came face-to-face with the sexiest stranger I'd ever met—and he wasn't going to be a stranger much longer.

"Looks like I arrived just in time. Because that's exactly what I intend to do."

I arched an eyebrow. "Excite me?"

The first notes of a sexy ballad sounded from the stage. "Yes. That's why I came here. Right now, however, I'd like to monopolize you on the dance floor, Miss Sophie Winston."

"You know my name," I said, shooting him a look that said I was impressed.

"I do," he said, holding me captive with his dark-blue eyes. "And I'd like to get to know more than your name."

"That sort of intel might be obtained with a dance," I said, clasping his hand and letting him lead me to the dance floor as the lights dimmed and the song wrapped itself around us.

5

RYAN

As the slinky, silky Vegas nightclub singer belted out a bluesy number from the stage, the lights in the ballroom dimmed. They turned the bright silent auction that I had caught the tail end of into a sultry nighttime affair. The chandeliers flickered, and violet lights shone on the dance floor. Men in tuxes and women in evening dresses moved and swayed, and the event reeked of old money and new money, mingling together. This was the cocktail mix of the Vegas built on the bedrock of Rat-Pack-era casinos, stirred up with the cool swagger of the sleek skyscraper crowds of today.

I led Sophie to the dance floor, my palm on her back.

Her skin was so soft. So bare. So fantastically naked in this backless dress as I pulled her near and we began to dance.

"So you made it," she said.

"I would have been here sooner, but I had to walk my dog."

She burst out in surprised laughter. "Really?"

"You don't believe me?"

"It's not that I don't believe you. It just came out sounding like an excuse," she said as we swayed in time to the jazzy number sung by the red-sequined woman on stage.

"He's a very demanding dog. Have you ever met a border collie mix? They can be quite needy. And I like to make sure he's happy."

"How good of you to think of him."

"I was thinking of you too," I said, my eyes fixed on her as I spoke. "I couldn't get you off my mind."

"Is that so?" she asked, but her smile made it seem less like a question. "I figured I'd read you wrong."

"You didn't expect me to show up?" I spread my fingers across the bare skin of her back. Goosebumps rose on her flesh.

"One never knows if a man has it in him to respond to an invitation on the street," she said coyly.

My spine straightened, and I stood even taller. "When a woman like you tells a man she wants him, that man should do everything in his power to show up."

She moved closer, her sky-blue eyes sparkling with mischief. "I don't believe I said I wanted you," she whispered.

I bent my head to her ear, catching the faint scent of her perfume. Something vaguely tropical. Something that suggested hot summer nights. I wanted to run my nose along her skin and inhale her. A groan worked its way up my chest. "You didn't have to say it," I said.

She shot me a sharp stare, but she didn't let go of me. "My, my. Aren't we a little over-confident?"

"Am I?" I asked, letting go to spin her in a circle then tugging her back as the music rose to a crescendo.

"Perhaps I just wanted to make sure the ballroom was

full," she said, gesturing to the crowd. "Maybe that's why I invited you."

"Is that what you wanted? One more attendee at your event?"

She swallowed and parted her lips. "Maybe I want other things."

She pressed her hand against my shoulder, and the pressure from that slight touch sent electricity flying through me. I stopped swaying and dipped her, holding her in that pose, her back bent in an arc, her body draped over my arm, trusting me. "Tell me, Sophie. What other things do you want?"

I watched her like that as I waited for her answer. Her eyes never wavered from mine. There was no shyness in her gaze, no nerves evident in her expression. Only confidence, which was so damn alluring. She licked her lips, then answered, "A man who can figure those *other things* out."

Oh, hell yeah. This woman turned me on fiercely. She was direct and naughty at the same time. I raised her up. Her full breasts were flush against my chest, and I was sure I could spend hours worshipping them. Or biting them. Or fucking them. "I can figure out all those things you want. I can deliver all of them too. But right now? Here on the dance floor? I presume this is when you need me to role-play being a perfect gentleman," I said, casting my gaze briefly at the crowds dancing alongside us.

"So you wouldn't be a gentleman if we weren't in front of all these people?"

"I would absolutely not be a gentleman at all," I said, letting my hand travel along her back. "But for the moment, you have your donors here to entertain."

She raised her chin and looked at me studiously. "You did your homework, Mr.—" Then she laughed and cut herself off, placing a finger over my lips. "Don't tell me your name. I prefer to think of you as Mr. Green Tie. So we can pretend we hardly know each other. We can be strangers."

"Strangers can make the best lovers."

"Are you? A good lover?"

"I don't really think you want me to answer that question."

"Why on earth wouldn't I want the answer to that?" she asked, toying with my tie, her voice a purr that lit up my organs, setting every last part of me on fire.

I shook my head, then pressed my lips near her ear and whispered, "I think you'd rather I show you."

She gasped, an enticing sound that ignited me. My body was strung tight, like a snare drum. I was torn between wanting to pounce on her now and drawing out the antici-pation. Making her want me. Making her beg. I was willing to bet she was a marvelous beggar, that she could get on her knees and say *please* in a voice that snapped all my restraint.

"Show me," she whispered, then her eyes floated closed as I touched her, fingertips brushing her back. They traveled higher, and she arched into my hand, like a cat being petted. I reached her hair, winding a loose blonde strand around my index finger, cataloging the expression on her face, the way her features were so soft, so open—her lips parted, her eyes closed, her breath gentle.

I let her long curls fall through my fingers as she molded to me.

Then I showed her what else I liked. That I wasn't soft. That I wasn't gentle. With my fingers gripping her hair, I tugged.

Hard.

Her eyes snapped open, and they blazed at me. "That wasn't gentlemanly."

"I know," I said, her hair still twisted in my fist. "And you liked it. Now, have you got any more questions about how I am in bed?"

She gulped. A touch of nervousness seemed to flicker across her eyes. "Not at the moment." She blinked and seemed to rearrange her features as I let go of her hair, smoothing it out as it fell along her neck. "So tell me, Mr. Green Tie, what did you learn about me when you went hunting for information?"

I learned she shared DNA with the lead detective reinvestigating my father's murder. But that wasn't exactly information that needed to be served up as small talk. "I learned you know everyone here, and can convince anyone to contribute to a worthy cause. Lots of money. Insane amounts."

She pursed her lips together. "That does sound like one of my skills," she said playfully.

"I learned you do it because you can. Because you made your mint already and now you give back."

"True, true. Does that bother you?"

"That you made a mint?"

She nodded. "Yes. That can intimidate some men. When a woman is successful."

I scoffed. "I'm not easily intimidated. And I happen to think successful women are"—I moved in closer, my lips daringly close to hers—"incredibly alluring." I skimmed my hand from her shoulder down her arm, unable to resist touching her. "But that's what I learned from your bio, Sophie. I know other things about you, just from these last ten minutes."

"What do you know?" she asked as the singer began a

new tune and the purple lights swooshed across the dance floor.

I ran a fingertip along her wrist, her chest rising as she drew in a quick breath. "That you like being touched."

She nodded. "If a man knows how."

"That you like to play games."

She frowned. "You make that sound bad."

"Games aren't bad." I lowered my voice to a whisper. "I bet you like to play pretend. Make believe. Role-play."

"I have an idea," she said with a purr, as she roped her hands around my neck and trailed her fingertips across the back of it, her touch a jolt of pleasure. "We could pretend, say, that we just met and I'm curious about the man who has been in my thoughts. So, since you know what occupied my time in college, why don't you tell me what occupied yours?"

That was easy. I could tell her my college major without giving up too much. "History."

"Why history?"

"I like to understand what motivates people. Why they do what they do."

"And did you learn what motivates people?"

"Usually it's a desire for property or money."

She smiled ruefully. "Sounds about right. What about sports? Did you play sports?"

"Yes. Hockey. Right-wing."

"Did you cause fights?" she asked, curiosity dripping from her voice.

I shook my head, my lips in a smirk, proud to be able to say no. "I was the one who stopped the fights."

Her eyes widened. "Interesting. Why is that?"

"I like to be in control."

She inched her hands up toward my hair, and I grasped

her wrists and returned them to my shoulders. "What line of business are you in?" she asked.

"Security."

"What do you do in security? Watch over banks? Guard the mall?" she asked with lightness in her tone.

I laughed and shook my head. "No. I run a security company."

"Do you love it?"

"I do. It's exactly what I want to be doing."

She danced her fingers down the front of my shirt. "I find men who know what they want a turn-on, more so than what they do."

"I know what I want."

"You do. You want me."

"So fucking much," I growled. I tugged her in closer, aligning my body to hers, letting her feel how much I wanted her already. A sexy sigh escaped her lips as I brought her near to me. She fit in my arms perfectly. Like that, we danced and moved under the dim lights to the next few songs, chatting about Vegas and the event and the silent auction, as I asked her questions about the gala and the hospital it benefited.

"See? You are a gentleman. Asking a woman questions. Getting to know her," she said, then touched a lock of my hair that had fallen on my forehead. I caught her arm, my fingers wrapping tightly around her flesh. I bent my head and brushed my lips against her wrist.

Our first kiss, and I was nowhere near her lips. But the skin of her arm had that same sultry, sexy scent as her neck. I let my lips linger on her wrist, then let go. "You taste fantastic," I said, holding her eyes, letting my meaning register.

"Do I?"

"Yes. You do. I bet you taste delicious everywhere."

She waved a hand in front of her face. "It's getting awfully hot out here. I'm afraid I might combust if we stay on the dance floor like this." She tipped her head to the bar. "Drink?"

I nodded and pressed my lips briefly to her neck, dusting a kiss on her collarbone. A soft moan floated to my ears. I was going to have a field day with Sophie Winston. She was a dream—every touch, every taste and she murmured, she sighed, she moaned.

I hadn't even properly kissed her yet.

We threaded our way to the bar, where I asked for two champagnes. As I reached for the flutes, a woman in a high-necked maroon dress and a severe bun zeroed in on Sophie, commanding her focus to ask her opinion on how the children's wing should be decorated. Sophie encouraged her to call her that week to discuss. As that woman finished, another darted in, declaring that she knew a building contractor, and she could up her donation if that would help secure the contract. Sophie was gracious with all of them, but after a few minutes, she tossed me a *save me* glance.

I stepped in next to her, handed her a glass of champagne, and flashed a smile at the two ladies. "I hope you'll forgive me for interrupting, but I have to leave shortly, since I've been called to the hospital to do an unplanned surgery."

The woman in maroon shot me a curious look. "Oh, you're a surgeon?"

I nodded. "I am. And I need two minutes with our Sophie before I have to go perform a bone graft."

The other woman eyed my champagne. I quickly thrust it at her. "Please. Take this from me. I can't drink on surgery nights, of course. I don't even know why the bartender gave it to me. But I hate to be rude," I said, shaking my head as if I couldn't bear the thought of turning down the man tending bar.

"Of course you don't want to be rude. You're a respected surgeon," the second woman said in a dramatic voice.

"And we don't want to be rude either," the maroon woman added. "Please. Go on. We don't want to keep you from your bone graft."

"Thank you so much," I said, and turned to leave, the beautiful bombshell by my side, her lips pressed together so she wouldn't laugh.

"Bone graft?" she whispered out of the side of her mouth as we walked off.

"I suppose bones, and the hardness of them, must be on my mind." Then I shrugged. "Besides, I needed to come up with something, or we'd never have a moment alone."

"You want to be alone with me?"

"Isn't it abundantly apparent?"

"From the hardness of your bones? Why, yes, it does seem quite abundant," she said with an amused expression as she cast her eyes to my pants.

I stopped at the side door, away from the crowds. I lowered my voice and spoke in a rough, husky tone. "You turned me on from the second I laid eyes on you this afternoon. You are gorgeous and beautiful, and everything about you arouses me. *Abundantly.*"

Her chest rose and fell, and she exhaled heavily. "Oh God," she whispered.

"Can you get away?"

She squeezed her eyes shut and shook her head. "I have to present a few awards on stage in—"

Out of the corner of my eye, I spotted a woman in a sharp black dress marching purposefully in our direction. She pointed at Sophie.

"I think someone's looking for you."

The woman stopped when she reached us. "Sophie, you have seven minutes before we need you onstage again."

"Thank you so much, Kelley."

The woman spun efficiently on her heel and walked off.

Sophie turned back to me. "I can't get away."

"No. You can't. Let me walk you backstage so you don't miss your presentation."

6

SOPHIE

The black curtain hugged the small stage, shielding us from the crowds still dancing and enjoying the music. Here, off to the side in this section of the wings, I was all alone with my stranger.

His eyes roamed my body. The look in them was predatory. He stalked me, and I backed up, step by step in my heels, until I hit the black wood wall. "You have six minutes now before you go out there," he said in a hungry voice, his fingertips brushing the fabric of my dress along my thigh. "Do you know what I can do to you in six minutes to make you feel amazing?"

The temperature inside me shot sky-high. A pulse beat between my legs. I was hot, and I was wet. I'd been turned on ever since he'd asked me to dance.

"What can you do?" I asked, feeling both utterly vulnerable and completely aroused. It was a matchstick combination for me.

"Do you want me to tell you?" He roamed his hand up the outside of my leg, reaching my waist, making me shudder.

"I do," I said breathily, my body on the cusp of something intense. Something I wanted desperately.

"What I've been thinking about since I met you." He raised his hand and cupped my cheek. His touch was both gentle and possessive. "First, I'm going to place my hand on your beautiful face, and your knees will go weak because I'll finally be touching you the way you've been fantasizing about since this afternoon," he said, his hot breath painting my skin.

"Cocky."

"Yes," he said with a nod as he ran his thumb along my jawline. "But also true. From the moment I met you, I knew I'd have my hands on you. You knew it too. Felt it too."

I nodded as I trembled from the trace of his finger. "I did feel it."

He brought his mouth to my ear and spoke softly. "If I ever do or say something you don't like, tell me. Or smack me. I only want to bring you pleasure." His words were both sexy and earnest. The combination sent flutters through my belly. "Immense pleasure."

"You already are. So tell me something else that's true. Something else you know," I said, loving the hot, dirty way he talked to me as he touched me.

"I'm going to look into your eyes like I want to take you," he said, his eyes blazing with desire. "That look will drive you wild. And you'll swallow nervously because you don't know me, and it's odd wanting a stranger as much as you do." He was reading me like a teenage diary. On the one hand, I was nervous. I didn't know him at all. But I was also aroused beyond words. Beyond reason. Beyond any normal limits.

For that same reason—because I didn't know him.

"Then, you'll run a hand down my tie," he told me, and I

reached out instantly, doing exactly as he said, loving the directions he gave. I craved this kind of interaction. So much time was spent deciding and doing and planning. It drove my brain batty, and I longed for this kind of release from my everyday.

"Do you know why you're so fascinated with my tie?" he asked huskily, his eyes pinned on me. He practically fucked me with his gaze. It was so intense. His confidence set me on fire. It torched a path across my body, sizzling my skin.

"Tell me," I said, eager for more of his words. "Since you seem to know me so well, tell me."

He brushed the backs of his fingers against my cheek. Oh God, I was dying for him to kiss me. I was so eager to feel those lips. To taste him.

He grasped my wrist with one hand, yanking it up his chest and loosely wrapping the end of his tie around my hand. "You want me to tie you up."

"How do you know that?" I asked, my voice stripped to the bone. He knew me. He read me. He could sense everything I wanted. He crowded me against the wall. Heaven Leigh belted out her song onstage while the inky black of the backstage cloaked us.

"Am I wrong?" he asked, arching an eyebrow. "If I'm wrong, tell me and I'll walk away."

I shook my head in answer, then glanced at his tie. "Are you going to take it off? Tie me up?" I asked in a voice that hardly sounded like me. It belonged to the part of me that had been untended for years.

He grinned wickedly. "No. I have other ways to tie you up," he said, and in a flash, he gripped my wrists in his big, strong hands, wrapping his fingers around me, binding me as he yanked my hands behind my back. Heat flared in my body, spinning through me, settling between my legs. My gorgeous, sexy panties were so damp right now they were useless.

I ached for his touch. And I could do nothing but wait for it, since I was his hostage.

He was so strong I couldn't wriggle away if I wanted to. His thumbs dug into my wrist bones, pinning my hands above my ass, rendering me helpless. The pressure from the twist in my arms bordered on pain, and felt oh so good.

There was no space between the two of us. Only breath. Only words and his bare, husky voice. "Do you know what else I've been thinking about all day?"

I shook my head.

He inched closer, his mouth mere centimeters from mine. My lips parted, so ready for him. God, I needed him to kiss me, badly, but he was making me wait for it, making me nearly ask for it. His mouth hovered so close I wanted to dart out my tongue and lick him. Draw him to me. His forehead brushed mine, and my breath fluttered.

Somehow I managed a *"Please."*

"Please kiss you?" he asked. "Is that what you want me to do?"

I nodded, too turned on to form another word, even a yes.

"That's exactly what I've been thinking about all day," he whispered.

Then he kissed me, and he wasn't gentle. He wasn't sweet. He was rough as he claimed my mouth, kissing hard. I moaned as he drew my bottom lip between his teeth then fused his mouth to mine.

His stubble rubbed against my chin. I'd have whisker burn later. I longed for the redness, the proof, the evidence of his bruising kiss.

The kiss lit me up. I felt it everywhere—in my toes, in my hair, in my belly.

And, deliciously, between my legs.

I ached for him there. I angled my hips closer as we kissed, desperately seeking contact with him. God, how I wanted him. And I didn't even know his name.

But he knew my body.

He knew my desires.

He held my hands so tightly they might as well be cuffed. In a flash, he changed his grip, holding both my wrists in one hand, keeping them pinned behind my back. He moved his free hand to the front of my dress and found his way up my skirt. He broke the kiss as his fingertips brushed above my knee, touching my stockings and garter. "Are you wet for me, Sophie?"

"Yes," I said on a pant.

"Are you hot for me?" he asked, racing closer to my heat.

"God, yes."

"Do you still want to ask me if I'm a good lover?" He flicked his finger against my clit. Ripples of pleasure spread through my body. I inhaled sharply and bit my lip so I wouldn't cry out loud.

"No. I don't need to ask you," I said as he stroked me through my black lace panties.

"Why not?" he asked.

"Because you're showing me."

His fingers glided across the wet panel of my panties, stroking faster as I rocked into him. He kept a firm grip on my wrists as I greedily sought his friction. "That's right," he said roughly. "I'm showing you, Sophie. I'm showing you exactly what I can do to you."

He ran his fingers across the wet lace, narrowing in on where I wanted him. I was so close to the edge, and I needed him to keep touching me. I needed his fingers flying across my clit, touching me until I fell apart.

"Beg for it," he commanded.

"*Please*," I whispered in his ear, my knees shaking, desperate for release. "Please make me come."

He rubbed fast and expertly, and I rocked into his hand as bright white fireworks blasted in my brain, radiating throughout my body. Faintly, in the back of my mind, I heard the song nearing the end, and I knew I'd have to come in seconds to make it to the stage on time.

But seconds were all this man needed.

"I want to taste your lips as you fuck my hand," he said, then dropped his delicious mouth to mine once more, kissing me fiercely as I rode his fingers. He wasn't even touching my flesh. He was getting me off through the lace. He was that good. I was that turned on. The tension in my body escalated, rising up like a roller-coaster car nearing the top of the hill. Then I reached it, hovered for beautiful seconds in that suspended state of bliss, then raced downhill as if it were an orgasmic joyride. As my own pleasure crashed into me, he ravaged my mouth with his lips, swallowing my moans, tasting my cries, and somehow it felt like kissing was coming, and coming was kissing.

Only it was more. It was also being held back, restrained—a hint of all that I craved.

I blinked and breathed hard as he pulled away. He arched an eyebrow, and let go of my wrists. My skin burned from his grip. I shook my right hand.

Gently, he brought my wrist to his lips. He kissed it softly, erasing the sting, his lips traveling across the same territory where he'd held me tight moments ago.

"Better?" he asked quietly.

I nodded as he gave the same treatment to my other hand. All these sensations both rattled and delighted me—I didn't know what to make of this man, and how he could talk and touch so roughly and harshly in the heat of the moment, then become so sweet in the afterglow.

He lowered my hands to my sides, then tucked a loose strand of my hair behind my ear. "Beautiful," he said, his eyes softer now as he looked me over.

I smoothed a hand over my dress. My legs felt wobbly. My heart roared loudly. My body still sang.

Clapping echoed loudly from beyond the curtains. The song was over. "Thank you so much," the singer said from the stage.

He tipped his head. "You better get out there."

I grabbed his tie and tugged him close. "Name. Tell me your name."

I expected a sly remark. A hint that gave little away.

"Ryan," he said with a glint in his dark eyes.

I scoffed. "Your name is not Ryan."

"Why not?"

"Ryan's a nice-guy name."

"Are you saying I'm not a nice guy?"

I shook my head and curled my hand around his shoulder. "You're not a nice guy at all."

He brought his palm to his chest. "I'm hurt. I'm a terribly nice guy. I saved you from those women who wanted to monopolize you at the bar. And I kissed you when you came so no one heard how loud you were."

"Then why are you leaving?"

"Because you have to go," he said, nodding to the stage.

"And why are you giving me your first name only?"

He brushed his lips against my ear. "What are you doing on Sunday at seven p.m.?"

I practically held my breath at the possibility unfurling before me. "What should I be doing Sunday at seven p.m.?"

"Be at Caesars. Outside the Fizz Bar. I want to see you again." He paused, then added, "*Badly.*"

I smiled. I wanted to see him too. "I'll be there."

I ran my hand along my skirt once more, then gently touched my hair, making sure it was still in place. My heart sped up in worry. I grabbed one of Ryan's strong arms. "Wait. Is my lipstick smeared?"

He shook his head. "No. It's all gone." He softly brushed the pad of his thumb along my cheek. "But you look perfect. Every single thing about you looks perfect."

"Thank you," I said, taking a deep breath as I left.

I walked on the stage, flashing a big, bright smile to the crowd. I thanked Heaven Leigh for her performance, praising how talented she was. As I spoke, I scanned the crowd and caught a last glimpse of the man in the suit, the man who'd made me come backstage. He was on his way out, but he stopped briefly and watched me. He didn't wave. He didn't chuckle. He didn't make a single gesture to say we had a secret.

But the way he stared made me tingle all over, and the way his lips curved up in a grin said he knew he had that effect on me, and that he had every intention of doing it again.

7

RYAN

I gripped the large tree trunk that had fallen on the roof, as my brother finished slicing through the last section of the wood. The chainsaw buzzed loudly in the midday air, then Michael turned it off.

After I let go of the wood, I grabbed the hem of my T-shirt and wiped the sweat from my brow. "You think it feels hotter, since we're closer to the sun, being on the roof and all?" I asked my brother.

"Absolutely. It's a proven scientific fact that working on someone's roof equates to a ten-degree increase in temperature," Michael said as he set the chainsaw on the tiles, resting it by his feet so it wouldn't topple into the yard.

I rapped my knuckles against the pile of wood we'd chopped from a large tree branch that had fallen on our friend Sanders's roof during a recent windy night. Sanders Doyle was a friend of our father's from long ago. Nearing retirement and damn ready for it, he was a mechanic at the limo company where our father had worked the last few years of his life.

"Did you meet with Winston?" I asked Michael as we walked to the edge of the roof, stopping when we reached the ladder resting against the house.

"Yeah. But I'm not supposed to say a word about what was said." He mimed zipping his lips.

I laughed. "He said that to me too. But what are the chances that we aren't going to tell each other?" I asked, though sometimes I wondered if my siblings had kept secrets from me, as I had from them. Would John Winston be privy to those secrets if they had them? "What did he ask you?"

With his sunglasses shielding his eyes, Michael answered matter-of-factly. "Any new friends. Anything I remember," he said, repeating what the detective had asked me. "But he also asked about Luke."

The hair on the back of my neck prickled at the mention of our mother's lover, a local piano teacher. "What about him?"

Michael sneered. "Wanted to know what I knew about their relationship. Like I had a clue about the affair. Isn't that the point of an affair? It was all in secret."

"Did Winston say he thinks Luke was involved?"

Michael shook his head. "Nah. That man just asks questions. Didn't share any details. And I have no idea if Luke was a part of it. They cleared him at the time, but who the heck knows?"

"Got any new theories on why they reopened the case?" We'd already speculated for hours after the detectives showed up at Shannon and Brent's wedding celebration at our grandparents' house a week ago and dropped the bomb about the investigation's new life. "It's frustrating that they know something but won't tell us."

Michael pushed down his sunglasses, meeting my eyes. "I bet they think someone else helped plan the murder."

"You think Mom will get out of prison?" My voice rose with a touch of hope that I knew would piss off my brother. Michael had cut off our mom. He didn't visit her. Didn't talk to her. Her guilt was crystal clear to him.

But the world wasn't black and white to me. I'd seen and heard other sides to the story. The side our mom hadn't told anyone else.

Michael scoffed. "Her fingerprints are all over everything. She's not innocent, not in the least. But there might be others who are guilty too, beyond her and Stefano. Murder for hire isn't a to-go order. You don't walk into a store and order a hit with fries on the side." Michael shook his head, as if to chase the thought away. "Now, let's get this wood down to your truck, so we can take it to green recycling."

That was apparently all the discussion Michael wanted to entertain about the investigation. But I wasn't ready to drop the subject. "You learned that from your police shows?" I asked, teasing my brother.

"Diehard CSI fan. Now let's get off the roof. I'm hot, and I need a beer."

I hefted a few chunks of wood under my arm. "You let me know when the next episode of *Law and Order* helps you solve the mystery, 'kay?"

Thirty minutes later, we'd finished loading the bed of my truck with the chopped-up tree trunk, and Sanders had come out of the house to survey our progress.

"Ah, youth. I remember the days when I could have done that," Sanders said wistfully, one hand parked on the side of the truck door.

"You pining for lifting tree trunks or other things we strapping young studs can do?" I teased.

"That part works just fine." His expression shifted to

gratitude. "But I appreciate you coming by to help out. Couldn't do this without you lads, clearly."

"You know we're always happy to help," I said.

At sixty-one, Sanders had spent his career as a mechanic bent over hoods or under engines, which had taken its toll on the man. With a bad back, and his own sons scattered across the United States and back home in Ireland, he leaned on us for heavy lifting from time to time.

"Let me treat you to a beer," Sanders said, clapping me on the shoulder.

"I'm always game for a brew. And Michael was already hankering for one."

"Wait till you experience the AC in my house. It was on the fritz, and I fixed it myself the other day. Impressed Mrs. Doyle quite a bit with that handiwork."

"And you need to with the way she was pissed about your speeding ticket the other month. You do know they have apps now that tell you where the speed traps are," I said as we reached the side gate to the backyard.

Sanders shrugged, a little helplessly. "I know, I know. What can I say? I was getting tired and was eager to get home, so I gunned the engine. The highway looked free and clear. You'd think four decades of driving would have taught me to look out better for a state trooper. Especially in California. They bust your balls there."

"There's a first time for everything. Congrats on your first speeding ticket."

Sanders quieted as we reached the deck where Becky waited, shielding her eyes as she waved. "I've got cold beer for my favorite handymen."

"You are the best, Mrs. Doyle," I said. "I'd give you a big hug, but I'm sweaty and gross."

"I'm not," Michael said, elbowing me as he moved in for an embrace. "I'll hug you."

Sanders stepped in front of both of us.

"Now, now. Keep your mitts off my lady. She's liable to leave me for one of you," Sanders said with narrowed eyes. "I'll be the only sweaty man touching her." He draped an arm around Becky and planted a kiss on her cheek. She smiled at him, then led us into the house.

Cool air blasted my hot skin. "This is heaven," I said with a relaxed sigh.

Becky handed beer bottles to Michael and me. "Glad you enjoy it."

"Now it's really heaven," Michael said, then knocked back some of the beer.

Sanders squeezed his wife's shoulder possessively. "Only four more months till I can spend my days drinking beer and lounging on the pool deck as we circle the Bahamas."

Becky smiled. "I can't wait. We're going on a cruise for three whole weeks. It's been a dream my whole life."

"Just make sure they don't make you do time for your speeding ticket before you go," I teased.

Sanders tensed, his spine straightening at those words. "Course not. It was just speeding."

"Sure. What else would it be?" I asked, with a laugh.

"Let's not talk about the trip to California right now," Becky said in a quiet but firm voice that brooked no argument. She turned away, the set of her jaw tight. I glanced briefly at Sanders, who was rubbing his wife's arm, then at my brother. Michael shrugged a shoulder.

I had no clue why the speeding ticket had touched such a nerve for the Doyles.

But the weird glances, the needy reassurance, the mix of worry and admonishment—those were all reminders of why I steered clear of relationships. They were trouble. Women needed soothing and tending to, and those were just not things I was good at.

I was, however, quite good in other areas, and there was a woman who seemed fond of those skills. A woman I'd be seeing tomorrow.

I couldn't wait.

8

SOPHIE

Ever dapper, always elegant, Holden played the final notes in a Beethoven Concerto on the grand piano.

I tapped my fingertips against the black lacquer of the piano in Holden's apartment overlooking the Mandalay Bay pool. Several stories below, hotel guests drank towering drinks and splashed in the cool water.

"Finito!" Holden declared with a flourish as he finished the piece, then stood up and bowed deeply.

I clapped and shouted my one-woman ovation: "Bravo!"

"Thank you, thank you to all my adoring fans," he said, then blew air kisses to the fictional crowd.

I wrapped my arms around him in a hug. "You're going to be amazing. Though that's not a surprise in the least."

"You really liked it?"

"Liked it? I absolutely loved it. It was . . ." I let my voice trail off as I searched for just the right word to describe his musical talent. I brought my fingers to my lips like a chef pleased with a dish. *"Magnifique."*

He sighed happily and beamed, placing his hand on his

chest as he mouthed, *Thank you.* He wore tight blue slacks, loafers, and a crisp striped button-down. My ex-husband had achieved some sort of pinnacle in male fashion—he never dressed down.

He was a lot like me.

That was the problem in our marriage.

He was a bit too much like me.

He liked clothes, he liked shopping, and he liked kicking back on the couch and gabbing over a glass of chardonnay and a pint of ice cream.

Best friends in high school, Holden and I were perfect for each other. I was the computer geek; he was the music geek. Together we were two peas in a pod, driven by our passion for machines or instruments. We connected, we laughed, and we had a grand old time. Our easy way together reminded me of what my parents had, and I wanted that kind of love. So after college, I married my best friend.

It seemed like a great recipe for a successful marriage. Everything between us had gone swimmingly as husband and wife, except in the bedroom. We'd learned we wanted different things from a lover. Fine, lack of bedroom chemistry wasn't the ultimate barometer for the success or failure of a marriage, but I didn't excite him, and he didn't excite me, and the things we tried to spice up our love life fell flat.

The time I'd asked him to pull my hair and talk dirty to me had resulted in him calling me a *hot bitch* as he tugged gently on my strands. He then broke into peals of laughter, clutching his belly as he said, "I'm sorry. I just can't say things like *I want you on your hands and knees now, woman.*"

That was where I wanted to be though.

And that was where he wanted to be too, because he'd

inquired casually one evening over our second pinot noir if I might want to try a threesome with another guy.

"Maybe someone who could say those things to both of us? Who could give all kinds of those sexy, dirty orders you like?" he asked.

My ex-husband went both ways, and when he went, he submitted. Which meant we didn't and wouldn't and couldn't ever gel. There was simply no room for two submissives in a marriage.

But was that the right word for me? I didn't really know if the term fit me, since I'd never been in that type of relationship. My experience was limited to Holden and to a college boyfriend who'd been rather "fratty" in bed.

Still, I knew what turned me on. I knew what I fantasized about.

Being dominated. Being taken. Being tied up. Even if I'd never fully experienced that type of lover, I was sure of what made my blood heat up and my body spark. Fantasies tripped through my mind late at night in bed, alone, and they often involved being pinned.

Bound.

Tied.

After struggling to make it work between the sheets, Holden and I had both agreed we'd be better off friends than lovers. The transition away from him wasn't wholly easy, and there had been times when I'd felt unsure of myself and my femininity. But we made a pact to stay the close friends we always had been.

A talented pianist, Holden had both toured the world and played in recording sessions for commercials and jingles, and he'd be joining the symphony at the concert I'd arranged in two weeks to raise money for the community center. "Do you think Clyde will try to marry you off again at the concert?" Holden asked.

I wrapped my fingers around the edge of the piano. "He's bringing a boy-child to the event. I have no doubt he wants to pawn me off on his lawyer grandson, and he thinks if he can just get us in the same room, we'll fall madly in love."

Holden shuddered dramatically. "Being the *glamorous divorcée*"—he sketched air quotes as he used the moniker that a Vegas high-society blog had bestowed on me—"isn't all it's cracked up to be, is it?"

I swatted his shoulder. "You're a glamorous divorcé too."

"Oh yeah. They're lining up in droves for a piece of me," he said with a wink.

Piece of me. My mind flashed back to a couple of nights ago at Aria, and to the commanding way Ryan Whoever He Was had controlled my pleasure backstage. A frisson of longing raced through me. I craved his touch again.

"Hello? Did you just drift off to la-la land?" Holden asked, waving his hand in front of me.

I blinked then grinned, caught in the act of remembering a hot encounter. "I did. Because I met someone the other night, and we had a fantastic time."

Holden patted the piano bench. "Sit. Tell me everything."

I sat on the bench and recounted the details. Not all of them. Not the particularly naughty ones. But the tidbits about how we met, and how he showed up at the gala, and how I barely knew anything about him.

"Which I like," I added. Perhaps I liked it so much because it was the opposite of my experience. I'd known everything about Holden, I'd gone in with my eyes wide open, and we hadn't worked out.

I knew virtually nothing about Ryan. Maybe the change was what I needed. To go into this thing blindfolded.

Wait. Add that to the list of things I wanted to try. *Blindfold.*

"Be careful," Holden said in warning. "He could be anyone."

"That's why it's fun."

"That's also why it's dangerous."

I nodded. "I know. I like danger."

"I just don't want to see you get hurt," he said, patting my knee.

"It's only fun and games. I'm not interested in anything more. In fact, I hope I never learn his last name," I said as I crossed my legs and kicked a foot back and forth, demonstrating how completely content I'd be in that scenario.

Even though, truth be told, I was terribly curious about the man behind the orgasm.

9

SOPHIE

So many sartorial choices.

On the one hand, the sun-yellow dress hugged my hips quite nicely.

On the other hand, the red one with the tiny white polka dots did offer a nice little cleavage peekaboo.

As I tapped my finger against my lips on Sunday afternoon, weighing the options for tonight in my perfectly organized, neatly arranged, color-coordinated closet, my phone buzzed from the back pocket of my jeans, signaling a text.

Absently, I reached for the phone, noticing the time. Seven more hours until my date. Four hundred twenty minutes. Twenty-five thousand, two hundred seconds.

Then I spotted the first line of the text.

Oh.

Oh my.

As I opened it, my belly flipped, my body lighting up simply from the intoxicating memory of his backstage skills.

Ryan: This is Ryan. Question. Are you afraid of heights?

A grin spread quickly across my face. I hadn't expected to hear from him until I saw him this evening. And he hadn't asked for my number either. He must have put those security skills to work to find it. I liked that he'd been hunting for me. I liked it a lot.

Sophie: What a lovely surprise to hear from you.

Ryan: I had your number thanks to the woman who tried to corral you at the event to talk about decorating. At one point you told her to call you, and she rattled off your number. I was impressed she remembered any number.

Sophie: I'm impressed *you* remembered it.

Ryan: It's only the number I wanted most in the world.

Sophie: And now I have yours too, so . . . lucky me. And no, I'm not afraid of heights. Should I be? Are you, say, taking me to the moon?

Ryan: Among other things, I will indeed be taking you on that kind of trip.

Sophie: Interesting. But how can you be so confident about this trip around the moon?

Ryan: Because I've already taken you there. And I'm glad you're not afraid of heights since that helps with what I have planned for tonight.

Sophie: Ah, we're going on a hot-air balloon ride over the Strip, right?

Ryan: Nice guess. Or maybe I plan to take you on the roller-coaster at New York-New York.

Sophie: Then why are we meeting at Caesars?

Ryan: To throw you off the scent of my plan, which is perfect, by the way. And because I suspect you like surprises. And roller-coasters too.

Sophie: Incidentally, I'm quite loud on roller-coasters.

Ryan: I have not yet had the pleasure of hearing the highs you can hit vocally. You came quietly the other night.

Sophie: And is that something you wish to know? My vocal range? Rather than my silent cries of pleasure?

Ryan: It's not just something I wish to know. It's something I intend to discover tonight.

Sophie: I suppose it is in your hands, then, to find out how high I can go.

Ryan: Hands maybe. Or could be other parts of my anatomy. Perhaps I should amend my plans for tonight and take you on that roller-coaster ride after all. On second thought, I'm just going to keep the plans to myself and surprise you. But wear a skirt tonight.

. . .

My pulse sped up at the command in his last text. I was about to reply with something saucy when his final text appeared.

Ryan: On a more serious note, it's not right for me to know your name and occupation and for you not to know the same. Not in this day and age. So, here's me. And I will see you in five hours, twenty-three minutes.

I hovered my index finger over the link at the end of the text.

The game had been fun, almost like a masquerade ball. Now he had changed the game and removed his mask. Asking me if I wanted to look.

How could I not?

I was a cat in front of an open box, and the cat had no choice but to slink inside and explore its contents. That man had sparked my mind and ignited my body, and hell, it was natural to want to know more about him. So, from the cozy cocoon of gold and cranberry-red pillows on my bed, I clicked on the link to his company website.

Sloan Protection Resources.

The site had a rugged, sturdy, and masculine look with black-and-gray colors and imposing fonts. Completely fitting with what the company was selling—armed private security, event security, bodyguards, guard dogs, and more. The mission statement on the home page read: "We provide secure solutions to a wide range of individuals, corporations, nonprofit organizations, and government customers. We are committed to helping businesses and individuals operate in a safe and secure environment that will enable them to prosper."

Interesting.

I vaguely wondered if any of my event organizers had relied on Sloan Protection Resources. Or if some of my wealthiest benefactors did. I suspected the answer was yes, and that Ryan Sloan and I trafficked in the same circles even though we hadn't met until the other day.

I clicked on the "About Us" page, and was greeted by a photo that made my heart stutter and other parts heat up.

The picture was of two strong, tall men—clearly related —in suits, with arms crossed and serious looks on their faces. My eyes were drawn to Ryan, with his slightly wavy light-brown hair, midnight-blue eyes, and firm, strong, toned body the suit didn't even try to hide. He was tailor-made for the part of strong, sexy businessman.

A murmur fell from my lips as I brushed my fingertip across his image. Then, clicking on his name, I jumped farther down the page and found his bio.

Ryan Sloan is one of the founders of Sloan Protection Resources. A native of Las Vegas, Ryan attended the University of Michigan, where he played on the hockey team. After graduating with a bachelor's degree in history, he spent five years in the United States Army, completing his service as a captain, like his brother Michael. The two of them founded Sloan Protection Resources six years ago. Together they are committed to ensuring the highest level of safety for their clients, and rely on trained teams of former law enforcement, military, and security professionals who are state certified and skilled in the latest tools and tactics.

My grin spread along with a burst of warmth through my chest. That was just . . . sexy.

And hot.
And so very dominant.

10

SOPHIE

I was early for once.

Only because I told myself over and over that our date started an hour sooner. I'd even set the alarm on my phone to leave my building at five thirty, which had given me the necessary thirty minutes to walk to Caesars and make it to the Fizz Bar

I didn't want to be late for my date, so I'd tricked my own overactive mind.

Now that I was here, I kept myself entertained outside the bar, playing the slots, settling in at the Wizard of Oz machine for several rounds.

The little hand on the clock landed on seven. On the dot.

"I see you didn't heed my instructions."

My lips quirked up in a wicked grin as the deep, sexy voice of my date reached my ears. I turned around and drank in the sight of Ryan Sloan, who looked just as lickable minus the tie and tailored suit I'd seen him in for our first encounter. Tonight he wore crisp charcoal pants that showed off a fantastic ass, the kind you could bounce a quarter off of, and a white button-down that demanded to be unbuttoned. Such a simple look, but a sexy one. Casual, but classy.

"Perhaps I was feeling a little defiant," I said playfully, taking the time to cross my legs and show off the skinny jeans I wore, in direct disobedience of his skirt request.

For some reason, the prospect of going against his fashion demand had felt like naughty mischief, and naughty mischief was irresistible.

I looked away from him and pressed the button once more on the one-armed bandit, hoping for a trio of glittery red slippers. "Over the Rainbow" played as the reel spun, and I awaited my lineup, eager for a winning jackpot. No such luck. Sliding into place were a tin man, a lion, and a wicked witch, who cackled in mockery. I pouted. "I guess my luck has run out on this machine. Are you a bad luck charm?" I teased as I glanced up at my too-handsome-to-be-believed date.

Ryan's hand came down on my neck firmly, but his voice matched my lighthearted tone. "I don't mind your defiance," he said, returning to my earlier comment. "As long as you don't mind having to wait longer for all the good things I have planned for you."

Instantly, my brain was awash with images, fantasies, and filthy scenarios I'd only dreamed of. I wanted *all the good things*.

"What sort of good things?" I asked, shivering as he touched me, his big palm wrapping around my neck. I closed my eyes as he traveled up to my nape. He threaded his fingers in my hair, gripping my locks. I tensed. His hand was sending a message, one that his mouth made abundantly clear when he bent his head to my ear and spoke.

"The kind that a skirt makes possible," he said as he tugged my head back so I had to stare up at him.

"You don't like the way I look in jeans?"

"I love the way you look in anything because you're extraordinary to look at, and even more phenomenal to touch. But I especially like the *access* your skirts give me." His lips were mere millimeters from my ear. He flicked his tongue against my earlobe, and I gasped. Then he drew the soft flesh into his teeth and bit. A burst of excitement whipped through me at his touch. Holden had never bitten me like this. Not with a sense of ownership.

Ryan ran a hand along the bare skin of my arm, on display in my black blouse with cap sleeves. The sheer material revealed a tight lacy camisole underneath, which pushed up my breasts, showcasing ample cleavage.

"Maybe I wanted to make sure you didn't forget about other parts of me," I said, casting a glance down at my chest, letting him follow.

Ryan laughed deeply then shook his head, seemingly in admiration of the view. He let go of his firm hold and kissed my neck, a soft and unbearably sexy kiss. I nearly squirmed on the plush red stool parked in front of the gambling machine. "Sophie, there's not a chance in hell I'd forget those gorgeous breasts, and I plan on getting better acquainted with them. Maybe even fucking them," he said as he dragged a finger along the bare flesh of my chest, and I nearly moaned out loud at the prospect of being fucked in the valley of my breasts by this dirty, dominating man. "Would you like that?"

I nodded as heat flared through my system. "I believe I would," I whispered.

"Excellent. Because I believe I would like to do that to you. There are many things I want to do to you, and I always want you to feel good."

"I'd say you're meeting your goal because so far it's all good," I said, pausing before I added, "*Quite* good."

He grinned. "And you should always tell me what you like and don't like. Does that work for you?"

"Yes." Anticipation bloomed inside me as we made some sort of impromptu pact to govern our pleasure.

"And I'll do the same," he said, bending closer to my head as he ran his nose along my hair, inhaling my scent. He murmured as he touched me, then kissed a curl on the side of my face. "Like right now when I tell you I really don't like that you didn't listen to me. And do you know what that means?"

I raised an eyebrow. I'd never experienced this sort of cat-and-mouse play before. By wearing jeans in defiance, had I violated some unwritten rule of the tie-me-up-and-take-me game? A squadron of nerves docked in my belly, and I wished I had more experience with men like Ryan. My knowledge of the opposite sex was woefully limited, and while I wasn't innocent by any stretch, I felt a bit like a wide-eyed woman recently freed from an unusual marriage and thrust into an unknown battlefield with this intense, commanding man.

That was the point, of course. Still, I was a traveler wandering through a lush new land without a map.

Whether I'd been *disobedient* or not, this back-and-forth we had going was intoxicating, especially since we were in public, ensconced in the middle of the Caesars Palace slot machines, amid the whir and jingle of imaginary coins falling as gamblers hunted for payouts in the games of chance.

The cowardly lion roared idly from my game, trying to entice me to play another round. I ignored it.

"No. Tell me what it means," I said, turning to face him and running my lacquered fire-engine red nails along his arm. I could feel the outline of his muscles, his strong biceps, his steely forearms, through the fabric of his shirt. "I'm dying to know."

"You want to know?"

I nodded, keeping my gaze firmly fixed on his. His dark-blue eyes were hungry. He looked as if he wanted to eat me. "Are you going to spank me?"

"Would you like that?"

A shiver of anticipation ran across my skin. "I think I would," I said in a whisper.

He knitted his brow. "You think? You don't know?"

I shook my head, biting my lip. "I've never been spanked."

He let out a low whistle of regret. "That's a damn shame, because you have a highly spankable ass. But this is music to my ears, because I fully intend to break it in," he said as he moved his hand down my back along the fabric of my shirt, heading in the direction of my, evidently, quite spankable ass.

"I suspect I'd like your hands on my ass," I said, and he groaned—a sexy, dirty rumble that turned me on. "So are you going to spank me on the roller-coaster? In the hot-air balloon? Or in the secret private jet you'll be piloting tonight?"

"None of the above. You're going to have to wait for all the good things now. That's what happens when you don't listen."

"Ah, so that's my punishment for my impudence. How long must I wait?"

He offered me a hand and pulled me up from my stool. "Until you're wearing a skirt," he answered crisply. The stern look in his eyes said he was serious, and that he could wait for me to change. He'd be waiting a lot less time than he thought.

"Right now, though, I want to spend some time getting to know you. That's why I bought tickets to the High Roller," he said, mentioning the Ferris wheel nearby. "So I can chat with you as we ride. Because you're far too classy a woman for me to get you off in front of all the other people riding in our pod."

"Why, thank you for opting not to get me off in a pod. But you know it's become a *thing* in Vegas now, trying to have sex on the Ferris wheel."

He nodded. "Yeah, and most people get busted. There's a difference between trying to get a tacky, tasteless notch on your public sex belt, and knowing how to pleasure a woman in public so that you're the only one who knows she's about to fall apart in your arms."

"And I trust you know the difference?"

He cupped my cheek, drawing my face near to his so his nose touched mine. How was it possible that touching noses was sexy? But even this made me sizzle. Then his words scorched my imagination as he said, "What I know, Sophie, is exactly what I want to do to you. And you'll just have to wait to find out."

He grazed his lips against mine, and I murmured as I melted into his touch. Our first kiss at the gala had been hungry and demanding. Ferocious and possessive. This was a soft, slow, unhurried kiss. It was an exploration, as his mouth caressed mine and my body turned soft and pliant under his touch.

His touch made me weak-kneed, hazy, and buzzed. And as he laced his fingers through my hair and held the back of my head in his hand, I gave myself over to him, letting him have me however he wanted.

When we separated, he whispered, "But kisses in public are good. They show everyone you're with me tonight, and that turns me on—having you with me." His tone, too, sounded thoroughly possessive. Then he laughed. "Which means I better sit and play a round, otherwise I'll be walking around with that fact on display."

He parked himself on the stool. In a flash, he pulled me back to him so I was seated on his lap. "Mmm," I said, wriggling against his erection. "Not sure this is going to help get rid of the issue."

He gripped my hips, the pressure pulling me down against his dick so I could feel his hard length lining up perfectly against my ass. Damn, he felt good.

He stretched out his arm and pressed the button on the machine. "Maybe you're *my* lucky charm."

I crossed my fingers in the air as we waited for the reel to roll through thousands upon thousands of permutations, and I rocked my rear subtly but insistently against his crotch. His breath hitched. He dug his thumbs harder into my hip bones, as if he needed to hold on to survive having me on his lap.

The reel slowed. One ruby red slipper. Then another. My shoulders tensed in anticipation and hope. "Please let it be another slipper," I murmured, then sighed when a witch's broom busted our chances. "Damn," I muttered.

"I don't mind losing. We can just stay here playing all evening because I like the way you feel sitting on me."

"You'll get no complaints from me. But we don't want to miss the High Roller."

He glanced at his watch. "We have time."

We played a few more rounds, losing every one. But it didn't matter, because his arms were wrapped around my waist and he held me close in his lap, a delicious start to my second rendezvous with this man who was not as much of a mystery as he'd been the first night, but who was now even more enticing. Perhaps it was knowing his name, or maybe it was our text exchange earlier. It might even be the naughty compliments he continued to rain down on me. It was all drawing me in.

"How's your dog?" I asked as the sound of a tornado grew louder from the machine. Dorothy's home was churning in the cyclone during this spin.

He chuckled. "You remembered I have a dog."

"Of course I do. You had to walk him—he's a demanding border collie. Is he totally adorable?"

"Ha. I suppose. Mostly I just think of him as badass."

"Got any pictures?"

He shook his head. "No, but if you're a good girl, I'll send you one."

"All the more reason to be good," I quipped. "What's his name?"

"Johnny Cash," he said, with the swagger it called for.

"That is a cool name."

"He is a cool dog. Loyal. Smart. Devoted. And a great listener."

"Sounds perfect. How'd you pick it?"

"My dad's favorite musician."

"Does your dad live in town?"

Ryan shook his head. I looked back at him. A kind of darkness had descended over him, and I processed quickly that he hadn't used a verb when talking about his father. "Oh, I'm sorry. Is he gone?"

Ryan nodded.

I sighed wistfully. "Mine too. Both my parents died two years ago."

He squeezed my arm affectionately. "Sorry to hear that."

"Actually, they were both older. Not terribly old, but late seventies. They met in their late thirties and had us in their early forties. They died within three months of each other. They were ridiculously in love even at the end."

"I can't imagine," he said, his voice hollow. The empty sound made me want to ask why he couldn't imagine loving someone until the end of your life. But it was too soon to press. Besides, I wasn't even sure I wanted to know his answer. Better not to go there. I danced away from the topic, returning to more comfortable second-date terrain as I pointed at the pair of flying monkeys that had landed alongside a shiny red apple in the last spin.

"So, Ryan Sloan, former Army captain, now head of Sloan Protection Resources . . . Flying monkeys." I tapped the screen. "Your verdict—are they fearsome or comical?"

He laughed, and in that sound, the tension deflated. "Absolutely fucking terrifying. When I was a kid, I ran from the room every time the flying monkeys came on." Then he squeezed the side of my rear lightly. "We should head to the High Roller."

I stood up from my seat on his lap and held up a finger. "Give me two minutes."

With my purple leather purse on my shoulder, I popped into the ladies' room at the other end of the slots, shimmied out of my jeans, and slid into a short, flowy pink skirt that hit me just above the knees and offered a perfect amount of lift if I twirled. I folded my jeans in half, then tightly rolled them and stuffed them into a side compartment of my purse.

I returned to Ryan.

And twirled once.

His jaw dropped when he saw the changeup.

"See? I'm not all naughty. I can be a good listener," I said with a flirty tilt of my head, as I jutted my hip out and ran my hands along the outside of the pink skirt with the white polka dots.

"You're the perfect amount of naughty," he said, his voice smoky as he drank me in from head to toe, from my black patent leather heels with the strap across the instep, to my bare legs, to my revealing blouse. "You're going to be rewarded so well for doing as you were told."

11

RYAN

With a hand on her lower back, I guided her past the lines at the High Roller Ferris wheel and straight to the head of the VIP queue. One of the highest Ferris wheels in the world, the ride circled to more than five hundred feet in the air and offered a majestic view of the skyline and bright neon lights of the city.

The attendant opened the door to one of the space-agey, glass-encased pods. Sophie and I weren't alone in the spacious capsule with the panoramic view, but it wasn't crowded either. We staked a claim at one end of the oval, and I leaned my hip against the railing, facing my date.

My stunning, gorgeous, sexy, naughty, and sweet date.

Soon, the observation wheel began to move, slowly rising higher as each capsule filled with passengers on the first revolution. "Hope you didn't mind too much that I sent you the link to my bio. That, coupled with my dog's name, means you know everything there is to know about me," I joked.

"Absolutely. I can't think of a single other thing that I'd be curious about."

I wiped a hand across my brow as if to say *whew*. "Okay, so we're done with the résumé basics and we can move on to favorite TV shows and movies, then?"

She laughed, a bright and pretty sound that seemed to match her personality and her bold sense of style. Not that I was well versed in women's fashion, but the way this woman dressed caught my eye and sparked my imagination. She had a va-va-voom look to her that was my kryptonite. She was all gorgeous, sexy, voluptuous woman, and she knew how to show off her assets.

I couldn't look away from her if I tried.

"Actually, I think someone's favorite show can be quite telling. I wouldn't mind knowing yours," she said, then did that utterly sexy thing she'd done at the slot machine, where she ran her hand along my arm. Okay, it wasn't, like, some signature move or anything. But the combination of her long nails, the glint in her blue eyes, and the wild flirtatiousness in her tone turned me on something fierce.

As she had from the second I met her.

"*Top Gear*," I answered easily.

"You like fast cars."

I nodded. "I do. And it's just a kick-ass show."

"I bet you'd like to drive my Aston Martin someday," she said, brushing her fingertips over my bicep now.

I nodded eagerly. "I'd love to get behind the wheel of that baby. What about you?"

"My favorite show?"

I shrugged happily. This was a simple enough topic. "Sure. Tell me."

"*The Marvelous Mrs. Maisel* for the fashion," she said, counting off one finger. "Dancing competition shows because they're gorgeous to watch. And *Orange Is the New Black* because it reminds me to always be a good girl."

I forced a laugh at the last one and decided not to touch

it, even though I was tempted to make a dirty comment about being a good girl. But I couldn't chance any conversation drifting into that territory—the behind-bars territory. I returned to the middle choice. "My sister is a choreographer. She's done some work on a reality dance show."

Sophie arched an eyebrow. "Ooh! Which one?"

"*Dance All Night*," I said, naming the show that Shannon had worked on.

Her eyes lit up. "Get out of here!" She slugged my arm.

I ran my hand over the spot where she'd hit me, pretending it hurt. "Ouch."

"I'll kiss it and make it better," she said, planting a quick kiss on my arm. Damn, that felt good, even through the fabric of my shirt. She raised her face. "I absolutely adore *Dance All Night*. There's a one-night reunion show coming up, and I already have it marked on my calendar to make sure I don't schedule anything else that night."

My grin spread, anticipating Sophie's next reaction. "I know about the reunion. She's choreographing that too. My sister is Shay Sloan. She runs Shay Productions," I said, using Shannon's business name.

Sophie grabbed my arm, wrapping her fingers around it and squeezing hard. "Are you kidding me? I *love* her shows. I've seen the live ones too. I saw her show at the Wynn. Please tell her I'm a huge fangirl."

"I will," I said, and the words surprised me. I didn't usually discuss my romantic life with my sister, or my two brothers either. I didn't usually date anyone long enough to mention them to the most important people in my life— my siblings. So it was odd that I'd so easily promised to tell Shannon about Sophie's adoration of her work. Odder still —talking about my family with Sophie didn't make me want to run for the hills. Even when we'd landed on the topic of my father earlier, I hadn't shut down as I normally would. Because I didn't share pieces of myself with women. I didn't like to get close. I didn't do relationships.

It was weird not to be breaking out in hives right now.

"I wish I knew how to dance," Sophie said wistfully. "I have absolutely no skills in that arena whatsoever. I'm pretty sure I can't even manage a basic fox-trot."

I leaned in and whispered, "Confession: I don't even know what a fox-trot is. Besides, I think you danced pretty damn fine with me the other night."

"Dancing with you was easy. I just aimed to press my body as close to yours as I could."

"Good rule of thumb. Keep it up, because you feel spectacular pressed up against me," I said.

"Imagine how spectacular I'd feel . . ." she began, then let her voice trail off as she danced her fingers down the front of my shirt and whispered, "*naked.*"

I drew in a hiss and narrowed my eyes. "You are too tempting." It was a warning, even though it was an invitation too.

"I think you like being tempted by me," she answered, licking her lips.

I liked it far too much. I was so damn hard there was no breathing room for my dick. Especially when my eyes landed on her pouty red lips, which would look so good wrapped around me. Her red lips meeting my dick . . . I nearly groaned out loud. I wanted that so badly. Wanted it from her. I couldn't imagine anything hotter than her gorgeous head bobbing up and down between my legs.

I shoved a hand through my hair, as if that would reroute my brain. "Talk about something else," I instructed with a huff.

She nodded. "So you've got one sister, and you have a brother too, your bio said. Three of you?"

Ah, nothing like family to make an erection vanish. I held up four fingers as the pod rose higher into the night, creating the illusion of floating above the brightly lit city and its landmark skyline. "There are four of us. Shay"—I used my sister's public name—"and Colin are twins. Michael and I run the security firm. Shay is the choreographer, and Colin is a venture capitalist. He lives here too."

"You all have fascinating jobs. That's so cool. And sounds like you're close."

I nodded. That was the understatement of a lifetime. In spite of my secrets, the four of us were as tight as any set of siblings could ever be. Our history, and our tragedy, had cemented our bond. The four of us had come to rely on each other, as well as the grandparents who had raised us after our father was killed and our mother was sent to prison.

"We're very close," I echoed, twisting my index finger around the middle one as if to show the connection between the Sloans.

"I'm close to my brother too. Especially since it's the two of us now. He's here in Vegas as well."

"Oh, is he?" I asked, keeping my voice even and normal, as if I'd just learned this fact for the first time.

"I basically adore him, even though I love to give him a hard time about his job and his coworkers. He's a detective with Metro so it's all very macho and guy-centric at his office."

I put on my best *isn't that interesting* face, feeling only the slightest bit weaselly at fishing for information. "That must be an intense job."

"Intense definitely describes John. He's a total workaholic. Honestly, he doesn't have to work as much as he does. He chooses to."

"What do you mean, doesn't have to?"

"He was my primary investor. He funded my company with his savings account. Basically everything he'd ever gotten as a kid—from the jobs he worked, his neighborhood lemonade stand, money gifts from relatives on birthdays—everything. He put it into my company when I started it—he was the seed investor. So, when I sold it, he profited too. I joked that he could retire like me, but he said, 'Never.' He has too much work to do putting criminals behind bars."

A tight line of tension coiled through me. I wasn't a criminal, but I'd been born to a woman branded as one. "He sounds pretty driven," I said, doing my best to refrain from prying. The less I said, the better off I'd be if Sophie ever found out I'd had business with her brother. Not that she would. I didn't date anyone long enough to meet their family.

She lowered her voice to the barest thread as we reached the top of the observation wheel. "John had a close friend who was an innocent bystander, shot in a drive-by gang shooting when we were younger."

"That's terrible," I said, a dose of rage coursing through me. He knew far too well, then, what it felt like to lose someone to a bullet. "How old?"

"David was fourteen when it happened. Same as John," she said, her voice breaking a bit. "He was a good friend of ours."

I gripped her hand tighter, and then instinct told me to drop a quick, comforting kiss on her forehead. Her skin was so soft. "I'm sorry," I whispered. "I was fourteen when—"

I cut myself off. Damn near kicked myself too. What the hell? I didn't go around offering up bits and pieces of my family story. I'd already shared more about my father than I ever had. I couldn't believe I'd been about to say more.

Something about this woman, maybe her willingness to share little details of her life, was working its way under my skin and tricking me into offering up more than I wanted to.

But closeness led to commitment, and commitment led to resentment, and resentment led to losing your parents when you were fourteen. And that led to your head and heart being fucked forever by not knowing who to trust or who to believe. To your mother telling you over and over she didn't do it, even as the cops arrested her and the jury sentenced her to life in prison.

And worst of all, it meant your father became faded photographs and memories that blurred around the edges. I was left with only faint reminders of camping trips and time spent traipsing around Vegas with my dad.

"Fourteen when . . .?" she asked leadingly. "Oh, when your dad passed away?"

Sophie was giving me a way out, unknowingly providing a safe landing. Hell, I needed one, given the way my mind had been spiraling, turning my insides into a treacherous knot. I nodded. "And your brother lost his friend too?"

She clasped her hand over her mouth and squeezed her eyes shut. "Oh God. I'm so sorry," she said when she opened her eyes. "I didn't mean to imply David was killed. I should have been more clear. David's paralyzed."

"Wow. And all because of a drive-by shooting," I said, shaking my head in disgust. No fake emotion there.

"It was some kind of retaliation shooting over territory. That's what really drove John to become a detective. Our dad was a fruit salesman, of all things," she said with a laugh. "Fruit salesmen don't usually have cops for sons. But then this happened to John's best friend, and it led him to want to clean up the streets."

I couldn't help but wonder if John had a personal stake in the investigation of my father's murder, if the gang connection had caught his eye because of his own goal to rid the town of street gangs. If that was the case, John must be betting on my dad's murder having deeper ties to the Royal Sinners.

Shit.

My gut churned, my emotions yanked in too many different directions. Desire to know more warred with the need to backpedal from this discussion.

"That is some heavy stuff," I said, staying vague. Even if I wasn't poking and prodding, I should know better than to try to glean a little bit of intel about the detective from his sister, who I was more and more drawn to.

But when your mom's in prison, and your dad's in the ground, and the men in charge think someone else might be involved, you don't always do the right thing. Sometimes you poke. "I bet he has some stories about what he's seen," I said, immediately wanting to zip my mouth shut for having led the witness.

"He hardly tells me anything. But when he does, it's usually laced with skepticism," Sophie said, tucking a strand of hair that had fallen loose behind her ear. So strange to have this conversation up here, surrounded by people chattering and watching the night sky pass through the glass windows.

"Why's that?"

"Detectives are naturally skeptical. It's their job."

"Ah. Of course," I said, and a bead of guilt gathered in my veins as I let Sophie continue to talk freely.

"Think about it. They spend their days getting lied to. By suspects. By criminals. Even by family members.

Almost all of the people they interact with hold back. No one ever offers the full truth to a detective. And if someone rolls over, they only do it for their own best interest, because they have information that might lessen their own crime. Not for altruism." She pinned me with a sharp gaze as she made her point, and the guilt inside me stirred. "Even witnesses who have some key piece of information will usually only offer it up if it helps them. It happens all the time. Just the other night, John mentioned he'd talked to someone who he was sure knew some key details in a case, but the guy wouldn't tell him."

Was John talking about me? Giving Sophie details of the case? The possibility was so damn enticing. I was dying to know. But guilt knocked louder inside me, telling me to stop hurtling down this path of deception with Sophie. She hadn't a clue that I was likely one of those witnesses her brother didn't trust.

I needed to focus just on this woman and forget the tenuous link between sister and brother, woman and cop. Besides, I had friends in the district attorney's office. My hockey buddy from high school was now an assistant DA, and now that Marshall was back in town from his vacation, I didn't need to sniff around this gorgeous woman and take advantage of her open heart.

I stared off in the distance, the city turning blurry as my eyes went out of focus, and I shoved off the questions running through my head about Jerry Stefano, the shooter, and the people my mother associated with, and anyone else who might have been involved in the murder. I blinked, refocusing to the here and now. To the best second date I'd had in ages. To the only one in a long time that made me want to have a third date.

"Do you like it up here?" I asked.

"The view is amazing," she said as she gazed at the endless sea of neon and night.

"I fucking love Vegas," I said, as I wrapped my arms around her waist and rested my chin on her shoulder, taking in the aerial show.

"You do?"

I nodded. "Yeah. This city will chew you up and spit you out, or it will embrace you and lift you up. Vegas always gives you the choice—to crawl in the gutter or soar in the sky."

"I choose soaring in the sky," she said softly.

"Me too."

So we soared, high above the city we both called home, hovering in the summer night sky as stars winked on and skyscrapers raced to the heavens. I loved this city. I loved my home, with all its troubles and problems and crimes. Maybe I wasn't that different from Sophie's brother. I wanted Vegas to be all that it could be.

I did my best to make that happen too.

She craned her neck to look up at me. "Would it be too bold to say I wanted you to kiss me again right now?"

"Kissing you is becoming a favorite habit of mine."

And so I kissed her. A lingering, luxurious kiss as the capsule swooped down toward the ground. But soon, the kiss climbed the heat scale, and by the time the observation wheel had completed its rotation, lust had camped out in my body and desire was ruling the rest of the night.

Good thing I'd booked a limo simply to drive around town. I needed to get her in it stat, and get her naked. Then, I'd regain some of the control I'd felt slipping away during all that talking.

12

SOPHIE

The gleaming white limo waited in the portico. The driver wore a black cap. A soft blue light glowed inside along the wood paneling of the bar where the champagne chilled.

That was all I saw in the three seconds after Ryan shut the limo door before he pounced on me.

There was no other way to describe it.

I was pinned on my back on the leather seat. His palms were planted firmly on either side of me, and he stared at me hungrily as sexy techno music played from a speaker near the bar.

"Are you still mad at me about the jeans?" I asked, my breathing coming quickly. The car began to hum as it pulled away from the hotel, vibrating gently as it rolled along the Strip in Sunday night traffic.

"Do I look mad?"

"A little."

"Does it turn you on if I'm angry with you?"

"Yes."

"I'm not mad. Because you have this," he said, lowering his hand between my legs and fingering the hem of my pink skirt. "If you hadn't brought it, I wouldn't do what I'm about to do. I'd send you home hot and bothered. Instead, I'm going to reward you."

"How will you reward me?" I asked, as anticipation flared through my nervous system. This moment was the cusp—the tantalizing precipice before we ignited. The way he gazed at me like a predator sent my temperature rising.

"Like this," he said, crushing my mouth in a kiss that scorched my body. He lowered himself onto me, and I moaned loudly at the delicious weight of his body. He was hard everywhere, and it turned me on beyond all reason, past all normal levels of arousal. His mouth was a hunter, marking me as his. He kissed me ferociously, and I could barely move underneath him, nor did I want to.

I'd never felt like this with my ex. Never. Our kisses had been playful and fun. Being kissed by Ryan was a mad claiming. His hand slinked down my side, and I gasped in pleasure, and that sound was swallowed up by his insistent lips on mine once more.

When he reached my ass, he squeezed one cheek, so hard I yelped. Then, in a flash, he'd moved from hovering over me to sitting. He pulled me on top of him so I straddled his legs, facing him.

"Change of plans?" I asked in between breaths.

"No," he said, pushing my skirt up so it bunched at my hips. "This is what I had planned." He gazed at my panties. Candy pink with a delicate heart-shaped bow. He ran his tongue over his top lip as he stared at my legs.

"They match the skirt," I offered, as if this detail was somehow vital.

"That they do," he said, and then I cried out as his hand landed on my ass. The sting radiated throughout my cheek.

"Did that hurt?"

"A little."

"But did you like it?"

I nodded. "A lot."

"Good. Because I loved it too." He rubbed his hand gently across my rear, soothing out the sting. "God, your ass is fucking perfect," he whispered with a kind of reverence that I'd never heard before. It thrilled me.

I tensed in anticipation as he lifted his arm again, and then his palm landed hard on my rear once more. I yelped as the sharpness spread. "Did that feel good too?" he asked.

I nodded on a pant, as he smoothed his hand against my backside, then he gathered the pink lace and tugged it inward.

My eyes widened in shock as it fully registered what he was doing. He'd turned my panties into a thong, wedging the material into a tight thread between my legs, so the front rubbed my clit and the back exposed my cheeks.

With his left hand, he gripped my chin roughly. The callous touch sent hot sparks down my belly on a mad dash to between my legs. "This is what you wanted, Sophie. You wanted to test me. To see what I'd do. To see what a man who loves taking charge of you would do."

I almost asked, *How did you know?* Instead, I asked something I longed to hear the answer to. "Do you love it?"

"I am obsessed with it," he said, his voice hot and filled with lust—a lust I'd inspired in him. That knowledge lit me up. I quivered, waiting for the next swat as he licked a path along my neck up to my ear, whispering with a dirty sort of awe, "I'm obsessed with your body. Your face. Your lips. Your ass. And I want to mark this beautiful, round, sweet ass with my palm."

He let go of my chin and looked in my eyes. He tugged on my panties, the tight fabric hitting my clit, setting off a chain reaction as he cracked his hand so damn hard on my ass that I flinched.

And grew wetter.

I was so immeasurably turned on from all these new feelings crashing into me, colliding inside my body in sweet, filthy bliss. My eyes fluttered closed as the sharp sting rippled through me. He rubbed his palm against my rear to erase the pain, and I whimpered at the quick shift from harsh to gentle.

Then I moaned loudly, because his hand was inside my panties.

"Seems you like it too," he said, and his fingers glided across the evidence.

"I do," I said, whimpering as he slid his expert fingers over me, then once again as he landed a biting slap on my rear with his other hand. Heat pooled between my legs from the hit, turning me into an inferno. I was learning that all my fantasies, all my dreams, all my wild imaginings of pain and pleasure were not only coming true, but I liked it.

No, I *loved* the mix of hurt and heat, of a sharp sting and a hot kiss. The evidence was on his fingers.

Then he gripped my hips and lifted me off him, laying me flat on my back again on the plush seats of the limo.

"Where's your purse?" he asked, glancing around.

I furrowed my brow, thrown off by the odd question. "My purse? It's over there," I said, pointing to the other side of the long car and the bench where I'd left my bag.

He stretched out and grabbed it.

"Why do you need my bag?"

"Do you trust me?" he countered, running his thumb along the slim strap of my purse.

I hardly knew him. But I'd already let him spank me, so I supposed in the context of the situation, the answer was that I did. The car slowed in traffic as I gave him a one-word answer.

"Yes."

His lips curved in a small smile, and he dropped a quick kiss on the hollow of my throat. Then he grabbed my wrists, held them together, and positioned them above my head so I was stretched out. When I turned my head to the side, I realized what he was doing—he'd wrapped the purse strap around my wrists and was tying the strap to the seat belt buckle. Next he reached for the hem of my skirt and gently tugged it down to ensure my punished ass didn't rub against the leather. Tied up and stretched taut on the seat, I was bound to his choices, yet somehow safe in his arms.

The prospect electrified me. All the planning and decisions and choices I managed all day long disappeared with this kind of letting go.

I breathed harder, lust and desire pent up inside me.

He kneeled at my feet on the end of the leather seat, his hands wrapped around my ankles. "I want to tie these gorgeous ankles too." He bent his head to my legs, dusting the bare skin of my calf with a kiss. My hips shot up.

He grabbed my panties, yanking them hard down my legs. "Say you want it too."

"I do, I do," I said quickly, the words spilling out.

With arms that moved like lightning, he had my pink lace at my ankles, and he turned the fabric in a knot, twisting the delicate lace. "I'll buy you new ones. Just like this."

He finished his work on my ankles and raised his head to meet my eyes. "You're so gorgeous, Sophie," he said, raking his eyes over my body. I was still fully clothed in my black blouse and pink skirt and black strappy shoes, but everything was in disarray and I didn't care one bit. He ran his hands up my legs, caressing the soft skin on the inside of my thighs.

"Look at you. So ready for me. So ready for however I'm going to take you," he said in a low, dirty growl. He reached the apex of my thighs, his thumbs brushing against my slick folds.

I gasped at his touch. "Take me," I whispered.

He was on all fours, bent over me, his face near my hot center, my trussed-up feet under his knees.

"Open your thighs as far as you can," he told me, and I did as commanded, parting my legs for him. In that position, I couldn't spread them in a V; instead, I opened into a diamond as one knee hit the side of the seat, the other the bottom.

"I love how turned on you get," he said as his gaze returned to my center. I ached. An exquisite, needy ache. He dragged one finger through my wetness, then brought that finger to his mouth. His eyes floated closed as he sucked off my taste, moaning as if I were his dessert.

I burned up all over from watching him savor me, from waiting for him to make contact.

He opened his eyes, breathing hard through his nostrils as he licked his lips.

Then he dropped his head between my legs, spread me open, and licked—a torturously slow lick up my center that had me singing his praises loudly, the music and the partition making the limo our own pleasure zone. He'd worked me up so much already that it wouldn't take long. He looked up. "You like that?"

"So much."

He brushed his finger against my throbbing clit, and I rocked my hips into his hand. "Say please," he said, his eyes blazing as he issued an order.

Oh God, we were playing again. I barely knew the rules. I was figuring it out as I went along. "Please don't stop. I'm dying for you. Please."

He dived back into my sex, licking and kissing and sucking. Making me tremble. Making me hot. Making me shudder. "Don't stop, don't stop, don't stop," I said over and over, and I meant it desperately. All I wanted was to come. To buck into his mouth and soar off that cliff of pleasure. To fall apart as he buried his face between my legs. With my arms stretched so tight I couldn't move, my ankles bound by my own panties, and Ryan kneeling over my hot, wet, pulsing center, I thrust upward.

He murmured and groaned, his hands curling around my ass gently, as if he was aware it still might hurt. But nothing hurt now. I only knew pleasure, only understood desire. Lust was our shared language, as his magic tongue drew wickedly wonderful lines up and down, flicking my clit, kissing my pussy. I screamed and writhed, calling out his name, shouting to the heavens that I was on my way to bliss. He sent me flying over that edge as I came hard.

A minute later, he'd untied my purse from the buckle. I lowered my arms to my waist—the strap was still wrapped around my wrists, my bag by my side.

"Sophie," he said, his voice gravelly and deadly serious. "I need something from you now. I'm desperate for it."

"Okay," I said, still loopy from the mind-blowing orgasm.

"Get down on your knees and suck me hard," he said as he stroked the thick bulge in his pants.

A fresh round of sparks rained down in my body at his dirty words. "Gladly," I said, so damn eager to taste him. "Want to untie me?"

He shook his head. "Yeah, that's the thing. I'm not going to."

Blow jobs were a hell of a good time, but I did a better job at blowing when I could use my hands. "But wouldn't it be—?"

He pressed a finger to my lips. "You said you trusted me, right?"

I nodded, even as a small swell of nerves rose up inside me. I could trust him, right? I wasn't being foolish, was I?

"Good," he said softly, running a hand through my hair. "Because I need you on your knees."

Oh Lord, how I'd longed to hear those words. How I'd craved to get on my knees for a man like this.

I dropped to the carpet, my hands tethered tightly to my own purse, which dangled in front of me, and I watched as he untucked his shirt and unzipped his pants. Arousal raced through me at the sight of him.

He pushed down his boxer briefs.

I drew in a sharp inhale at the sight of his gorgeous cock. My lips parted instantly, and my mouth watered with want. His dick was thick, hard, and long. He stroked it with his right hand, and the fire inside me roared. "Come here. Take me in," he whispered, and with his free hand, he grasped the back of my head, guiding me to his shaft. A drop of liquid was on the head, and my tongue darted out to taste it.

He grinned. "You like that?"

"I do," I said.

Gently, he tugged me closer. I opened my mouth wide, my lips tightening over my teeth as he fed me his dick.

"Yeah. Just like that, beautiful. Just like that," he said, his voice rumbling.

I'd never done this hands-free, but he tasted so good—the perfect mix of clean and musky, of sex and freshly-showered male—that I let go of my worry about not using my hands. Besides, I had no choice. I had only one instrument. My mouth.

He gently guided my head up and down, moving my

mouth along his cock at just the right speed. All I had to do was suck. I tightened my lips as he rocked into me.

"I pictured this the day I met you," he said on a loud moan.

I raised my eyebrows as if to say, *You did?*

"You were so stunning. In that dress. Those tits. That hair. The whole Marilyn Monroe thing you have going on," he said, roping his fingers through my hair. "I've wanted to have you from the second I laid eyes on you."

I sucked harder, listening to him tell the story of wanting me.

"I've wanted to fuck you from the second I saw you," he said on a thrust, filling my mouth. "I wanted to make you come," he said, as he curled his fingers tighter around my skull. "And I wanted to come in that pretty mouth of yours." And as he squeezed his eyes shut, he did just that.

13

RYAN

I scooped her up and set her down on the seat, still woozy from my own climax. But I wasn't so sex-drunk that I couldn't focus on taking care of her. Before pulling up my briefs, I unknotted her panties from her feet, untied her from her purse, set the bag down on the seat, and held up her wrists.

"How do they feel?"

She shot me a sly grin. "The purse is made of only the finest vegan leather, so they feel quite fine."

I laughed and dropped a kiss to her forehead, then tucked myself back in. She pulled her panties on, glancing down at them. "Hmm. They are a little stretched. But I don't regret it."

"Neither do I. And I promise to replace them immediately." I tipped my head to the bar. "Champagne?"

"I'd love some. You should have some too, especially since you don't have to do bone graft surgery tonight. Or so I presume."

"No. I don't. Lucky me," I said, then poured two glasses from the bar, handing one to her. I clinked my flute to hers then wrapped an arm around her, rubbing her shoulder and her neck as we chatted and drank the bubbly beverage while we rode around the city in the long, sleek car with no destination and no goal but time together.

Later, I had the driver take her to the front door of her building. I stepped out of the car with her, and before she left, I reached for her hand and kissed the top of it.

"You're beautiful. And dirty. And clever. And you take direction like a very good girl."

She batted her eyes in an over-the-top way as she sidled up against me. "Does that mean I've earned the dog photo?"

I squeezed her ass, savoring once more the way it felt in the palm of my hand. "You have absolutely earned it." Then I let go and looked her in the eyes, surprising myself a bit with the next words that escaped my mouth. "So, what would you think about a third date?"

For a moment I was nervous. I desperately wanted her yes, even though I was as sure as a man could be that I'd get it.

She shot me that bright, gorgeous smile that could light up a night sky. "I think I'd wonder how you plan on topping the first two, because they've both been spectacular. So I'd say yes out of curiosity."

She blew a kiss and left.

As the driver headed for my house, I tried to keep my mind blank to avoid the litany of questions I wanted to ask myself. But when Johnny Cash greeted me at the door, the questions tumbled free as I petted the dog's head. "What am I doing? What the hell am I doing? Because I am counting down the hours till I see her again."

The dog thumped his tail on the floor and whined. A sign he had to pee.

I took him to the backyard and wished I didn't like Sophie so much already.

* * *

The next morning, I sent Sophie her promised reward—a photo of Johnny Cash at his finest.

Ryan: Took this just now after our morning run. Hence the tongue lolling out of his mouth. And yeah, you can say it. He's adorable.

Sophie: He is so cute. I'm in love with your dog.

Ryan: He has that effect on women.

Sophie: He's not the only one. Johnny Cash is so handsome. If he were mine, I'd dress him in a cool leather jacket. Or maybe a trendy sweater, like a cardigan. With an elbow patch.

Ryan: He will never wear clothes, I promise you.

Sophie: You know, I once thought I wanted to be a fashion designer rather than a geeky coder.

Ryan: More like a pinup girl coder. How on earth did the computer science guys get any work done with you around?

Sophie: I assure you, I was quite geeky in college. I *never* wore skirts or dresses or high-heeled shoes.

Ryan: I refuse to believe you were geeky. Prove it with a photo.

Sophie: See? Case closed.

I groaned as I stared at the photos she sent. They must have been taken ten years ago, and yeah, she had the whole casual Converse-sneakers-sweatshirt-knit-cap look going on, the complete opposite of the woman I knew now. Still, she was hot then, and she was hot now, and no matter what, she turned me on. Fucking hell.

Ryan: Hot as hell. Gorgeous as heaven. Sexy as sin. You are just as deliciously enticing in jeans and a hoodie as you are in a tight dress. Everything looks good on you because you look good in anything. And everything. And especially in nothing.

Sophie: Same to you.

* * *

After a lunch meeting with a new client later that day, my phone rang. My spine straightened as I headed to the parking lot of the restaurant and answered John Winston's call.

"Hey," I said.

The detective said a quick hello then slid into business. "Mr. Sloan," he began, and I found it vaguely amusing that Winston was so formal with the way he talked. "I hope you don't mind, but I had another question for you."

"Sure," I said as I unlocked my truck and turned on the

radio. It was an old habit to have a little background noise during a private conversation.

"Luke Carlton. The piano teacher your mom had an affair with," Winston began, and I clenched my jaw, a visceral reaction to that name and that description. There was so very little anyone could say of my mother that was good. She'd had an affair, she was in prison for murder, she'd been a—

But I couldn't even say those words in my head.

"Was he ever at your home?" John asked. "Did your mom spend time with him at the house?"

I took a deep breath, letting the air work its way through my frustration at having to discuss her cheating. As if that was the worst thing. "Not really. She kept it pretty secret."

"Sure. Of course. I get that," the detective said, and I forced myself to compartmentalize, to see John solely as the detective and not as the brother of the woman I'd taken on a limo ride up and down the Strip last night. "Did they ever meet on James Street?"

I furrowed my brow. "James Street? Not that I know of. But that's a pretty long street. Cuts through a lot of town."

John laughed lightly. "Yeah. I know. That's the problem."

"Why are you asking?"

"Just trying to put some things together."

"Man, I wish I could help, but I sure as hell wasn't privy to the details of her affair," I said, though that wasn't entirely true. My mom had told me how much Luke had helped her to come out on the other side of the trouble she was in. But all that data fell under the *don't breathe a word* category. She'd warned me before she left for prison to guard those secrets, and I did—to keep her out of more trouble and to protect her honor, even from behind bars.

I'd buried that secret and hadn't breathed a goddamn word.

"Listen, I would really appreciate it if you could give me a call if you remember anything about their relationship."

I shoved a hand through my hair and nodded. "Of course."

The call ended, and I banged my head on the steering wheel.

What the fuck was I supposed to say to Sophie? *Your brother called me today to ask about my mom's lover from eighteen years ago?*

The last thing I wanted her to know about was my shit-storm of a past. I'd never met a woman I'd wanted to tell, but Sophie was already starting to feel different, and I had no clue how I'd even begin that conversation. I wished, I really fucking wished, that I could just be the man I was now. Not the guy whose family story had been dragged through the headlines in all its salaciousness years ago.

I only wanted the woman, not for the past to spill over into my present with her.

14

RYAN

The puck screamed across the ice, streaking right through the goalie's skates and smacking into the back of the net.

I raised my arms and cheered. My teammates echoed my excitement, skating over and clapping me on the back for putting us ahead with five minutes to go in the game. I skated off the ice with the line.

Breathing hard, my muscles working overtime from the intensity of the game, I grabbed my water bottle and gulped down some liquid. I momentarily parked myself on the bench with the line change.

"Good job," Marshall grunted with a pat on the knee.

"Gotta keep up with you," I said, since he'd scored the first goal in this game for the recreational league team we played on. We'd been playing together for years—all the way back to varsity high school. Marshall was as close to my inner circle as anyone could be.

"Hey, need to ask you a question," I said, lowering my voice as I tugged off my bulky gloves. "You told me a few weeks ago about Stefano being questioned by some of your attorneys for other crimes." Marshall had tipped me off about the visit before the investigation had reopened, but he'd been away on a family vacation for two weeks so this was the first time I'd been able to catch up on the details.

"Right," he said as he tightened his skates. "Some of my colleagues are working on that."

"Do you know anything more about it? Because a detective brought me in for questioning a week ago. He talked to Shan, Colin, and Michael as well. My grandparents too. He asked a lot of the same questions that the guy who investigated the first time around did, but some different ones as well. He really seemed to want to know who my mom was friends with and if there was anyone new in her life at the time," I said, speaking as casually as if we were catching up on the latest sports scores. It was damn nice, in a strange way, not to have to dig in and serve up my messy family story to someone. Hell, I couldn't remember ever having to tell Marshall at all—he simply knew because we'd grown up together.

Marshall gestured with his clunky gloved fingers for me to come closer. I scooted over as he spoke low. "Listen, you didn't hear this from me," he said, beginning with his usual caveat when he shared something he wasn't supposed to. I never violated that trust. "But Bianca Rosa came to us a few months ago. She told us she had some information."

My eyes widened at the sound of that name. I hadn't heard it in ages, hadn't thought of her since way back when.

Now I was damned curious what Jerry Stefano's girlfriend had had to say to the authorities.

15

BIANCA

A few months ago

My mother extended her arm and unclasped her gold bracelet with the bunny charm. "Here. Take my bracelet. For luck."

My stomach churned as I sat in the front seat of her parked car outside Applebee's, my knee shaking. "Do you think I need luck?"

"Baby," she said, stroking my hair, "we all need luck. You already have guts." She poked my stomach for emphasis.

I clicked on the bracelet, hoping to channel her strength. I raised my face. "I'm doing this, right?"

She nodded. "You're doing it. I've got your back. Just like I always have."

"You always have. Even when I didn't deserve it."

"Not true. You always deserved it. I always believed you'd come home."

"And I did."

Still, nerves skittered through me. I tried to ignore them, but I knew I'd only be able to let them go once I met with the authorities about what I'd heard.

My gut churned and my head ached with the sick, twisted realization of what I'd unwittingly been tied to for years. Decades, even.

I opened the car door and gave my mom one last look. "Wait for me?"

"Always. I waited for you when you were sixteen and confused and scared. I'll wait for you now," she said, and my heart squeezed. She'd welcomed me with open arms after I'd run away as a teenager—then returned just having given birth to a murderer's child. "And don't you worry. We will do everything we can to make sure Lee stays away from those guys. Whoever they are."

My son, nearly eighteen. The reason I was here. But not the only reason. I was here because, well, I liked to think I was a decent human.

And decent humans needed to tell the cops what they'd heard.

What they'd suddenly put together.

Head high, I strode across the parking lot and walked into the cool, air-conditioned Applebee's on the outskirts of Vegas, near my new home. I scanned the establishment, wondering briefly if there were any other recently minted paralegals meeting with law enforcement.

Maybe that table over there had a thirty-four-year-old mom telling a detective that she feared her former boyfriend had associates who were still in a gang, men whose names she didn't know, but who'd called and said they had been looking out for her son. Maybe in that booth there, a woman was revealing all those years ago she'd overheard her then-boyfriend making calls to meet with friends about a *job*.

And maybe at the counter, a woman was telling a local deputy, a DA, or a cop that she feared that said long-ago boyfriend wasn't the only one who ought to be behind bars.

Or, as I sat down across from the detective, maybe I was the only one here about to tell that story.

I extended a hand and introduced myself, saying the words I'd practiced with my mom: my rock, my strength. "I'm Bianca Rosa. I was involved with Jerry Stefano at the time of the murder of Thomas Paige, and I have new information that may be useful to the authorities."

The detective's blue eyes were caring, his voice gentle. "I'd love to hear it."

"I don't think Jerry acted alone. I don't know who his partners were, but we've been getting calls that make me believe he asked someone to look out for us when he went away." I swallowed roughly. "And I believe that based on things I overheard at the time, it's possible there were others involved."

"And why didn't you share this eighteen years ago?" It was a question, but not an accusation.

"I didn't fully realize it. I was sixteen and had run away from home. When Jerry told me he was meeting with some of his friends about a job, I didn't ask questions. He told me it was an honor thing. They worked together. They did everything together. *Honor*—he kept talking about honor and protecting each other on the job. I thought . . ." I paused, shook my head. "How stupid of me to think this, but I figured he was talking about tree trimming of all things. Like, they protected each other and looked out for each other on *those* jobs. It didn't seem like a big deal at the time, and then as soon as he was under arrest, I did what I knew how to do. I left."

"Where did you go?" he asked in that same calm tone.

"A woman's shelter in Idaho. Until I gave birth."

"Your disappearance was one of the unsolved mysteries of the case," he said.

"I know," I whispered, my voice cracking. "I was sixteen. I was a baby, and I was having a baby. That's all I could focus on."

"That's very young." His tone was sympathetic. "How is your son?"

I shrugged. My throat tightened like a noose. Tears pricked the back of my eyes. He'd been great, so great.

But then, he had too much of his father in him.

He was drawn to trouble, lured by the wrong side of the law.

Or maybe by bad people. I had a hunch he was starting to spend time with the same men who I feared had played a part in the murder Jerry went to prison for.

I only wished I knew their names.

But maybe this man could figure out that piece of the puzzle. Maybe then he could keep them away from my son. For now, I shared what they'd told me on the phone.

"'Jerry asked us to look out for you and for your son. We're bound by honor to do him right,'" I said, telling him exactly what they told me.

"That's why you called us? That's why you wanted to talk?"

I nodded fiercely. "That's when I started to think the code of honor extended to the job Jerry was serving a life sentence for."

16

RYAN

I couldn't believe what Marshall had just told me.

The cops had tried to talk to the shooter's girlfriend at the time of the murder, but she'd skipped town. No one had found her, and Colin had told me at the time that there were rumors that Stefano had had her killed.

I never believed those rumors. Skipping town when you found out the guy you loved was going to prison? That was much more believable. Turned out it was all too true.

"Apparently, that's why he took the job from your mom. Needed money for the kid. Bianca said she didn't know at the time that he was doing *those* kinds of jobs. She thought they were tree-trimming jobs, like he'd claimed at the time," Marshall said. "Anyway, once he was behind bars and the investigation was over, she went back to her family in Reno with the baby, and only moved back to the Vegas suburbs a year ago when she became a paralegal. Some of Stefano's friends have looked out for her and the kid over the years, a code of honor thing, unbeknownst to her, until they called to tell her they were looking out for her son. A code of honor thing, only it's hard to say what their honor truly means. And it's likely those friends were in the Sinners."

"Are they still?"

Marshall shrugged. "My guys don't know yet. All we know is Stefano asked them to keep his kid away from the Sinners. He wanted his son to have a shot at a new kind of life, different from his. But lately, he's been getting into trouble. Bianca's not too happy about them breaking their promise to keep her son safe from the gang, being in that world themselves."

Something about Marshall's info aligned with John Winston's questions. If the girlfriend was talking after all these years, maybe mentioning names that had been off the radar during the first investigation, it would make sense that Winston had been asking about any other people in my mother's life. "Were these buddies involved in my dad's murder?"

"That's the part we're trying to figure out. It's not even my case. It's not even at the level of a case yet, to be honest. Just an investigation. All I know is the detectives are looking into it. And you did not get this from me."

The coach slapped the white wood of the bench then pointed to the ice.

Marshall and I, along with the rest of the line, hopped over and went out on the rink, returning to the game. As I skated, I mapped out a plan. No reason I couldn't try to work the case too. John Winston might be the lead detective, but I could play that role on my own. It was my family, my life, and my story. I knew how to figure things out, and how to put two and two together. And I had a damn good notion of some of the people I needed to go see.

Later that night, I scheduled a piano lesson with a local teacher for later this week.

17

SOPHIE

"Wish me luck," I said as I pushed back from the table after a fantastic sushi lunch with Holden and my good friend Jenna.

Holden stood first and cupped my shoulders. "I know you can do this. Everything is going to go great with Clyde. Just tell him to keep his grandson's paws off my ex-wife," Holden said with a wink.

"If only you'd kept *your* hands on me, I wouldn't be worrying about my biggest donor to the community center trying to pawn me off on his grandson," I teased, squeezing his arm. Holden swatted my rear with a light touch.

"Like that? Is that what you want?"

"No. Put some gusto into it," Jenna said, with a playful note.

I waved them both off. I wasn't sore, per se, from my spanking two nights ago, but I was keeping this patch of bodily real estate for Ryan's possessive hands only. Actually, *all* of my body. True, we'd made no such promises. But after the time we'd spent together, the things we'd done, the messages we'd exchanged . . . well, there was no way in hell I wanted to even dabble with anyone else.

"No gusto, please," I joked, then glanced at my watch. "I'm off. Enjoy your green tea ice cream."

"We will," Jenna said, eyeing the dessert dishes the waiter had just brought the two of them. "Just remind Clyde how important the community center is in and of itself. And that building the new additions is not dependent on you dating or not dating his grandson."

"Absolutely." I gave a big thumbs-up. I knew what to do. I certainly knew how to handle myself in front of old, rich men, in front of young, rich men, and in front of nerdy, rich men. I'd handled myself just fine when I ran InCode. I'd made pitches. I'd stood up in front of groups of people. I'd asked for funding. And I'd presented on the strength of my vision.

That was what I would do with Clyde. Besides, I didn't feel my romantic life, one way or the other, needed to be a part of my conversations with him. If I were a man, surely no one would expect me to date someone's daughter.

I hopped into my Aston Martin and headed to Clyde's office. He greeted me with a handshake that lasted too long, then a kiss on the cheek that left too much whiskery scratch on my skin. I wished he wasn't so touchy, but I reminded myself the man hadn't crossed any lines. He was simply more affectionate than I would have liked. No crime in that, just a wee bit of discomfort.

In his office, I reviewed the final plans for the Beethoven concert benefit as well as the community center. When I was through, Clyde smacked his palm in approval on his grand oak desk. "I am delighted to be able to help fund this. It is so great to have a place for young people to be able to go to stay off the streets and out of trouble," he said, and I couldn't deny that I loved his giving heart and spirit. He reminded me in some ways of John, with his mission to help make the city safer and better. They each had their own style of going about it, but the goal was the same.

A better Las Vegas.

Clyde stroked his chin. "Say, do you know who's here today?" There was a glint in his gray eyes.

I cringed inside, then I plastered on my best smile. "I can't even begin to guess."

Soon he was escorting me to an office where a young blond man was bent over his laptop.

"Taylor, my boy. I have someone I want you to meet," Clyde said, and the young man looked up. He was handsome, sported a nice smile, and boasted straight white teeth that could only be courtesy of the best orthodontia money could buy. "This is Sophie, our city's leading philanthropist, who is spearheading the plans for the community center fundraiser."

"That's so great. I'm one hundred percent behind that." He pushed back from the desk in his rolling chair, walked over to me, and extended a hand.

He had a strong grip, and I cataloged that as a good thing. "Pleasure to meet you, Taylor. Clyde raves about his favorite grandson, and I promise I won't tell the others he likes you best."

Taylor laughed. "Excellent. I won't tell the other fundraisers that you're his favorite, then, either," he said with a *we've got a secret* wink.

"You've got a deal," I said with a cheery smile for the fresh-faced law school graduate. "How are you finding the transition from law school to the corporate world?"

"My grandfather works me hard. The other day, for instance, he only let me take a one-hour lunch to play cards at the MGM instead of the two hours he gives the senior partners."

"I'm so cruel," Clyde said with a hearty laugh.

After another minute of casual chatter, I said goodbye, and Clyde saw me to the lobby.

"That went quite well didn't it?" he asked, a huge grin on his face.

"He is lovely indeed," I said. *Also six years younger than me.*

"Perhaps the two of you could attend the concert together," he said, then snapped his fingers. "Wait. I have a better idea. Why don't you go out before? Have a nice dinner. On me."

I wanted to put my foot down, but I also didn't want to offend this man who I needed in my court by turning down his grandson. Nor did I want to lie to him. I wanted to live a life free of lies and free of trickery. I also wanted to operate on my own terms, not conform to the expectations of the men I worked with, whether they were the geniuses in the tech world back then or the titans of industry with fat wallets now.

"Oh, Clyde, you are such a darling," I said, stalling for time.

"What do you think about that?" he asked, undeterred.

"Why are you so eager to set him up? He's a handsome, smart, sweet man. Seems he could easily find a date on his own."

Clyde lowered his voice. "I want to leave him the firm. And I want to know he's with a woman who's not going to try to take all my money," he said in a *you get my drift* voice.

Oh, I got it. I definitely got it. Because I had money, I wouldn't *need* his. Clyde assumed I was the type of woman who'd sign a prenup. Well, maybe I was that type of woman. But still . . . the notion of *why* I was his top choice made me feel greasy.

"Also, you're the most delightful young woman I know," he added, as if suddenly that reason would hold water. "The two of you could be a wonderful match."

I had other ideas about what made a good match. Besides, who said I was looking for something serious? I was quite content with my life as it was, thank you very much. If I wanted anything right now, it was passion. It was sparks and fire.

It was Ryan Sloan, and the way he commanded my pleasure.

Oh God, just his name in my head sent heat flaring in my body.

Which meant it was time to nip this thing with Clyde in the bud. I'd run a multimillion-dollar company for several years, and I hadn't gotten to that position by letting the men I worked with try to set me up.

"Clyde, you know I adore you. And I could humor you right now simply to stay in your good graces, but I want to be totally honest. Your grandson is lovely. However, I've started seeing someone, and it's going quite well so far. So I'm not really on the market at the moment."

He frowned. "Is it serious?"

"Clyde," I said softly, "it's not a matter of whether it's serious. It's a matter of choice. I'm choosing to see someone right now, and I'll likely be bringing him to the benefit. I hope this won't affect your support of the center, but it's important to me to be honest with you."

Clyde took a deep breath and nodded, as if he was processing this news. I mentally crossed my fingers, praying I hadn't messed up by being too frank. I held my breath, hoping he wouldn't snatch away his funding.

"I've been too presumptuous," he said, contrition in his

tone. "And I respect you for saying that. And of course I remain a committed supporter." Then he fixed on a cheery smile. "And I look forward to meeting this man at the event."

Oh shoot. Now I had to deliver Ryan in the flesh to back up my *thanks, but no thanks* and to prove I was an honest woman.

"You will definitely meet him then," I said, my businesslike bravado hiding my worry that I'd been too bold to assume Ryan would be my arm candy.

I was going to need to ask Ryan to be my date. The possibility thrilled me, but he seemed to be taking it day by day. Would he even want to plan that far ahead?

As I drove to my next meeting, I ran through the best ways to invite Ryan to the event. What was happening between us was new and tender, and I didn't want to ruin it by asking for too much. Would this type of date imply we were more than merely lovers? Was I ready to state that so boldly?

I shut off the questions momentarily when I arrived at the community center, parking behind a brown Buick. I rushed inside for a quick visit with Elle, who ran the center, updating her on the status of the fundraising.

"So glad it's going well. We are lucky to have you behind this," Elle said, gesturing broadly to the broken-down building and the basketball court with its cracked concrete surface, all badly in need of the repair and revamp we hoped would soon be possible.

"It thrills me to help," I said as the dark-haired and insanely gorgeous Elle walked me back to my car at the end of our meeting.

"Thank you again for everything. I know we can do so much more for these kids when this comes together."

"We have great donors behind this. It'll happen."

As I said goodbye, backing away from the Buick then heading in the direction of the Strip, my damn brain went haywire again trying to figure out what was happening with Ryan. I muttered a curse as I turned onto the highway, dropping my shades over my eyes to shield them from the sun. I gripped the wheel tighter, trying to focus solely on driving. But still my mind whirred and raced as I played out scenarios and cycled through relationship permutations, just as I had with computers.

The questions rattled my brain and drove the tension in my body sky-high.

By the time I returned to my building, I felt like a radio station tuned in badly—all warped, fuzzy, and off-kilter. I was frazzled by what I might possibly do next—push Ryan into something that might feel more serious, when he hardly seemed the type.

But then I shoved all those feelings aside once the front desk attendant told me there was a delivery for me. He handed me a silvery gift bag with slim handles, and instantly I was sure it was from the man I had a third date with. Desperate to open it, I clutched it tightly as the elevator shot me up to my floor.

The second I opened my door, I tore in and found a small white box, tied with a white bow, nestled inside the red tissue paper. I pulled off the bow and removed the lid.

Wow. I lifted the satiny fabric. The panties were dark pink with sheer lace in front. But it was the back that knocked the breath out of me. The rear was comprised solely of crisscross satin pieces of fabric that fan out and would leave most of my bottom exposed. An open cage back, it was called, according to the tag.

I called it a prelude to multiple orgasms.

I owned many pairs of pretty panties, but these were by far the most alluring, taking sexy to new heights. Moments later, my phone pinged with the notification that a message had arrived.

Ryan: I hope you'll forgive me that they aren't pale pink.

Sophie: I do forgive you. I forgive you so much I promise to be wearing these next time I see you.

Ryan: Don't tease me like that.

Sophie: Good things come to those who wait . . .

Ryan: How's 7:00 tonight? I can't wait longer than that.

Sophie: You can take me for that drive you wanted in my car. I'll see you then.

Looked like that third date would be happening sooner than expected.

18

SOPHIE

It didn't matter where we were going tonight or what we were doing.

I was wearing a dress. I was not toying with him today, because I wanted what he wanted.

Access.

I adjusted the slim orange shoulder straps as they curved into a tight white bodice that was practically fused to my breasts. Just enough cleavage to ensure his eyes would pop out of his head, then the skirt itself would pretty much blast all his brain cells away. Full and gathered, the white skirt with oranges printed on it swished as I walked. The waist cinched with a slim belt, and I wore matching orange pumps with a strap over the instep. The cotton sateen fabric of the dress wasn't see-through, so I could wear the pink panties he'd sent, no problem.

As if I'd wear anything else right now.

This was a sex date, wasn't it? Oh yes, it was, and I wanted it, needed it, and was damn eager to have it.

Ryan was an enticing mix of enigmatic and open, of caveman and gentleman. The combinations I saw inside him intrigued me, body and heart. His quickness with words and the ease of his flirty banter ignited my mind. There was something else in him too that simply gripped me—the man had a magnetic intensity. It drew me to him, lured me under his spell.

That was where I wanted to be tonight.

I grabbed a small white handbag, dropped my wallet, lipstick, and phone into it, then realized I didn't have a condom. I laughed when I couldn't even remember how long it had been—not only since I'd needed one, but also since I'd bought one.

It would be up to Ryan, and he sure seemed like the kind of man who came prepared.

One more check of my reflection told me everything was neatly in place, including the soft curls I'd styled into my hair after I showered. I ran a shimmery red lip gloss wand over my lips, then tucked that into my purse too.

I tapped my chin, cycling through my mental to-do list. I'd been to the office, I'd seen Clyde, I'd visited Elle, I'd confirmed some items for the concert, and then made a number of phone calls for other fundraisers I was working on. There was so much in motion, but right now my plate was clear. My list was emptied. Time to have fun.

Then the sound of a lock in the door caught my attention.

19

JOHN

I'd say I walked in, but it sure as hell felt more like I'd been dragged. Weariness was my middle name.

But the second I spotted my sister in the kitchen, my tired eyes lit up, I was sure. She had that effect on me. She was sunshine and oranges, and I loved my kid sister something fierce. Wished I had some of her optimism. Some of her *the world can be better* beliefs. "Hey, Soph," I said.

"Hey you. Long day?"

I dropped my keys on the table by the door and headed to the kitchen. "Too long a day. Got the runaround from everyone," I said with a sigh, trying to push back the memories of today and the goddamn merry-go-round of the Thomas Paige case.

"The life of a detective," she said, then held up a finger in the air. "But I have just the cure for a long day."

I arched an eyebrow as my sister walked over to a black marble table at the edge of the kitchen and held up a sturdy glass bottle.

Ah, the antidote indeed.

She removed the stopper and poured some amber liquid into a glass, then grabbed an ice cube from the freezer, dropped it in, and handed it to me. "There's never been a long day in the history of the whole world that Macallan can't make better."

"I see I've taught you all of life's most important lessons."

She tapped my shoulder playfully. "Yes. Always keep a Maglite flashlight by the side of the bed, don't trust anyone, and savor the good stuff."

"You're covered." I raised the glass and knocked back half of it. With a satisfied sigh, I set the drink on the counter. "That does make my day suddenly better."

She laughed. "I knew it would." Then she took a beat, her brow knitting. "Are you still working on that case?"

Was I ever. That case and others. But *that* case had a way of making my head spin and my brain hurt. "Yeah. Today was like a goddamn puzzle," I said, dragging a hand through my hair, wishing I could put all the clues together, assemble the intel from years ago into something that made sense. "You know the math problems you can't solve? If a train is traveling at a speed of—" Then I stopped and shook my head, bemused. "Look who I'm talking to. You never had problems solving math puzzles."

She laughed. "True. So if you ever run into any impossible math or code-breaking with your cases, just let me know."

I took another drink. "This had to do with addresses. Fucking addresses from years ago."

"Sounds more like cartography than math," Sophie said.

"Well, both are vexing my partner and me," I said, then waved a hand as if to dismiss the day. At least for these few minutes here with my sister. Because I knew myself. I could let this case spill over into all aspects of my life. That was a good thing, in a way—show me a detective who's not obsessive and I'll show you a detective who's not doing his fucking job.

But right now, I needed a break.

A break before I spent the rest of the night trying to figure out if there were others, where they were then and now, and how and why they were involved.

And that break came courtesy of my fantastic sister. And her clothes. She killed me with her outfits. "What's with the dress? Wait. You're probably just going grocery shopping like that. Am I right?"

She made a funny face, sticking out her tongue. "Haha. And yes, I *would* wear this grocery shopping. But if you must know, I have a hot date."

I covered my ears. "La la la. I don't want to hear about hot dates." I took my hands off my ears, arching a brow. "Are you done now?"

"Why'd you ask, then, if I had a date if you didn't want me to tell you how fabulous this new man is?"

Scrubbing a hand across my chin, I groaned. Fine, she wanted to tell me. Least I could do was hear her out. Sophie loved to share, God bless her. "Like I said, long day. It fries my brain. Who's the date with?"

"As a matter of fact, it's someone I met—"

But her words were cut off when my phone bleated loudly from my back pocket. "Manny," I said when I saw my partner's name flash on the screen. "Got to take it."

She waggled her fingers. "Toodle-oo. Don't wait up for little old me." Then she whispered, "Hot date and all."

I rolled my eyes then pressed the phone to my ear, switching right back into work mode, eager to know what was cooking. "What's the latest?"

What he told me gave me a burst of hope. Because ever since Bianca Rosa came to me, I'd been trying to learn who else was involved. I'd always figured Dora Prince and Jerry Stefano hadn't acted alone. And now it appeared, we were inching closer to two more.

20

RYAN

I leaned against one of the stone columns of the portico, sunglasses on, tailored shirt tucked into my crisp pants, and a suit jacket tossed over my shoulder.

Patiently waiting.

The second I saw her, my breath fled from my lungs. She was impossibly beautiful.

"You," I began, and my voice sounded dry. "Are you?"

"Am I what?" Sophie purred.

I needed to know. I was already picturing her in what I'd sent. "Are you wearing them?"

With a sexy grin, she leaned closer, her lips mere millimeters from mine as she grabbed my hand and pressed her keys into my palm. "Take me somewhere and find out."

* * *

The car hummed. Adrenaline surged through me as I drove into the dusk, heading for the mountains southwest of the city. There was still unchartered land in that area.

Clearing had just begun, which meant miles upon miles of roads were still bare.

As I shifted on an uphill stretch, the engine roared. The feel of the luxury automobile she owned was absolutely extraordinary, blurring into some kind of gorgeous harmony between car and driver and road.

Not to mention the incredible woman in the passenger seat.

As I accelerated, my chest vibrated with a purpose—find someplace and fuck her.

I stole glances at Sophie during the drive, wishing it were possible to stare at her and keep my eyes on the road at the same time.

"Have I mentioned you look good enough to eat?"

"It's the oranges, isn't it?" she asked, running her fingers along the pattern on her dress.

"You had cherries on your dress when I met you. Now oranges. What will it be next time?"

"Do you like peaches?"

"I love peaches. I love peach ice cream. I especially love peach pie."

"Then maybe I'll have peaches on me next time," she said with a sly look in her eyes.

I laughed, then tapped the steering wheel as I turned onto a two-lane road at the base of the mountains. "So, what's the deal with you and this car?"

"What do you mean?"

"Is this like a James Bond thing you have going on?"

She laughed and shook her head. "He doesn't drive this model. Lately he's been driving the DBS. This is a Vantage GT."

"I know. It just seems very Bond."

"Maybe I'm a spy," she whispered in a sultry voice, winking as she spoke.

"Are you a good spy or a bad spy?"

"I'm whatever kind you want me to be," she said, and the innuendo in her words heated me up. The notion that she'd play whatever role I wanted intoxicated me.

But then, everything she did turned me on. My attraction to her ran red-hot and burrowed deep into my body. It operated on some kind of elemental level that at times I felt powerless to resist or deny. My fingers gripped the wheel harder as lust thrummed through me.

But even so, I remained curious about *her*. The woman who generated all this heat in my blood. I wanted to understand her. "What I mean is," I said, trying again, "what's the story with you and this fancy car, and the gorgeous building you live in, and the way you dress like you stepped off the pages of a magazine?"

"The answers are simple. I give a lot of my money away, and I give all my time away. But I still like having nice things. And I like to reward myself for hitting milestones in charitable fundraising. Like this car—it was a gift I gave myself after my first big event. And this dress I picked up when I started working with the children's wing. Besides, I like dressing nice. Is that a crime?"

I shook my head. "Hell no. You wear it all well. Do you like being pretty?"

She laughed lightly. "I'm glad you think so."

"Answer the question," I said firmly, since she'd just danced around what I considered an immutable truth of the universe—she was beautiful.

"*Ryan*," she said, and I heard her embarrassment in her tone. I was having none of that.

"Sophie," I said in a firm voice. "You're gorgeous. Don't deny it. Now tell me, do you like being so gorgeous?"

"To you—yes," she said, managing once again not to

answer completely. But her answer was completely satisfying.

Briefly, I ran my thumb over her bottom lip. "Stunning. You are fucking stunning." I turned my eyes back to the road that curved up into the hills. "Even in that picture you sent me of you in a hat and hoodie."

"I told you I was a nerd in college. I mean, total nerd," she said, slicing her hands through the air for emphasis. "I had a weird haircut. I dyed my bangs blue. I was bent over a desk coding all the time."

"I wouldn't mind seeing you bent over a desk."

She shot me a naughty grin. "Why does that not surprise me?"

"Did you like having blue hair?"

I shrugged. "I did it to fit in. There's a certain geek culture, and I had to work hard to conform to it. I already had a strike against me being a woman, so I tried to at least look the part of a computer nerd."

If she hadn't sent that photo, I'd never have believed it. "And now that you've left that part of your life behind, you embrace this other side of yourself," I said, gesturing to the pinup dress, high heels, and styled hair.

"Exactly," she said, her eyes lighting up.

"Was that part of you untended to? The woman in you?"

"For many years," she said, almost to herself. I was about to follow up and ask what she meant, but she kept talking. "But there are always parts of ourselves we don't take care of. I could ask you the same. Are you the same person you were when you were in the Army?"

As I hugged the side of the road on a turn, I eyed my tailored pants, button-down shirt, and leather shoes. "Well, I don't wear fatigues anymore," I said dryly.

"Did you wear fatigues then? Were you actually in battle?" she asked, worry in her tone.

"I did wear fatigues. But I wasn't on the battlefront. I was in Germany. Stationed in Wiesbaden. Not far from Frankfurt."

"I know where Wiesbaden is," she said quickly, a flicker of excitement in her eyes. "I'm having some work done on a new car at a custom shop in Rüsselsheim, not far from there."

"Yeah? What kind?" I asked, figuring she'd say Audi, BMW, or Mercedes—luxury autos with high-end options for the discerning buyer, like Sophie.

"It's a Bugatti," she said breezily. "I've always wanted one."

My jaw dropped. There was no hotter make or model of car to a *Top Gear* fan than a Bugatti. "Yeah, me too. You're really getting a Bugatti? I thought they were made in France."

"Mine was made there. But I've contracted with a specialty shop in Rüsselsheim to make it more eco-friendly. And the paint job they're doing is divine. It's going to be a lush *green*," she said, stretching that last word out as if it tasted like honey. "It's going to look like an emerald."

"That's pretty hot. Can't wait to see it."

"Me too. I should get it in a few weeks. I bought it when I hit another goal for charities. But enough about me. Tell me about Wiesbaden. What did you do at the base there?"

"Army intelligence. The 66th Military Intelligence Brigade."

"And I suspect your career path now is a pretty typical one after working in Army intelligence?"

"It is. Military to security. Natural fit."

"So perhaps you aren't that different now than in your previous job."

"Maybe I'm not."

"Maybe you're not," she echoed. "Or maybe you are. I don't really know."

"Do you want to know?"

"I want to know what makes you tick now," she said, her gaze fixed firmly on me as I drove. She was so straightforward, and I couldn't deny that I liked her directness in conversation as much as I liked her willingness to bend to me in the bedroom.

Besides, it was a good question, one I was rarely asked but one I could reasonably answer with the truth. "This car," I said, tapping the dashboard. "My dog. My job. My family. Living the life I choose. Keeping people safe. No, I'm not that different than I was before."

"You're like my brother in some ways," she said. Guilt burned through me at the mention of John, and I tried to shove it aside. There was no space tonight for the things I hadn't told her about how we met. "He's got the same focus," she continued, then looked at me and rested her hand briefly on my leg. "I admire it."

I gritted my teeth. *No, you don't. You can't admire me. I'm a liar and you're a truth teller, and I don't deserve you. But I still want you. Desperately.*

Sophie leaned back in the passenger seat, lowered the window, and let the wind whip through the car until I turned a corner at a lookout halfway up the mountain road and pulled the gleaming silver beast to a stop.

I cut the engine and stared at the windswept woman by my side. Maybe I wasn't a liar. Maybe I was simply a man who hadn't yet told the whole truth. There'd be time for that when I needed to offer it up. Then it hit me—I was thinking about the next time with her, and maybe even the one after that. Which wasn't like me at all. I didn't move beyond short-term, so why was my brain all of a sudden thinking differently?

I had no answers, only a stark certainty inside me that I wanted this woman all to myself.

"Do you like the way she handles the curves?" Sophie asked, patting the dashboard.

"So fucking much," I said, then nodded to her door. "Wait for me."

"I've been waiting for you," she said, tilting her head, locking her eyes with mine, and saying everything in her gaze. My breath stopped short at the way she looked at me. So guileless.

I never thought I'd been waiting for anyone. Given the walls I'd erected and the foundation of privacy I built my life on, I never imagined I'd be captivated this quickly. But Sophie had me bewitched—from her beauty to her spirit to her wide-open heart.

Maybe I had been waiting for *her*.

My muscles tightened. Something that felt like fear raced through me—the fear of feeling something.

But goddammit, I didn't want to think about matters of the heart.

The physical was so much easier.

The physical paid better dividends.

I walked behind the car then opened her door, offering my hand.

"Get out of the car and show me," I said, issuing a command. "Show me how you look in my gift."

Sophie's eyes widened, and she unhooked her seat belt in one second. Damn, this woman loved to be told what to do, and I loved being the one to do it.

I tugged her out and spun her around, lining her back against my front. Sex. Contact. Connection. I needed it to wipe my mind of all the dangerous little details I kept locked up. I moved her body closer to the hood of the car. I tested the metal with my palm—warm, not too hot. "Bend over."

She placed her hands on the hood and flattened her back. My God, she took orders like a dream. "Raise your skirt for me."

She reached a hand behind her and grabbed the orange hem. She lifted it up, and a groan ripped from my throat when I saw her in the panties I'd bought for her.

The hottest item of clothing in all of creation.

"Nothing has ever looked better on any woman in the world," I said, as I fell to my knees in the dirt and pressed my face against her rear. I flicked my tongue through one of the crisscross sections that exposed her creamy white flesh, and she gasped. I gripped her cheeks in my hands, squeezing her as I smothered her barely-covered bottom in kisses. Oh, the things I wanted to do to her. The ways I wanted to touch her with my tongue, fingers, and cock. Lick her, touch her, fuck her, and taste her.

My dick throbbed in my pants, begging to be set free, to be inside her gorgeous body.

"They were made for you," I whispered as I worshipped her ass with my lips, and she squirmed under my touch, rocking her body back into me. I licked the outline of one of the diamonds, flicking the tip of my tongue over her skin, and she moaned my name.

"I bet you're soaked right now," I said in a hungry voice.

"I bet you're right," she answered in between erratic breaths.

The world around us was dark and quiet. There was only the slightest rustle of an evening breeze. We were all alone on the turnout at the side of the road, and I was going to fuck her good and hard.

I slid my fingers between her legs and groaned when I felt how damp she was. Nothing was better in the entire universe than when a woman responded to a man like this. Her body told me everything—from the way she stretched her arms, to how her belly pressed flat to the metal, to how her ass was raised in the air, the skirt all bunched up by her hips.

Sophie wanted me. She gave herself freely, and I was utterly consumed by a deep and potent longing for her. I'd intended to fuck her, but with my face so close to her sweet center, I decided on an appetizer first. "Don't move," I said, as I pulled the panel of her panties to the side. Keeping her in place would keep me in control of this ravenous desire that raged inside. "Stay still while I eat you."

"I won't move," she answered, digging her heels into the ground.

I stared between her legs, where she glistened. My breath came fast as raw desire overtook me. "You're so fucking delicious," I said, then licked.

She trembled and sighed sexily. The most enticing sounds floated from her lips as I licked her sweetness. Her clit was a hard stone under my tongue, and with each flick, she trembled but remained still. She'd taken my order to heart and hadn't moved an inch. She could follow directions like a perfect student, and she tasted like heaven on earth. I buried my face in her slickness, my hands gripping her luscious ass as I devoured her.

She flooded my tongue and moaned her pleasure. "I'm so close, Ryan. I'm so close. Can I please move?"

Please.

Oh hell, it was like a direct line of desire to my cock. I ached to fill her. That simple word spurred me on, making me want her even more. "Yes," I said roughly, then gave her an order. "You have permission to fuck my face now."

She followed it to the letter. I continued my assault on her pussy with my lips, thrusting my tongue inside her heat, as she rocked into me madly. She went from frozen to frenzied in no time. Her thighs tensed, and as soon as I felt her quiver, I slid a finger inside her.

Her soft walls clenched around me, and she cried out into the night as she came on my tongue, my lips, and my chin.

She tasted divine. Absolutely intoxicating all over me, and I was hooked on her, on her taste, her scent, her body. Everything. I lapped up her wetness as the aftershocks moved through her. I placed a palm on each thigh, steadying her as I kissed the backs of her legs, then lapped up a bead of wetness that had slid down her skin.

I stood up and raked my eyes over the gorgeous sight of her bent at the waist, soft and warm from her first orgasm. "I'm just getting started, beautiful. There's so much I want to do to you."

She looked back at me and smiled, a tipsy grin that made my heart pound and my dick ache. Rabid desire raced through me again, and the need to take her overwhelmed me. Her feet were planted on the ground. I nudged the inside of her right leg with my foot, then kicked her legs open wider.

"Spread your legs for me," I instructed, and she inched her feet apart into a more perfect V.

My fingers traveled along her spine and up her neck to her hair, grabbing it, turning her head so she looked up at me. Her eyes were hazy and full of a lust that matched mine. "Do you have any idea what you do to me?" I asked harshly.

"I think I do."

"You are under my skin," I whispered, as I kept her pressed against the warm hood with one hand, then slinked my other hand down to her waist and unfastened the slim orange belt. "And in my head," I continued as I snapped the belt free. "And I can't fucking stop thinking about you."

"I can't stop either," she said, and in a flash, I wrapped the belt around her wrists, knotting it, twisting it, and tying her hands together with her own accessory. She allowed me, offering up her wrists to be bound. She was a willing hostage.

"That turns me on even more," I growled in her ear, as I stretched her tied arms along the silver hood.

"Tying me up?"

"Yes," I said, pressing my erection against her ass. "But what makes me rock hard is the way you let me. The way you want me to. The way you give your body to me," I said as I grabbed a condom from my pocket, unzipped my pants, and pushed down my briefs.

"Take me," she said, meeting my eyes as she lay vulnerable and completely open to me.

I rolled on the condom. Then I placed my hands on that perfect ass and dug my thumbs into her cheeks, spreading her sex open. I rubbed the tip of my dick against her wet heat.

Lust crashed over me like a wave beating the shore. I returned my right hand to her neck, held her in place, and sank into her in one swift move.

Then I stilled inside her, inhaling deeply as I savored the intensity of this moment—the feel of her luscious body drawing me in for the first time. I'd craved this from the second I'd met her, and now I knew why.

She fit me perfectly.

"You feel fucking amazing," I groaned. "I knew you would."

She moaned. She whimpered. She cried out my name. "*Ryan.*"

The sound of my name falling from her red lips made me want her more than I'd ever thought possible. She'd seduced me with her willingness, she'd lured me in with her sweet naughtiness, and she'd captivated me with her mind.

I was mesmerized by this woman. Completely spellbound.

And so I did what I came here to do.

I fucked her. Deep, hard, and feverishly. I swiveled my hips and thrust into her, her sweet, snug pussy taking me in all the way. I breathed heavily as I stroked, one hand squeezing her ass. She gave me everything I wanted—complete control of her body—and it annihilated my brain. It scorched a path of pure pleasure through me. I was driven with need for her, by the sheer ecstasy of fucking this woman on the hood of her car in the desert, under the sky, under my command.

"It feels so good," she said on a pant. "Oh God, I'm going to come," she cried out, then screamed my name. The sound of it echoing in the night made my balls tighten and pleasure ricochet through me, sweeping over my entire body, obliterating everything else in my world but this pure and perfect moment with this magnificent woman.

I grunted, calling out her name as I came, then slumped over her back and wrapped my arms around her.

She sighed happily.

I damn near did the same. "I can't get enough of you. I just fucking can't."

She shot me the sweetest smile. Then in a soft voice, she said, "I'm hungry. Care to take me out for a bite to eat?"

I'd already eaten, but food sounded good.

21

SOPHIE

The dry spell had officially ended, so I ordered french fries and a chocolate milkshake.

Because the combination felt like a celebration, and I was celebrating not only the first time I'd had sex in a few years, but also the best sex ever.

Make that Best. Sex. Ever.

We'd stopped at a roadside diner on the return to the city, and he ate a burger and shared my fries. I reached for one at the same time as he did, and our fingers bumped. He laughed. "We could fight for it. Or I could let you have that one," he said.

"I trust you'll let me have it," I said, then snatched the fry in question and dragged it through ketchup. As I brought it to my lips, I glanced down to make sure my napkin was spread across my skirt. Damn. I'd missed a loop when I'd put my belt back on. Wait. I hadn't. One of them had split.

That was some hard loving.

"Looks like I ripped a belt loop," I said after I finished chewing.

"I'll have it fixed for you. Pretty sure I'm responsible."

"I'm pretty sure I can fix it easily with a needle and some thread." Then I noticed the dress was streaked along the bodice and the skirt—the danger of sex on a car in a white dress. "Oh no. My dress is dirty too," I said, gesturing to the marks on the front.

He frowned. "My fault as well. I'll pay to have it cleaned."

I scoffed. "No. You're not paying for my dress." Funny, how I consented so easily to his orders during sex, but the rest of the time I had no problem holding my own.

"But I made it dirty," he said, then took a bite of his burger.

"You didn't make it dirty," I said, correcting him. "Fucking you made it dirty."

He set his burger down on the plate and narrowed his eyes, giving me a purposeful stare. "Sweetheart, *I* fucked you. You didn't fuck me."

I grinned wickedly, loving teasing him like this. "I know." I leaned closer to him across the table. "And I loved it. I loved how you fucked me," I said, and even just saying that word—*fuck*—turned me on. Holden had never been one for *fucking*. Bless his heart, but Holden was a *let's make love* type of guy. Then there was my college boyfriend, Zach, my one and only other lover. There was no finesse. No attention to detail. And no more than two minutes, tops.

I couldn't even compare Ryan to those guys. He was in a class by himself. Everything about him—that soft brown hair, those dark-blue eyes, his hard body, the way he took me—he was fantasy material.

But real.

Add in the easy way we were able to talk, toss in the intensity of the connection, and mix in the sweet little gestures, and I was dangerously close to feeling something more.

Ryan reached across the table and tucked a strand of hair behind my ear. "I've never met a woman like you, one who's so strong and direct everywhere else, but able to turn over the reins in bed. It's addictive," he said, his eyes fixed on me the whole time, the look in them earnest and truthful. My heart swooped in a daredevil loop the loop.

Correction: I was *already* feeling something more.

Which meant I wanted him to know more about me. I brought the straw in my milkshake to my lips and swallowed some of the delicious chocolate ice cream concoction. "Confession: I've never had the chance to be like this."

He arched an eyebrow in question.

I put the shake glass down, keenly aware of the sounds of the diner—the cooks frying up bacon for patrons ordering breakfast for their late-night dinners, the twang of a country tune playing softly overhead, a waitress taking an order a few booths away. "This isn't some big secret. I know you looked me up before the gala, so you might have learned this, but I was married for five years." At this point it would be odd *not* to tell him this fact about my romantic past. Now, on the third date, after hot sex on my car, seemed the right time to mention my former marital status.

The surprise in his eyes told me he hadn't known this. "No, I wasn't aware. How long have you been divorced?"

"A little over two years. I was twenty-four when I married Holden," I said, sharing the details matter-of-factly, because there was nothing to hide.

"That's young. Did you go to college together?"

I shook my head. "We were best friends in high school, and we stayed close. He went to Berkeley and I was at

Stanford, so we weren't far apart. I didn't date much in college, except this one guy, Zach, who was a computer geek too. Truth be told, Zach was kind of a competitive ass who thought his tech start-up would blow mine out of the water, and he told me as much every day."

"Did it? Blow yours out of the water?"

"As if." I was pleased, and not a bit guilty, to share this next tidbit. "He never even got funded. He actually applied for an engineering job at my company two years after graduation."

"Did you hire him?"

"No. But it had nothing to do with our past relationship. It had to do with him rushing through things, including his work. He was always cutting corners." His work ethic was similar to his sex ethic. "Anyway, we only went out for a few months during college, and even though it wasn't a tough decision to end things, he was quite insulting at the time. Holden was there for me when I broke up with Zach. And soon enough after college, marrying each other just seemed to make sense."

He furrowed his brow, as if marriage didn't truly compute for him. Perhaps it didn't. "Make sense?"

He reached for a french fry as I nodded. "We were great friends. And we actually still are. He's probably my best friend."

He dropped the fry. "I don't get it. How can you be best friends with your ex-husband? If you're that close, why aren't you with him?"

I inhaled deeply. Okay, telling Ryan I'd been married wasn't hard in the least. But explaining why we'd split up was a bit tougher. I lowered my voice. "We weren't compatible in the bedroom."

"In what way?" he asked.

"Well, he likes girls and boys."

"Ahh, so he's bisexual."

I nodded. "Yes. And he was interested in sharing me with boys."

He drew a deep breath and straightened his spine. "Did you?"

I studied his face, unsure if the uncertain look in his eyes suggested that a past ménage was a deal-breaker. I didn't want to be judged for my past, even though I hadn't had one. I needed to know Ryan wasn't that kind of person. "Would it bother you if I had?"

"No," he said immediately, then waited for my answer.

I shook my head. "I didn't have a threesome. I don't want to be shared."

He pushed away from his side of the booth, stood up, and moved in next to me. Draping an arm around me possessively, he pulled me close, then brushed his finger along my jawline. "If you were mine, I'd never share you," he said, his deep, sexy voice sending goosebumps over my flesh.

"Is that so?"

He cupped my shoulder in his strong hand, his fingers brushing along my bare skin. "I'd never let anyone else touch you. The thought of it already drives me mad. And I'd never stop touching you," he said, then dropped his mouth to my lips and kissed me hard, as if he were marking me.

My mind went hazy, and sparks raced madly through my bloodstream—all from a kiss.

He pulled away. "If you were mine, you'd only be mine. And I'd satisfy you every night. Every day. Every morning. Every single time," he said, claiming my lips once more. Roughly.

I *felt* like his. It was crazy to feel that way so soon. But tell that to my heart, which was beating furiously at his possessive words. "You would satisfy me every time. You already do," I said in a breathy whisper, my voice feathery soft now, as he crowded me in.

His throat rumbled. "If you were mine, I'd never let you want for anything. I'd take care of you and all your needs. Whatever you needed, I'd give you," he said, and his words set me on fire. They made me want him again.

They gave me confidence too. I knew this was as good a time as any. "Ryan?" I asked carefully.

"Yes?"

I swallowed. "There's an event I'm organizing for the local community center. Another fundraiser next weekend. One of the donors wanted to set me up with his grandson," I said, and he clenched his hand around me tighter as I said those words. His eyes seared me. "But I told him I was seeing someone, and I was hoping that someone would take me to the event."

The corner of his lips quirked up in a knowing grin. That smile settled the anxiety. "And who is this someone you want to take you to the event?" he asked playfully.

I rolled my eyes. "You. Obviously."

"And do you want me to act all possessive, so everyone knows you're taken?"

"Would it be an act?" I asked, countering him.

He shook his head. "No. It's not difficult for me to feel a sense of ownership of you," he said, brushing his hand along my bare arm. "So when I take you to this event—because I will be taking you – it will be clear to everyone that you're with me."

His commanding tone lit me up, and a fresh wave of longing rolled through. "Am I? With you?"

He nodded. "Yes." Then he took a deep breath, becoming even more sober. "I'm not good with serious relationships, Sophie. But there's something about you—I want more."

I beamed. "I can handle that."

22

RYAN

"Tell me about this event. What should I wear?" I asked, as I turned onto the Strip to drive her home.

"Tux. Do you own one?"

I laughed softly. "Of course I own a tux. Where is it?"

"The Venetian."

"And who are the sponsors?"

"Well, *me*, for one," she said, then rattled off a few names of local companies, including a law firm, an insurance company, and a national sporting goods chain. "And Redwood Mountain Ventures too. A venture capital firm."

I jerked my head to look at her as I pulled to a stop at a red light. "Redwood Mountain Ventures?"

She nodded. "Yes. Why?"

"That's my brother Colin's firm."

"Oh, that's great. I've been dealing with one of the other partners. A woman. I didn't make the connection that your brother the venture capitalist was at this firm. But how wonderful that he's a supporter. It's a great cause."

"Interesting," I said, wondering why Colin never mentioned anything about such a hefty donation. But then again, my youngest sibling had never been one to brag about all the ways that he gave back. "I wonder if he'll be there."

"You should ask him. It would be nice to say hello. I'm hoping John can make it so perhaps you can meet him too," she said, lightness in her tone because, of course, she had nothing to hide.

Unlike me.

My chest clenched. I muttered a silent curse as I reached her building. Now would be a good time to admit I'd already met her brother, had been questioned by him at police headquarters about my father's murder, and then received a phone call from him, hunting for more details about my mother's affair.

Honestly, though, telling her about the connection to her brother wasn't the hard part. What felt insurmountable was what it meant—if I told her I knew John, I'd have to tell her about my parents. I'd have to explain how my family had been blasted to pieces one night when I was only fourteen.

I'd never told anyone I'd dated. I'd never wanted to.

But here in the driveway of her building, at almost midnight, after the most mind-blowing sex of my life, was not the moment to dive into the past. I needed to figure out how to tell her without fucking everything up. My experience in saying the right thing was terribly limited for many reasons—I didn't get close to people, and I didn't speak of matters no one else needed to know.

Trust was a screwed-up promise.

Intimacy was a lie.

Love wasn't real.

She'd shared so much, though, and I had to figure out how to do the same.

I said good night and headed for my home, taking my

dog for a midnight run in an effort to glean some answers. But an hour of hard exercise under the stars didn't illuminate my own path any better, so when I got into bed with my dog curled up on top of the covers, only one thing was clear.

I was fucked.

Because I liked her more than I'd ever intended. That first night with Sophie I'd gone in armed with every intention of keeping things only physical, because I couldn't stay away. The second time too. Hell, I'd tried to do as much tonight. But my intentions were futile. I wanted this woman with a desire that burned away everything in its path. That consumed my brain cells. That chained up my heart. And for the first time ever, I felt the flicker of something awfully dangerous. So dangerous it'd made me start to use words.

Words that mattered.

Words that came from that organ inside me that had gone on lockdown many years ago.

Words that could mean the start of something more.

I ran a hand between Johnny Cash's soft ears. "Where do I go from here, buddy? Tell me that."

RYAN

I slapped the contract on my brother's desk on Wednesday morning. "Boom. Done. Another deal for us," I said, parking myself in the black leather chair in Michael's office. Guitar-heavy rock music pulsed from his laptop. My brother used to play the electric guitar and had dabbled in rock bands in high school and college. A workaholic with little time to play now, he compensated by assaulting his eardrums with his favorite tunes.

Michael arched an eyebrow. "You don't say. Maybe I should keep you around."

I rolled my eyes. "Hey, fifty-fifty, I could say the same of you," I said, referring to our joint ownership of Sloan Protection Resources.

"As you often do." Michael cast a cursory glance at the pages on his desk. He tapped his index finger against them. "Looks good. I see White Box is getting a full suite of security services. This is the company you met with in San Francisco a few weeks ago, right?"

"Yep, Charlie's on board for the whole shebang." I'd been slated to visit my mom in prison then, but she'd gotten the dates wrong, and Shannon wound up going solo, while I'd been meeting with the head of White Box. Charlie had owned some restaurants, but converted them to private clubs, the kind that catered to gentlemen with big wallets and hearty appetites—for both women and bets. That kind of business needed security, and since White Box was expanding from San Francisco to Vegas, the firm had reached out to us.

"And you said the VP of biz dev is coming in to sign the papers?"

"One p.m. today. Guy named Curtis," I said, tapping my watch. "He's local here in Vegas. It's on you for the final signatures. I worked on that deal all day Saturday and Sunday."

"Aww, poor baby," Michael said, breaking out an imaginary violin and running the bow across the strings.

"Whatever," I said, waving a hand dismissively. "Point being, I'm out of here the rest of the day."

"You going to see 347-921?"

Michael didn't even use our mom's name, just her inmate number. At first it had rankled me, and I'd told my brother as much, but I had learned to let it go. Now, I was used to the way Dora Prince had been reduced to digits.

"I am."

My brother made a scornful sound as he shook his head. "Why do you waste your time with that?"

"*Why?* You're seriously asking why?"

Michael nodded as a guitar riff played through the speakers. I rose, planted my palms on Michael's desk, and stared at him, wondering if he was crazy. How did he not get it? "Because I want to know why the hell the case has been reopened. Don't you?"

"She won't tell you shit."

I stabbed my index finger against my sternum. "But I'm

the only one she *might* tell something to. That's why I'm going. Because I'm the only one who sees her, besides Shan. So if there is something to say, or someone else involved, I'm the one she's going to talk to."

Michael softened his tone but still held his ground. "Look, man. I get it. I understand she did some kind of number on you and convinced you she might not be guilty —but she's so damn guilty, Ryan. Day is day, and night is night, and our mother had our father killed. Maybe there was someone else involved, maybe Detective Winston is sniffing around for a middleman, or for something more between her and Stefano, but I guarantee you're not going to exonerate inmate number 347-921."

I gritted my teeth as frustration seared my nervous system, running a wild course through my body. "Here's the bottom line. Someone knows something about our family that we don't," I said through tight lips. "I want to know what that something is, and I'm not going to stop until I find out."

Michael stood up and clapped me on the shoulder. "You're a determined bastard, I'll give you that. But don't speed like Sanders. We need you squeaky clean here at the company. No tickets, no record, nothing."

"Don't worry your pretty little head. I'm never dirty," I said with a wink.

Michael tugged me in for a quick hug. "Love you, bro."

"Love you too," I grumbled.

This. My brothers and sister. My grandparents. My dog. That was the only kind of real love I knew I could trust for sure.

24

RYAN

But first I had to see Luke. I bounded up his steps, ready to know, when an elderly woman with curly gray hair opened the faded red door of the ranch-style home and waved goodbye to the man inside. "See you at the recital."

"You're going to be great. Your 'Für Elise' is fantastic."

The voice blasted me back in time, like a slingshot to the end of junior high. Luke Carlton, older, grayer, and paunchier, turned to me as the woman ambled down the steps on the way to her car.

"Ryan Sloan," Luke said, extending a hand. He wasn't surprised to see me, nor should he be.

I had made an appointment for a piano lesson. I hadn't used the name I'd had growing up—Ryan Paige-Prince—but Luke clearly knew who I was. He obviously suspected this was a result of the reopened investigation.

Even so, my legs felt wobbly and my stomach plummeted. It was as if I was having an out-of-body experience and someone else was grasping the palm of this brown-eyed man in khaki slacks and a sky-blue Tommy Bahama shirt.

My mother's ex-lover.

"Come in," Luke said, letting go and gesturing to the home he'd lived in for the last five years. Before this meeting, I had run a security check on Luke Carlton. He was only a few years older than my mother, and he'd bought this home with his wife, a woman named Angie. I didn't know how long Luke had been married though.

"My kids are at camp," Luke said as we walked through the living room. Okay, he'd been with her long enough to procreate. "Wife's out grocery shopping. I take it you're not really interested in a piano lesson?" His question was wry, but I didn't need to be buddy-buddy with him.

I answered him without a note of sarcasm. "Sometimes I think about taking it up."

"Lots of adults do. Half my business these days is from adults who decide they've always wanted to learn how to play." He guided me through the kitchen, and my eyes gobbled up every detail. The sink was stacked with plates. Eggs had been served for breakfast. A loaf of rye bread was on the counter, a twist tie keeping it closed. An odd sense of the surreal descended on me. Everything about Luke's home was so . . . normal. From the blinds that hung on the living room windows, to the beige couch with an indentation on it in front of a large TV screen, to scattered pictures of his wife and kids, many of them on the beach, playing in the sand and surf.

But what had I suspected? He was just a regular guy. A regular guy with a whole lot of issues who'd had an affair with a married woman once upon a time. Guys like Luke were a dime a dozen.

He led me to an office area, with a baby grand piano, a couch, a chair, and a writing table.

"We might as well chat here," he said, then claimed a spot on the piano bench, gesturing to a wooden chair.

I hardly wanted to sit. I didn't want to stand. I didn't know what to do with my hands, so I stuffed them into the pockets of my pants. I was used to talking to clients, to pitching the need for security services, to giving orders to troops in Europe during my days in the Army.

But talking to my mother's former lover from eighteen years ago gave *uncomfortable* new meaning. My throat was parched, and my tongue barely worked. But somehow I found the ability to speak, because I had to know what he'd told Detective Winston. I had to know if Luke had revealed anything about the intel I kept locked up tight. I swallowed roughly. "My dad's case was reopened. The detective asked me about you and your relationship with my mom." I jumped right in, hitting the key points without mincing words.

Luke nodded. "I am aware of that. I met him too. Winston. Seems sharp."

"Yeah," I said, but Winston's skills at his job were beside the point. The point was *this*, so I asked firmly, "What does he know? Did you tell him how you knew my mom?"

"I told him we were in love, yes. And that it had been a mistake, since she was married," Luke said, clasping his hands together. "I still ask God every day for forgiveness for having fallen in love with a married woman."

I gritted my teeth. We all knew that. "That's not what I meant," I said, because I wasn't here to talk about contrition for cheating. This was bigger. Heavier. I clenched my jaw, then took a breath, pushing on, speaking words aloud I hardly ever said. "I'm talking about her drug problem. *The cocaine.* That she got it from Stefano. Do they know?"

This was the first time I'd said those words aloud in nearly twenty years. *Drugs. Cocaine. That Stefano was her dealer.*

This was the secret she'd begged me to keep since I was

thirteen—a year before the shooting—and had come home early from school on a half-day she'd forgotten about.

The day I found her cutting lines at her sewing table. With a rolled-up dollar bill, she'd leaned in and inhaled a line of white powder off her Singer machine.

The secret I'd kept.

25

DORA

More than eighteen years ago

He wasn't supposed to be here.

No one was supposed to be here.

Just me, my machine, and *this*—the means to work faster, make more.

But when I looked up from the machine, there was my baby. My Ryan, his jaw hanging open. His eyes were ringed with disbelief, his voice wavering as he asked, "Mom?"

I froze, stunned for a split second, maybe fifty. I didn't know, but I had to act fast. Think fast. Because no one was supposed to be home.

No one was supposed to see me.

Not my sweet Ryan, not any of my babies.

I couldn't think. Emotions took over, gripping me.

"Please don't tell anyone," I said, as the tears started to flow. I got up quickly, rushed around the machine, and clasped him in an embrace. "Please, this is my last time. I'm trying to stop. I swear I'm going to stop. I promise."

I clutched him as if my life depended on it, and begged him to never breathe a word.

No one could know. Not my husband, not my other babies, not a soul.

I couldn't let anyone know.

He nodded, his mouth tight, his chin strong.

My tough, brave boy. He would always be my toughest.

And I would prove him right for trusting me.

And for looking out for me.

Over the next few months, I was determined to prove myself to him.

I told him I'd joined Narcotics Anonymous, and had found a sponsor for counseling and guidance. And in quiet moments, I pulled Ryan aside, reassuring him. "Please, Ry. I'm trying so hard, baby. I'm trying so hard to fight these demons," I said to him. "Don't tell your daddy, please. He'd just worry. And don't tell your brothers and sister. I'm so ashamed, and I want to get well again. I've got a sponsor and I'm going to meetings, and I swear I'm going to kick this habit. I owe some money to the guy I used to buy from, and I'm working extra for the local gymnastics team to earn enough to pay him back. Once I do, I swear I'll be free of this."

"I won't tell anyone," he said.

He never did. He was so good. He kept it all locked up like I'd asked him to. Thank God. Thank the Lord for my Ryan.

He was the best at keeping secrets.

That's why I knew I could ask him for one last favor when the cops were questioning me after my husband's murder. I could ask him for the biggest one of all.

26

RYAN

When she'd told me to never say a word, I took that to heart. I put my brain on lockdown, some sort of self-preservation kicking in. It was all I'd been able to do. Zip it up, keep it quiet, and never speak of what I saw.

I never said a word.

Even when she met Luke at those meetings. Even when she fell for another recovering addict. Even when she was first questioned by police, and it all came to light that she'd not only been having an affair with that former addict at the time of the murder, but that she'd made a string of phone calls for two months to a man named Jerry Stefano. Why was she talking to him so much, the cops wanted to know.

She wouldn't tell them.

She'd begged me again to stay quiet once more. She'd shut the door to my room, planted her hands on my shoulders, and given me instructions. "They haven't found the person who shot your daddy. And they're asking me all kinds of questions, and I'm petrified they're going to try to frame me for his murder. You know what we talked about?"

Her green eyes were wild as she'd begged me, gripping me so tight as if that would ensure my silence, her hands curled around my shoulders. "If the police know I used drugs, if they know I bought them from Jerry Stefano, it will look so much worse for me. They know I've been on the phone with Jerry for months. I'm going to have to tell a lie about all those phone calls. He's been calling to collect money, and if they know I was buying from him, they'll paint me as a druggie murderer wife."

I tried to connect her dots, but I spotted holes. There had to be a better way to prove she was innocent of the crime. I had to get her to see it. "But, Mom, wouldn't they see you're innocent if you tell them about the drugs? Wouldn't it be better to have them know you bought drugs than to have them think you planned a murder?" I'd asked, trying desperately to understand why she didn't confess her secret. She had to get it. I could see it easily—what she should do. Confess to the drug use, confess that was how she knew Stefano, confess that's why she had called him.

Not to hire him to pull a trigger.

She shook her head. Vehemently, like she was snapping it back and forth. "No. Never. Trust me. It will only look worse, and I have to beat this rap. So I have no choice but to lie about Jerry. Luke is the only other one who knows the truth about those phone calls."

Luke and me.

The weight of that resonated with me, like a door shutting.

Her lover and me.

Her two secret keepers.

Now, years later as an adult, I was asking the only other person who knew if he'd broken the code of silence.

I drew in a breath, looked at the man who'd had an affair with my mother, swallowed down the ancient disgust, and zoomed in on what I needed to know.

"Did you tell the detective that Stefano was her dealer?" I asked crisply, coolly, keeping all my emotions under control as I damn well knew how to do.

Luke shook his head, rose, and turned up the air conditioning in his piano room. The sound of the whirring grew louder, as if Luke was using it as a buffer to cover up this conversation. I bristled inside, because I so often did the same thing. I'd cranked up the tunes in my car when Winston had made his follow-up phone call a couple of days ago.

Luke held up his palm, as if he were swearing in court. "I did not say a word. Her last wish before she went away was for me to keep that secret," he said, his voice trembling. "She was terrified of Stefano. You never met him, Ryan, and I pray you never do. Bump into a guy like Stefano on the street and you run the other way." There was rabid fear in his eyes as he offered this strange piece of advice.

I crossed my arms. I didn't want advice from my mom's lover. Besides, I wasn't afraid. Not of Stefano—the scumbag who'd killed my father—and not of men like him. "I'm not scared of men who deal drugs to mothers and children," I said, practically spitting out the words.

Luke's gray eyes widened, and he reached out to grab my arm. "She was petrified of what would happen if people knew she was connected to him," he pleaded.

I stared at him, impervious to his plea. Uninterested in anything but the full truth. "But their plan didn't work. Their cover-up failed," I said, reminding him that the lies my mom had told didn't save her from jail. The truth would have tethered her more closely to the Royal Sinners, so she'd fashioned a fable. She'd said all those phone calls to Stefano were for tree trimming, and I'd said the same, following her lead. That was Stefano's day job—a laborer at a tree-trimming company—so when she was asked about the string of calls, she'd claimed she'd hired him "under the table" to clean up some overgrown branches. It was the kind of work she couldn't have her sons do, since it required specialty saws and tools. That was all true and completely plausible.

And the tale seemed to work at first for both Stefano and my mom. For a brief while, their story did the trick. Botched robbery—that was how the murder looked to authorities, and Stefano seemed clean. My mother seemed clean. Some unknown assailant had tried to rob my father and killed him instead, the cops had believed.

It was on its way to becoming an unsolved murder.

Until the detectives found Stefano's fingerprints on the gun he'd disposed of. The gun the cops found.

Everything turned with that tide.

There was no botched robbery in the driveway.

Because Stefano confessed.

He started singing about how he'd been hired for much more than tree trimming.

Stefano served it all up, and the lies he and my mother had concocted unraveled.

He told the cops he'd been contracted to kill. He said the calls to my mother weren't to cut overgrown branches —they were to plan the murder of my father and to make it look like a robbery gone wrong. He alleged he'd been promised 10 percent of Thomas Paige's life insurance policy if he pulled it off.

The life insurance company went next, supplying more evidence. They confirmed that Dora had called a few months before the death to make a "routine check" on the beneficiary information on behalf of her husband, then again six days after the murder to try to liquidate the funds.

All the dominoes fell in her direction, pointing clearly at her.

In her defense, she'd maintained her husband had asked her to check on the policy and that was why she'd phoned the company months before his death. *For him,* she'd said. He was busy working and asked her to check up on various pieces of paperwork. As for accessing the payout, she pointed out that if she'd killed him for money, wouldn't she have called hours later for the cash? No, she'd waited a week.

A week. She hung her hope on a timeline.

The jury didn't buy it.

She could have admitted to the drugs then, but it was too late for her. The case was so far beyond drugs. The state had Stefano and his testimony, they had the life insurance proof, and they had circumstantial evidence— she was having an affair at the time of the murder.

They had her, beyond a reasonable doubt, the jury said.

Admitting to drug buying and using, to money owed to dealers, wouldn't have done a damn thing to change the fate of either Stefano or my mom.

"Don't mention the drugs," she'd begged me before she left for Stella McLaren Federal Women's Correctional Center. "It won't make a difference now. I will keep fighting to be free, and it will look worse for me if this gets out. I'll try to find a way to get the guys who really did it. I have to take the fall now, but please know I will be appealing. I will do everything I can to be with my children again."

I did as she asked—I protected her lies.

But now, eighteen goddamn years later, why was Luke still covering everything up?

I shrugged off his grip, my jaw tight, my hackles raised. "Luke, let's get real here. Let go of the song and dance. The lies didn't work." I licked my lips, drew in a breath, and asked the question I needed to know the answer to. "So why are you protecting Stefano?"

"I'm *not* protecting Jerry," Luke said in a wild hiss, pointing to the door, waving desperately beyond. "I'm protecting my family—my wife and kids—from Stefano's friends on the outside. His friends protected him, Ryan. That's what a Royal Sinner does. The goddamn ink on their arms says that. *Protect Our Own.* He has friends who have been looking out for his interests, and I am not about to serve up any more details on him and have those friends come after my family now." Luke rubbed a hand across his jaw, glanced away, then turned his gaze back to me. His eyes were softer now, and in them I read honesty, truth. I hated it, but that's what I saw. "Look, I made some mistakes when I was a younger man. I made some terrible mistakes. I left town to start fresh after Dora was gone. Moved to San Diego and met my wife there. We returned to Vegas five years ago. My job now is to protect my family, and Jerry Stefano is not a man to be messed with, so I never talked then and I don't intend to now. He told us to never say a word, so I didn't. He made it clear the people we loved would get hurt. That's why your mother kept it quiet, and that's why I did too. I love too many people to take that chance."

I sighed heavily, a long, deep, frustrated sound filled with years of regret, years of anger, years of locking up all these awful secrets.

There wasn't much else to say. He had nothing more. And I was in the same damn boat too.

I thanked him and headed to the front door. On the way, I spotted a framed wedding photo of Luke and his wife. The man didn't look much younger than he did today. I peered at it. "How long have you been married?"

Luke glanced sheepishly at the floor. "Only a year. But we've been together for a lot longer. Anyway, don't tell the church I had kids out of wedlock."

"Your secret's safe with me," I said, wishing it were the only secret I shared with this man.

As I headed for my truck ready to hit the road to Hawthorne, a fresh wave of loathing rolled through me. I was in a pact with the man who'd fucked my mother behind my father's back.

The one bright spot was the message on my phone from Sophie.

27

SOPHIE

Red. Ripe. Juicy.

The peaches looked mouthwateringly good.

"One pound of peaches coming right up."

"Thank you, Marietta," I said, flashing a bright smile at my favorite employee at my parents' former fruit stand at the farmers' market.

"You will love these. They're divine. My God, they melt in your mouth—and in a peach pie," Marietta said, bringing her fingers to her lips and pressing a kiss to them before setting to work bagging up my fruit.

"Nothing is ever as good as a pie made with summer peaches kissed by the sun," I said as I pushed my big white sunglasses on top of my head.

"How's John doing?"

"You know John. He's as busy as ever. Work, work, work. And he has these dang termites, so he's been staying at my place. Talk about cramping my style," I said in a faux whisper. "But he'll be gone tomorrow night. So I think . . ." I trailed off to tap my nails against the red-checkered cloth that covered the table filled with baskets of peaches, cherries, plums, and all sorts of summer fruit. "I might invite over this man I've been seeing."

Marietta wiggled her thick black eyebrows as she wiped a hand across her apron. "You know that's how your mom wooed your dad," she said, winking.

"Oh, stop."

The woman nodded enthusiastically. "It's true. She lured him with a pineapple. You've got peaches."

"How many times did my parents tell you that story?"

"Countless," she said with a laugh, then tapped the counter. My parents had operated this fruit stand for many years, and Marietta had taken it over when they died. "This stand has some sort of magic to it. I met my husband here too, and we're going on twenty-five years."

"The magic of fruit," I quipped, then stopped for a second to gaze heavenward. "You know, maybe that's why I have so many dresses with fruit patterns."

"You're trying to attract love," Marietta said. "Draw it to you. I think that's brave and hopeful."

"Is it crazy?"

Marietta shook her head. "Nothing is ever crazy when it involves love," she said, handing me a sturdy brown paper bag. "Go make a peach pie. It's always the way to a man's heart."

That made me hopeful, so I sent Ryan a teaser.

Sophie: Know what's really exquisite? My peach pie. So exquisite you should come over for dinner and dessert, and peaches and me. Friday night?

Ryan: Yes and yes, and yes and yes.

My phone rang as I turned on the engine in my car.

"Tell me more about these peaches," he said, his strong, sexy voice making my belly flip.

"They're ripe and juicy, and they taste like sin," I said, taking my time with each word, letting them fall from my lips like sugar.

"Mmm," he said in a sexy growl. "So, just like you, basically?"

"I'll have to take your word on that."

"Oh, you can definitely take my word on that."

A robotic female voice sounded from his phone. *"You are two hundred miles from your destination in Hawthorne."*

I furrowed my brow. There wasn't much in Hawthorne. That was a small town with a big prison. "What are you doing in Hawthorne?" I asked curiously as I pulled onto the road. "Do you do security for the prison?"

He didn't answer at first. "Yeah. Shit, Sophie, I need to pay attention to the road, but I can't wait to see you Friday. I'll be there. It's the only thing making this drive better."

Then he hung up.

28

———

RYAN

Halfway there.

The sun glared at me as I played The National on repeat. My favorite band. Dark and moody. It suited me after seeing Luke, then lying to Sophie.

I gripped the wheel tighter. What choice did I have? Was I supposed to tell her about my mom over the goddamn phone? I was flying blind when it came to sharing this emotional stuff about my family history. I'd had no training in how to open my heart, or my life, or my past. And I'd never been a practitioner of closeness or commitment.

But I couldn't seem to stay away from Sophie.

So I'd need to do it right. Tell her when we were sitting down, face-to-face, not over the phone.

As the road echoed its sameness for miles, I dialed my sister's number. After a quick hello, I put her on speakerphone and jumped right into the matter at hand, because I had a special request.

"Where do I find a dress like the kind movie stars in the fifties wore? Like a pinup dress?"

Shannon laughed. "What's going on?"

"I want to get one as a gift. For a woman."

She whistled, then I hear her rustle around, and she said to someone, "Ryan is shopping for a dress."

A woman chuckled.

When Shannon returned to the phone I said, "Who are you with?"

"Mindy. Brent's friend. We're having lunch and she's telling me funny stories about what he was like in high school. Say hi to Mindy. I'll put you on speaker."

"Hi Mindy," I said, suspecting I was about to get a double dose of woman advice.

"Hi Ryan. Tell us more about this dress," Mindy said.

"Yes, Is Mr. Always Single dating someone? Details," Shannon demanded.

"I can't get into them now. I'm sure it's fascinating and all, but I'm driving. Just tell me where I can buy one. Is there a store on the Strip that sells them? She told me they're kind of specialty items."

"Well, they are very boutique-type dresses. You don't really find them at the department store. But maybe Rockin' Bette or Viva Las Vegas might have them. Do you want me to call around for you?"

I breathed a sigh of relief. "That would be awesome. But I want one with peaches on it."

"Ooh, peaches," Mindy said as if peaches were a dirty word.

Shannon chimed in. "You're not going to find that off the rack, even at a boutique. You need to go to Etsy and hunt online for something that specific. I'll look for you. Tell me what size to get."

"Um . . . I don't know what size she is," I said.

"Well, what's her figure like?"

"Perfect. Curvy. Sexy."

"Hmm . . . pinup, you said? Like Marilyn Monroe?"

I snapped my fingers as I drove. "Yes. Exactly."

"Okay. I'll see what I can track down for your pretty lady. How's her personality?"

I smiled, a grin that seemed to come out of nowhere, one that I had no control over when I thought of Sophie. "Brilliant, clever, sweet, fun."

"That makes me very happy to hear."

"Ditto," Mindy said. "And you better treat her well."

"Of course I will."

Shannon clicked off the speaker, from the sound of it, then said in a quieter voice, "Brent and I are coming by on Saturday for lunch, so you can tell me all about her when I see you in person." She paused before she added, "By the way, have a good visit with Mom."

"Thanks, Shan."

I hung up, and a little later I drove through the gates and into the visitor lot at my mother's permanent residence.

29

DORA

I had important things to tell Ryan.

The breakout in New York State.

The guy who made it out through a manhole.

How Kelsey in the cell next to mine can't eat bread, so now she gets gluten-free accommodations. If they could make exceptions for her, they could make them for me.

Wasn't that fair? After almost eighteen years in this joint, didn't I deserve a little fairness? All I had were a few visits here and there in these concrete rooms with only a table and chairs.

Ryan had to be able to help me. "Can't you talk to them? Ask them to give me something better to eat?"

He heaved a sigh. "I love you, Mom. But you gotta fucking focus."

At that word, my gaze snapped up. My eyes narrowed. He was still my baby, and I'd taught him better. "Watch your mouth," I chided him.

"Sorry," he muttered. "I'll try to do better." He tapped his watch. "But time is running out, and I want some details."

Glancing at the clock, I noticed he'd been here for a while.

Time.

It slipped by me. It fell through my fingers.

Time was all I had. Endless time.

Time to think. Time to plan. Time to wonder.

And now I was wasting time with my baby.

I had all the time, and I had no time.

"What? What is it?" I asked, trying to focus. Telling myself I could focus on him.

He reached for my hand, squeezed it. "I've held on to your secrets. Can't you tell me a damn thing? The cops won't say a word about the evidence they have. You've got to know, Mom. I'm sure they've been here to see you about the case being reopened."

Fear raced through me. I pursed my lips together.

He held his hands out wide, waiting for an answer. "So?"

I shook my head.

Don't say a word, don't say a word, don't say a word.

He closed his eyes and sighed. "Mom, c'mon. I'm trying to help, but you've got to give me something. Does it have to do with Stefano's kid?"

My head jerked. What did he say? I'd never known. Never heard. No one told me. "What?"

He squeezed my hand harder. "He had a kid. His girl-friend was pregnant at the time of the murder. Bianca Rosa is her name. Supposedly, his friends were supposed to look out for the kid, but they apparently haven't followed through. I think that's why the case was reopened."

This was huge.

Oh God, this was so big, bigger than I'd imagined.

I lowered my voice to the barest whisper, my eyes fixed intently on my Ryan. "*Who* was supposed to look out for the kid?" That was all that mattered. Jerry was on the inside. But who was on the outside looking out for the kid? Who, who, who? Was it them? Was it those guys? "*Who* was supposed to look out for the kid?" I asked again, my voice shaking.

His brow knit, and he shook his head. "I don't know, Mom. Who do you think is looking out for the kid?"

Don't say a word, don't say a word, don't say a word.

The words though. They were in my gut, lodged in my head, locked up in trunks I couldn't let open. But I had to know. I simply had to. I opened the trunk a smidge. "Was it TJ and K who—?"

No! I couldn't do that. Couldn't say more.

I smacked my hand over my mouth and dug my fingers into my cheekbones. Dug them so deep to remind me to shut up. Shut up. Shut up.

"Who are TJ and K?" Ryan asked, reaching across the table to gently pry my hand from my face. I didn't want to let go. Didn't want to have the use of my mouth again. Didn't want to risk speaking.

But Ryan was stronger, and soon he'd peeled my hand away.

"Who? Who are they? Who are TJ and K? Are they Royal Sinners? Were they involved?"

30

RYAN

Talking to my mom was like trying to capture a hummingbird with a thimble.

But for the first time in ages, she'd said something.

Something that could be valuable.

But once I pulled her hand off her jaw, that focused look vacated her eyes. Her gaze turned glassy again, exhausted. "I'm tired. I'm so tired. I'm so incredibly tired."

No way. That was not okay. I was not giving up so easily.

"Mom, c'mon," I said, begging. "I've done everything you asked. I can't help you unless you tell me. You begged me to never say a word about the drugs, and I never did. I never said a thing, just like you asked. I followed your word to the letter. For eighteen goddamn years. But, Jesus Christ, I miss my dad. Okay?" My voice rose as I pleaded with her to just tell me everything. "I miss him every day. If you know something you've never told me, now would be a really good time to share it, since there's a chance of justice being served."

Her lips curved down. She reached for my hand and

clasped her bony fingers around it. "I have to protect you. I swore I'd protect you. I will till the day I die."

I leaned back in my chair and shoved a hand through my hair. "I can protect myself. I'm not fourteen anymore. I'm not a kid. I'm a thirty-two-year-old man. So tell me. Who are TJ and K? Did they kill Dad?"

"I'm protecting you and your brothers and sister," she said, sticking to her party line.

I tried again, hoping to rattle her this time. Press her buttons. "Then did you do it? They all think you did. Everyone thinks you did. The state sure as hell does. Did you kill Dad?"

She narrowed her eyes. "*No.* I've told you I didn't."

"You better not have lied to me. For years I have believed in you."

"Everything I've done is for all of you. I love you all so much."

I was a powder keg, about to go off. "You gave this to me—don't you get it? You gave me this obsession over what really happened," I said, grabbing the sides of my skull for emphasis. "It's like a sickness in me now. You asked me to cover up the drugs when the cops were investigating my father's murder, and the details and secrets eat away at me. It makes it hard for me to have a normal fucking life. Tell me, who are they?"

Her eyelids started to close. "I need to sleep," she mumbled. "I can't sleep at night. All I do is lie awake and stare at the ceiling and wish for the light to come. Wish for time. Wish for less time. Wish for it all to make sense." She rested her cheek against the table. In a minute, she'd fallen into slumber.

And I was hardly any closer to knowing *why.*

I sat there in silence till the hour ended, and the sturdy brown-haired corrections officer returned to the room.

"Hey, Clara," I said to the woman in the beige uniform.

She smiled. "Hey, Ryan. How's it going?"

"Keeping busy. Trying to stay out of trouble. How about you? How's the family?"

"My oldest starts high school next month. Time flies, huh?"

"I remember when you were telling me about him starting kindergarten," I said, because it had been that long since I'd known her.

Clara patted my sleeping mom. "C'mon, Prince. Visiting hour is over."

Dora raised her head an inch. A line from the table's edge was pressed into her cheek. Her mouth was open and saliva had pooled in the corner of her lips. She blinked, then she rose and held out her arms.

With a lump in my throat and a hole in my heart, I hugged her. "Bye, Mom. Get some sleep."

"Come by again, please. And stay safe. Stay away from the Sinners. Just stay away and you'll be safe then."

"I will," I said, and kissed her forehead. The Sinners, it was always about the Sinners.

I gave a quick wave to Clara. "Take care of yourself, Clara."

"You too. Will we see you later this month? She earned some more visiting hours. She started volunteering in the library."

"That's good. The library and the hours."

"It is good. Reading helps them. So much more than TV."

"That's the truth. When are her hours?"

"End of next week, I believe."

I nodded. "I'll do my best. Can't seem to stay away from this place," I said with a wry smile, and Clara patted me on the shoulder.

As I left, I wished I could simply google "TJ and K" and know what the hell my mother had been talking about. Spend the night searching for them. Track them down. Confront them. But who the hell were they? I didn't know, and I didn't know how to find out.

But as I closed the door to my truck, it occurred to me that I could do something else with the information. I was grasping at straws, but maybe someone else could make sense of this. Maybe it was time for me to ask for help, to turn to another person who was trying to solve this case.

I was never big on asking for help.

But this time, I had to.

This time I had to reach out.

I dialed Detective John Winston and passed on the initials TJ and K.

"I really appreciate that," John said.

"I don't know that it means anything."

"I don't either. But it might, and that's what matters. A lead is a lead, and I'll see what I can do."

For the first time in a long time, I felt unburdened.

31

SOPHIE

The scent of roasted rosemary chicken wafted through my penthouse on Friday night as I turned off the oven and set the roasting pan on top of the stove. I leaned in to the bird, cuddled by potatoes and carrots, and inhaled the delicious scent.

"Mmm," I said aloud, enjoying the savory aroma almost as much as I delighted in the yummy smells emanating from my second oven as the pie baked. I'd also made a summer salad, which was staying cool in the fridge.

Since Project Termite had been officially terminated and my brother had returned to his own home last night, I wore red lace panties and a matching push-up bra, barely covered by the flirty apron I had on and finished off with black strappy pumps on my feet.

A timer dinged, and I pulled the mouthwatering peach pie from the oven. A sultry Billie Holiday number played in the background, and now all I needed was my sexy date to arrive.

Soon my buzzer rang, and my heart sped up in anticipation. I pressed the button to respond. "Hello there."

"Ryan Sloan is here. May I send him up?"

"Absolutely," I said, and within minutes there was a knock on my door. The sound made my chest tingly. I was so damn ready to see him.

I opened the door, and he nearly stumbled.

He opened his lips to speak, but no words came. His jaw simply hung open.

I fought valiantly to contain a victorious grin. Inside, though, I wanted to pump a fist for having rendered him speechless.

He had a bottle of white wine and a bouquet of peach tulips in one hand, so I grabbed his free hand, tugged him inside, and shut the door behind him. In seconds, he'd backed me up against the wall, set the wine and flowers down on the entryway table, and placed his hands on my face. "How is it possible that you are more stunning every time I see you?"

I jutted out my hip and winked. "It's the apron," I said, gesturing to my skimpy attire.

He dropped a hand to my back, running it along the bare skin above the waist. "It's not the apron. It's how *you* look in it. Every time I see you, you're wearing something that makes me rock hard," he said, yanking me close so I could feel the evidence myself.

"I like you hard, Ryan Sloan," I said, meeting his gaze, and he smiled at me, then grasped my ass, grinding his erection against my belly.

"You're all I thought about all day," he murmured.

"What were you thinking about specifically? Wait. Don't tell me." I leaned back to tap my finger on my chin. "Was it the food? You were so damn curious to know what I was cooking for you—admit it."

He shook his head.

"So it was the peaches, then?"

Another shake as he rubbed his hard-on against me.

"Maybe it was getting a tour of my home?" I craned my neck, gesturing with my eyes to the living room.

"Nope," he said with a sexy grin.

"Oh," I said, my lips forming an O. "Was it this?" I spun away from his grip and ran my hands along my breasts, down to my belly, letting one hand rest between my legs. Then, I took slow, measured steps into the open kitchen that looked out onto my living room.

His eyes prowled over me as he followed, unknotting his tie and tossing it on the floor. He undid the top button on his crisp white button-down. I reached a metal stool in my kitchen, bumping it with the backs of my legs. His arms darted out, and he grabbed my waist, lifted me up, and set me on the stool. He skimmed his fingers down my bare arms. "Let me just look at you," he whispered, raking his eyes over my figure from head to toe. His dark gaze made me feel not only naked, but dirty. Filthy. Wanton.

His chest rose and fell as he drank me in. He wasn't even touching me, but my skin sizzled. I felt *touched*. Then he brushed his fingertips along my sides. I let my legs fall open for him, spreading myself, as I hooked my heels onto the bottom rung. Pressing my palms on the back of the stool to hold on, I arched my spine, offering my body to him.

Placing myself in his hands.

Giving myself to him.

"Look at you. Just fucking look at you. You are killing me," he murmured as he cupped my cheek in his right hand. "You're all I thought about all day. Seeing you. Touching you. Tasting you. Having you," he said, stroking my cheek. He paused, his voice rough with desire. "And fucking you."

He swept his lips over mine in a deep, devouring,

hungry kiss. His tongue searched mine, and I let him lead. When he broke the kiss, I said softly, "Do whatever you want to me."

He pressed his forehead to mine. "Everything," he said. "I want to do everything to you, Sophie. I want to explore every inch of you. I want to taste all of you. I want to fuck you *everywhere*. But right now? I want your sweetness on my tongue."

I gasped as heat raced through my body. "I want that too."

"Keep your hands right where they are. Behind you," he said, and I nodded.

Dipping his hands under the front of my apron, he tugged at my panties and pulled them to my ankles, then off. He hooked my high-heeled shoes more firmly back onto the rung, a clear sign I had to keep them in place. "I need to taste you every day. I can't go this long without you on my lips," he said, kneeling on the floor then burying his face between my legs.

I squeezed my eyes shut and cried out in pleasure, my voice becoming the harmony to Billie Holiday as Ryan licked and sucked and tasted. If I wasn't allowed to move my body, I could use my mouth. I could rely on my voice. I could scream and moan and groan. And so I did, because every lick, every touch, every press of his tongue drove me wild.

He moaned against my center then pulled back. "Grab my head. Use your hands. Do whatever you want," he said, giving me a command. Somewhere in the house I heard my ringtone. "Fly me to the Moon." Seemed appropriate.

My hands flew into his hair, and I laced my fingers through those soft strands, for the first time touching him as he licked me. I'd longed for this chance. I loved being restrained, but I loved his hair too. I grasped harder, my nails curling into his skull. He groaned, a mad, feral sound as I dug into his head, and I knew that he wanted me to be rough right now. That he wanted me to show him how I felt about the way he touched me.

I felt like an animal.

Wild and crazed.

I held on to his head, yanking his mouth closer. I was on fire, a white-hot path of flames tearing through my body, burning everything in sight, turning me into an inferno as he fucked my pussy with his lips, his mouth, his tongue, and I rode his face until I saw stars, until the heavens fell from the sky and I came in his mouth.

Shuddering.

Trembling.

Shaking from head to toe.

Clutching his face between my legs as I rocked into him.

Soon enough, I uncurled my hands from his hair. Everything around us smelled like food, and sex, and chemistry, and peaches.

He reached into the bowl on the island that held the few extra peaches I'd sliced, grabbed a slice, and brought it to his lips. He ate it, and then said, "It's good."

He grabbed another piece of peach. He pulled down the top of my apron, exposing my red bra then unhooking it. He dragged the peach slice across my breasts. "Let me taste it like this," he said, then licked up the juice from my body.

"So good. But it doesn't even compare to you," he murmured against my chest, and I moaned happily from his words and his touch.

I'd never been one for food play, only because I'd never had this type of sex. But Ryan licking the taste of a ripe peach from my pale skin felt like the way sex should be. It felt primal, an elemental connection between a woman who wanted a man and a man who had to have her. Nothing else at play but this red-hot, sinful desire that burned between us. I grabbed his head and pulled him to my breasts.

"That's enough of you being able to use your hands," he said, narrowing his eyes as he picked me up and carried me to the dining room table. He set me down on it and began undoing my apron strings.

"Ryan?" I whispered.

He looked at me, waiting.

"Do you remember what you said at the slot machine, what you wanted to do to me?" I gazed down to my breasts.

He pressed a finger to my lips. "I told you I would never forget your perfect tits. Do you think I have?"

I shook my head.

He dragged a finger between my breasts. "You want me to fuck these beautiful tits?" he asked. "You want to watch me come on them, don't you?"

I inhaled sharply. "Oh God, I do."

He got on the table and straddled me as I scooted back. "You need to do something first."

"Anything."

"Take off my shirt," he said.

I sat up, thrilled to unbutton his shirt, pushing it over his chest then down his arms, murmuring as I felt how strong he was. He was so toned and muscular, so hard and fit. He shrugged off the shirt, and I splayed my hands across his chest, dragging my nails through the soft little hairs. He breathed deeply as I explored him.

"Unzip my pants," he said, and I raced to unbutton then unzip them, pushing them down to his ass, freeing his cock. I ran the tip of my tongue over my teeth as I gazed at him. The head was swollen and pulsing, and I was dying to feel him. He untied the red ribbon behind my neck, letting the fabric of the ties fall. He pushed the material below my breasts, but I caught the ties and wrapped them around my own wrists.

I held them tight like that, savoring his reaction as he saw my breasts rise up more, creating an even deeper valley between them, from the tug of the fabric and my own hold on the ribbons, restraining myself as I waited for his next instructions.

32

RYAN

She'd offered her own bound body to me, and lust burned through me like wildfire. She was the most enticing woman I'd ever known.

A bolt of desire slammed into me at the sight of her sweet pink flesh. So slick and ready. I slid a finger through her folds, then dipped it inside her, watching her thrust up into my hand. Then I brought that finger to her perfect tits, spreading her wetness between them.

Her eyes widened as she watched me prepare her. I could have fucked her without lubrication. I could have taken her and just thrust my dick between those gorgeous globes of flesh, the friction spurring me on. But it would be better like this.

Better wet. Better slippery.

I gripped my dick, sliding a bead of liquid over the head and closing my eyes momentarily as the sensations roared through me. Fuck, I needed to come. I needed release.

I planted my knees by her ribs, then lowered myself to her chest, sliding my hard cock between her lush breasts, as I parked my hands on the table.

Then I ravaged her tits.

I groaned as I felt her soft flesh press against my dick. She'd inched her arms closer to her body, making a warm, snug tunnel for me. Her breasts caressed my cock as I thrust, my balls slapping against her chest. Her mouth parted, her lips open. Such an eager one, she flicked out her tongue and licked the tip on several thrusts.

"You like that, don't you?" I asked, panting as heat spread through me.

She nodded. "I want to watch you get off on me," she whispered as she held on tight to the ends of the red fabric, her firm grip on the ribbon giving me all the friction I needed. "I've never seen your face when you're coming. I want to know what you look like when you come all over me."

Desire surged in me, like white waters raging, as I pumped between that perfect flesh. I jammed my hands harder against the table. "Tell me how much you want it," I growled, my voice ragged.

"So much," she pleaded, her blue eyes shining with desire. My God, I had unleashed a wild woman in her, and I fucking loved it when she talked dirty to me, saying, "I want you all over my neck and my chest and my tits. Please give it to me."

My spine ignited. My balls tightened, drawing up closer as I rocked through the slick, hot valley of her breasts. That first neon burst of pleasure roared in me, then climbed higher as I pumped. Keeping my dick where it was happiest, I sat up so she could see my face as I gave her what she wanted.

"Now. Fucking now. Watch me come on you," I groaned, fighting to keep my own eyes open, wanting to watch her as she savored the sight of me straddling her chest, rocking into her tits, and spilling hot white streams onto her breasts, all the way up to her neck and her chin, even the ends of her hair.

I shuddered.

A total body release.

She let go of the hold on one of her ribbons, dragged her finger between her breasts, and brought it to her lips, licking me off.

"Oh, beautiful. You deserve another orgasm for that," I said, then fucked her with my fingers until she came riding my hand on her dining room table.

33

RYAN

Hot water rained down on us in her luxurious shower with glass brick walls. I poured some of her shampoo into my palm then lathered up her soft hair, taking my time working it into her wet strands. She closed her eyes and leaned her head against my chest.

"Your dinner's probably getting cold," I murmured in her ear as I turned her around and rinsed the shampoo from her hair.

"I know. But that's what rewarming in the oven is for," she said.

I looped an arm around her waist, tugging her soft, wet body against me. "I know this sounds crazy because it was only a few days ago when I saw you, but I did miss you," I said, planting a kiss on her neck, then traveling to her lips, kissing her softly, slowly, taking my time. She whimpered sexily against my lips, and I let go. "That dinner is really going to get cold."

"And I am really going to get hot the longer I stand here naked in the shower with you," she said, and I eyed her all over, keenly aware that this was the first time she'd been completely naked in front of me, and I with her.

I held up my finger. "Let me go get a condom." I turned to the shower door, when I felt her grasp my arm.

"I'm on the pill," she said. "And I'm kind of ridiculously clean."

I laughed. "Ridiculous is good. And same here. Clean, that is."

I backed her up against the royal-blue tiled wall, hitched up her right leg around my hip, and guided myself into her.

There were no words to describe how fantastic she felt. So I didn't say anything. I simply moved inside her, getting to know her body even more intimately as twilight fell and she wrapped her arms around my neck and whispered my name.

Soon, she was saying it louder, in an orgasmic shout, and I chased her there.

34

SOPHIE

Ryan pointed admiringly at the chicken, polishing off his second serving. "This is delicious. You sure can cook."

"Just wait till you have dessert, then," I said with a smile as I brought the glass of pinot grigio to my lips and took a sip of the wine he'd brought. The peach tulips blazed brightly in a vase in the middle of the table. After cleaning up—and heating up—in the shower, I'd changed into a short yellow sundress and had combed my hair into a clip. Ryan had dressed again, but the ends of his still-wet hair gave away what we'd just done, sending sparks swooping through me. I was damn near ready for another round. But I also enjoyed talking to him, and we'd had a nice chat over dinner.

"Tell me more about your company, and what it's like working with your older brother," I said.

As he talked about his work, and both the joys and pitfalls of working with a sibling, a realization landed front and center in my mind.

I liked him. A lot.

No, that wasn't it. It was way more than like.

I was falling for Ryan Sloan. That was what the sparks in my belly were. They weren't *sex* butterflies. They were *falling for you* butterflies.

Ryan set down his fork and cleared his throat. "So, there's something I've been wanting to tell you."

My shoulders tensed instinctively. Nothing good ever came from those words. "You're married?" I asked, panic seizing me. I wasn't sure why that was the first thing that came to my mind. But I was sure something bad was about to come out of his mouth. Especially given where my own mind and heart had just gone.

He laughed and shook his head, and his response made me feel the tiniest bit better. "No. It's about—"

But his words were cut off by a knock on the door. I stood up quickly. "It's probably just a delivery or something. Dry cleaning maybe," I said, and walked to the door. I peered through the peephole and beamed when I saw my brother.

I turned to Ryan as I opened the door. "Oh. You can meet John."

Ryan's face froze, and so did my brother's when he made eye contact with the other man in the room.

Then John said my lover's name like a hiss.

35

SOPHIE

"You two know each other?" I gestured from my brother to Ryan.

Ryan nodded as John said, "Yes."

John went next, pointing to Ryan. "Why are you talking to my sister?" His voice was accusing. The tone was enough to send hackles up my spine.

I held up both hands. "Wait," I said firmly. "Someone tell me what is going on."

Ryan pushed back his chair, the wooden legs scraping loudly against the floor. "We know each other because he's working on a case that involves my family." He took long strides to me. "My father's murder."

I clasped my hand over my mouth. I shuddered, but then blinked when I realized something didn't add up. "You said you were fourteen when he died?"

"I was," Ryan said, standing a few feet from me. He pressed his fingers against his temple, speaking the next words as if they pained him. "He was shot in the driveway of our home one night. Both the gunman and my mother are in prison for the crime. The case was just reopened."

My mouth fell open, and the earth ceased rotating as the enormity of his statement rocked through me. Slowly, I let each word sink in. That was a hell of a hand of cards to be dealt. I couldn't even imagine what he'd gone through, living with that kind of tragedy.

"Oh my God, I'm so sorry," I said, reaching for him, stepping closer, my natural instinct to comfort surpassing all else.

He shook his head. "It's okay," Ryan mumbled, his body language telling me he didn't want soothing.

"I had no idea," I said softly.

"I've been trying to think of the right way to tell you, because I don't really talk about it," he said.

I was floored, but as I took it all in, I was starting to understand all his walls now—and oh hell, did he have them.

"We reopened the investigation a few weeks ago because of new evidence," John added, stepping closer to me, flanking me, as if he needed to protect me from Ryan.

It suddenly seemed like I hardly knew the man I'd just spent the evening with. But then my mind galloped over the last several conversations I'd had with John. I spun to face my brother, adding up the clues. "This is the case you've been working on?"

He nodded. "One of them. One of the big ones."

I turned my gaze back to Ryan, and for the first time ever, he didn't look in control. He didn't appear cool or confident or passionate. He seemed rattled, as if he'd been knocked out of orbit.

Something clicked in my head. "*Hawthorne*," I said under my breath. "Is that why you went to Hawthorne?"

John cut in before Ryan could answer. "He visited his mother on Wednesday at Stella McLaren. He actually passed on some info to me later that day that may wind up being useful," John said, a bit grudgingly, but still with some gratitude in his tone.

"You don't do security for the prison, like you said?" I asked Ryan as I furrowed my brow. He'd lied. Maybe it was a small one, but it was still a lie.

He shook his head. "The prison's not a client. I went there to see my mom. She's been in since I was fourteen," he said, his voice heavy, laced with shame and sadness.

I felt confused, overwhelmed, and . . . *fooled*. Ryan had always been mysterious, but now he felt like a stranger. I was grappling with the fact that I was finding out like this, from my brother, that my lover had this monumentally dark past, rather than him sharing it directly with me, as I'd done with him.

"I have a question, and it's pretty important, as far as I can tell," John said, cocking his head and staring at Ryan. "How long have you been involved with my sister?"

"Over a week. I met her the day I went to—"

"That's why you were at the municipal building?" I asked, crossing my arms. "The day I met you? You were going to see my brother?"

"I didn't know he was your brother then," Ryan answered defensively. "I didn't have a clue you two were connected. All I knew when I met you was that I wanted you."

John cleared his throat. "I left my phone charger in the guest room. That's why I stopped by. I'm going to get that right now," he said, then stopped to look at me. "Unless you want me here in this room."

I waved him down the hall. Once I heard the door to the guest room shut, I spoke. "When did you know the detective investigating your father's case was my brother?"

He gulped. "When I looked you up before the gala," he

said, and my blood turned to ice. Now that I'd moved beyond the initial desire to comfort him, I felt . . . *used.*

"Did you pursue me to get close to the investigation?" I whispered, dreading the answer.

He shook his head several times. "No. No. No."

That was a few too many *noes* for my taste. "Maybe a little?"

He shoved a hand through his hair and sighed heavily. "Sophie, I can't stop thinking about you. It's that simple. It has nothing to do with your brother."

I held out my hands in question. "Then I just don't understand why you didn't tell me."

He shot me a quizzical look. "Uh, maybe because it's not that easy for me to say."

I barely registered his words as the memories of my own admissions reared to the surface. I'd shared so much with him. He'd shared so little. He'd had so many opportunities to tell me. "Ryan, I just went on and on about John and his work so many times. And you knew who he was. You even made remarks like 'I bet he has some stories about what he's seen.' You said that on the Ferris wheel," I reminded him, my near-photographic memory coming in handy. "I just feel stupid."

"Did you want me to drop this on you on the Ferris wheel?" he asked, his tone turning heated. I could practically feel the frustration burning off him. "That your brother is investigating a fucking murder in my family? Just weave it in as we gabbed about our siblings. *Oh, it's great that you're so close with him. By the way, he asked me the other day if my mom happened to be associating with anyone new at the time of the murder.* Is that what I should have said?" But he didn't give me time to answer. "We don't even use the last names we had when we were growing up,

Sophie. Everyone had heard of us in this town. It was all over the news. Everyone fucking knew us. And we were the kids left behind—mom in prison, dad in the ground, Royal Sinners gang gunman behind bars. We were the poor Paige-Prince kids from the shitty section of town, who everyone felt sorry for," he said harshly, and I let out a surprised squeak.

I'd heard the story when I was finishing junior high. It was one of the biggest news stories in town at the time. "That's you?"

He nodded. "Yes. That's us."

He'd lost so much. So incredibly much. A father. A mother. A normal childhood. Everything. My need for self-protection took a back seat to compassion, and I tried once more to comfort him. I wrapped my arms around him and hugged him. "I am so sorry for what happened to your family, Ryan. I'm sorry for what happened to your dad, and to your mom, and to you and your brothers and your sister," I said softly. He said nothing, but he let me hold him, even leaning into me. He sighed softly, and that sound, that vulnerable sound from this strong, sometimes standoffish man infiltrated my heart and soul. Somehow, in that brief exhalation, I felt him inching toward me.

Not physically. But emotionally. I wanted to be the one there for him. I ran my hands through his hair, wishing I could erase the tragedy.

John's footsteps echoed across the hardwood, breaking the moment. He cleared his throat. "Sophie," he said, and I separated from Ryan. "Is everything okay?"

I nodded. "It's fine."

"Do you want me to stay?"

I shrugged. I didn't know what I wanted anymore. Everything that had felt so certain before John knocked on my door had been uprooted in minutes. "No. Yes. I don't know," I said helplessly.

He pointed his thumb at the door. "I'm going to go wait in the hall. Give you some privacy, but I'll be nearby if you need me."

After he left, I looked at the man I'd been falling for. He had the same brown hair, the same blue eyes, the same strong build as an hour ago, but he *wasn't* the same, because I didn't know how to see him the same way. "I feel like I barely know you. I don't even know where you live."

In a monotone, he said his address.

But it didn't change anything. Knowing the numbers and street name didn't give me any greater insight.

I didn't know what to make of this revelation. Maybe I was overreacting to this news. Or maybe I was underreacting. Was I supposed to feel hurt? Or outraged? Be sympathetic? Care for him?

I had no idea what to do next.

This new wrinkle was so strange, and my chest was knotted up, my head fuzzy. "I like you, Ryan. I like you so much, and I am falling for you. And I understand it's not easy to talk about what happened to your family. I get that, and I wish I could take away the horrors of what you've been through. But aside from that, when I analyze what's been happening with you and me, the reality is this—I've been completely open. I told you at the diner about my marriage. I didn't wait for you to uncover it. I put it all on the table. I told you about my parents and my brother and myself. I can't help but wonder what else you haven't shared, or said, or didn't want to deal with when I've tried to be forthright with you."

"Look, Sophie. I don't tell anyone. I don't get *close* enough to tell anyone. But I knew I needed to tell you, and it's not the kind of thing I wanted to tell you on the phone, so I was planning to tell you tonight. I was starting to at the table . . ." He waved his hand in the direction of the dining room.

Maybe he had been planning on opening up. But I had no way of knowing if he was being truthful now. I tried a new tactic. "Why was the case reopened?"

"I don't know. He won't tell me. I think he thinks there were others involved."

His words sent me back to the night I left for the gala, and my conversation with John beforehand.

Talked to some guy today who I'm sure knows something, but he won't let on what it is.

What do you think he knows?

Something that would help me find the other guys I think were involved.

John was my brother, my flesh and blood. He was the man who'd supported me and helped me build my business, who would take a bullet for me. He had a reason to suspect Ryan was hiding something, and I'd be a foolish woman to wave that off and carry on as if nothing had changed.

"I need you to believe me. I wanted to tell you," he added, and I desperately wanted to trust in his words.

But I'd relied on my instincts before, in my marriage with Holden, and those instincts had been wrong.

Maybe I needed to use my head more. Not my heart. Not my body. "I don't really know what to think. I want to believe you, but I need to sort this out. I've been letting my heart lead instead of my head, and my heart feels pretty foolish and stupid right now." I walked over to the dining room table, picked up the peach pie, returned to my kitchen, and covered it in tinfoil. Then I handed it to him.

He shook his head. "I can't take the pie."

"I need you to. I made it for you. I need some space to think, and I can't do it if I'm surrounded by this dessert I wanted to give you."

I showed him to the door.

36

RYAN

My grandmother dug her fork into the pie on her plate. She rolled her eyes in pleasure.

"Let me tell you something. You don't give up a woman who cooks like this."

"Yeah? That's the bottom line, Nana? How she cooks?" I asked, and grabbed a fork from a utensil drawer, stealing a bite from my grandma's plate.

She smacked my hand, then eyed the ceramic pie pan. "Get your own, young man. This is all mine."

"That's all I wanted. One bite," I said, thinking the sentiment might be apropos for Sophie too. Maybe all I'd take of her would be the one bite I'd had. Then I'd walk away. It was better like that, wasn't it? Leave before your heart gets mangled. Enjoy it while it lasts, like this dessert. This absolutely scrumptious dessert.

My grandma scooped up another forkful, then answered my question. "When she bakes like this, yes. You don't give her up. This pie is *divine.*"

Funny, I had used that same word to describe Sophie.

Divine.

As well as exquisite. Not to mention delicious.

Sophie was a peach pie.

And I wanted the whole damn pie.

I wanted all of Sophie.

But what was the point? Tonight's argument was further proof that intimacy was too dangerous. I had to protect the secrets I'd locked up. When secrets were cracked wide open, you were left far too vulnerable. And when you were vulnerable, you could wind up dead in your own driveway.

"Yeah, it is, but . . ." I said, letting my voice trail off.

"You like her," my grandma said.

I shrugged. "What does it matter?"

She set her fork down and parked her hands on the counter. "It matters because this is all we have," she said, tapping her chest.

"It's not like that." I tried valiantly to deny that there was more to the empty ache I felt right now other than missing great sex. "We were just having a good time."

She screwed up the corner of her mouth. "If it was just a *good time*, why are you here?"

"I wanted to bring you the pie."

"You could have eaten it yourself."

"Nah, I can't finish that," I said.

"Sure you could. You're a sturdy man. You can handle a peach pie."

I patted my flat stomach. "Gotta watch my boyish figure."

She shook her head and rolled her eyes. "You're not fooling me."

I held my hands out wide as if to say I was an open book, even though that couldn't be further from the truth.

"Ryan," she said gently, walking around to join me on

my side of the counter. "I worry about you. You're so private about everything."

"I'm fine."

"You're not. You brought me this pie because you wanted to talk, and you have never wanted to talk about a woman before. So I'm saying perhaps you should consider talking to *her*. Sharing some of your heart," she said.

"What would I even say?"

"Just talk to her. Tell her why you didn't say a word. Tell her what's on your mind. What's in your heart. Women often like that."

But did they? I flashed back to Sanders's wife and her weird glances at the mention of the speeding ticket. I hardly knew how to do what my grandma was prescribing. "Is it even worth it?"

"Is it?" she echoed. "Only you know the answer to that. But Ryan, you think you have to manage everything perfectly because your life spun out of control when you were younger. Here's the thing you need to see—you can't control everything, and you also don't have to. The only things you can take charge of are the choices you make, and if Miss Peach Pie is a choice you want to make, then you should let her in." She paused, then added, "Besides, you've never shown up at my house at ten p.m. to talk about a woman. So think about that, my love."

I wasn't sure I agreed with her.

Hell, I wasn't sure about anything. Except tonight seemed to prove it was a good thing I generally didn't make it beyond a third date.

Just look at the mess I'd made of the fourth one.

37

SOPHIE

I scrubbed the island for a third time. John finished loading the last plate in the dishwasher. "Look, men are pigs," he said in a matter-of-fact tone.

I shot him a sharp-eyed stare. "That makes you a pig too, then."

He nodded vigorously. "Takes one to know one. Men are horrible."

I grabbed a dishtowel and swatted him on the shoulder with it. "Stop. You're being ridiculous. Men aren't pigs. Not all of them, at least," I said softly. "You're not. Dad wasn't. I don't really think Ryan is either."

John said nothing, and I returned to cleaning the marble countertop of the island. I wasn't trying to erase the evening, or the man. I was merely trying to keep my mind busy, so I'd be less apt to rely on my heart.

My heart was a puppy, happily trotting in a field of poppies.

That was the problem.

"Does your silence mean you think he's bad news?" I

asked John. I didn't know anybody else who'd even met Ryan. At least my brother had spoken to him.

"I don't know enough about him to say if he's bad news or not," John said carefully as he poured dishwasher soap into the machine.

"You don't trust him though."

"It's not that I don't trust *him*. I don't trust anyone."

I shoved the sponge roughly back and forth. The repetitive motion was strangely soothing. "But is your distrust of Ryan more or less than your baseline level of distrust?" I asked in a clinical manner.

"It's higher, but that's because we're talking about *you* now. And I don't want you to get hurt."

"You think I'm foolish."

"No," he corrected as he shut the dishwasher. "I think you love easily. Maybe too easily for your own good."

"I'm not in love with him," I said quickly, dropping the sponge and meeting his eyes.

He arched a brow, questioning me with his steely stare. "It sure looked like that. Or like it was heading in that direction."

"When? When did it look like that?"

"When I walked back out and saw you holding him."

I shut my eyes as I slipped back in time to those few seconds that felt like a slice of possibility. My arms around him. His cheek on my shoulder.

"Also, you believe in love so strongly because of Mom and Dad, and you think you're going to have that," John continued. "But most of the world isn't like that. Some of the world is like Ryan's parents."

"What happened with them? Beyond the news. Beyond what I could find on the internet," I asked. I was dying to know. Curiosity had me in its grip.

"Soph," he said in a chiding tone. "You know I can't say."

"But you think he knows something that will help you in the investigation? You said that. You said that the night I went to the gala. I know you had to have been talking about him then."

He huffed. "You're too smart for your own good."

"I'm just a good listener. So what do you think he knows? You don't think he's a suspect, do you?"

He laughed and shook his head, leaning his hip against the counter. "No. Absolutely not. But everyone has an agenda, and I think Ryan Sloan has his own, which for some reason involves protecting his mother."

"But she's in prison. How can he be protecting her?"

"I think he's protecting things she won't tell us. But the good news is he told me something that I think will be helpful, if I can just connect all the dots."

"Can you?"

He shrugged. "That's the million-dollar question. And you know I can't say any more. If I do, I'd compromise the investigation, and all investigations matter, but this one is a big one, Sophie."

I had a sneaking suspicion John wasn't merely looking into an eighteen-year-old murder. I had a feeling he was hunting for something that went much wider and bigger.

"And if you crack this one? You can keep the streets safe?"

"That's always my goal." He nodded to the door. "I should go. Unless you want me to stay."

I shook my head. "I'm fine. Just tell me—is there anything about him you think I need to know? Would I be a fool to see him again?"

He tucked his finger under my chin. "Sophie, I can't make those sorts of promises or guarantees about anyone. Let alone someone I barely know. What I do know is this—

he is focused and intense, and his mother adores him, and he loves her too."

Was that such a bad thing? Was there some law that said you were supposed to become a hater if someone you loved killed? I shuddered at the thought. Was the world that black and white? I had no clue how I would feel in Ryan's shoes, which was why I didn't want to judge him.

I said goodbye to John then went to bed.

When I woke up the next morning, my phone bleated loudly—a reminder of my meeting in a few hours with Clyde. I groaned because the man would surely ask me about my date for the fundraiser, and I didn't know if I had one still.

Or if I wanted one anymore.

38

RYAN

Pool cue in hand, I stared down the eight ball and the corner pocket. I tapped the ball lightly then followed its path as it rolled across the green felt, hell-bent on its destination and impending victory.

C'mon.

The ball veered to the right, bumping the edge of the table and missing the mark by an inch.

"Damn." I let out a long, frustrated sigh.

Brent pulled back on his stick and knocked the eight ball in flawlessly.

"You're killing it today," I said, extending a hand to congratulate my brother-in-law on his third win of the afternoon.

Brent shook his head then waved his hand as if my utter demolishment in a game at which I usually excelled was no big deal. "Just lucky today, that's all," Brent said.

There was a time when I hadn't been a fan of Brent Nichols, because the man had broken my sister's heart long ago. But that was then, and as I had gotten to know Brent anew these days, I'd let the past go. Brent made Shannon immensely happy, and I loved seeing my sister like this—*glowing*.

"Go again?" I asked, holding up my cue.

"You're a glutton for punishment, aren't you?"

"Seems that way," I said. But I was determined to right this ship. I never lost three games in a row. Never ever. This was unprecedented, and I had to get my act together, because I didn't like being so off my game.

I racked the balls as Shannon walked into the den, holding up soda bottles for the crew. "Are we ever going to eat lunch?" she asked as she doled out drinks to Brent and me. She had one left for Colin, since he'd texted that he'd be there any minute, and she set it on the edge of the table. "Or are you boys going to play all afternoon?"

"I'll stop when I break my streak," I said, as Johnny Cash barked happily from the other room. He must have spotted one of his favorite lady dogs walking along the sidewalk from his perch staring out the front window.

"Brent, please let him win. I'm hungry," Shannon said to her husband, who simply laughed.

I shot a sharp-eyed stare at Brent. "Play fair and square."

"I'll play."

I spun around to see Colin walk in, with Johnny Cash trotting by his side. "What the hell? You don't knock?"

"Yeah, some asshole who owns this house didn't lock the front door. I was able to wander in and your guard dog greeted me with a big lick," Colin said with a mischievous glint in his eyes as he petted the dog's furry black head. Then he looked at me. "You'd think a man who works in the security business would lock his door."

I rolled my eyes. "Whatever. I know you used your key. Don't even try to pretend that stuff slips by me."

Colin grinned widely and held up his key. "Ha. Got you. Where's Michael?" he asked, looking around.

"He said he'll be here soon. Just finishing up some work on this new client deal we signed this week," I said as I clapped my brother on the back in greeting. "How's it going? Haven't seen you in a few weeks."

"Good. Busy. Been training for the Badass Triathlon next month."

"You are hard-core. Is that the one where you do some crazy rock climbing too?"

Colin nodded. "Yup. Was up at sunrise on a climb. Gotta go for it after the last time I tried to do it. We all know what happened then."

"You're going to do great this time, man."

"I hear you're busy too these days." Colin wiggled his eyebrows. "Getting it on with some new lady."

I swiveled around to face Shannon. She held up her hands. "Ryan, you had me get her a dress. It's not a state secret that you're seeing someone. But I don't even know her name."

"I really don't want to talk about it," I said, cutting this conversation off at the knees. I missed Sophie like a hungry man misses food, and it had been less than twenty-four hours since I'd seen her. I missed every single thing about her, from her clever banter, to her sexy winks, to her giving heart, to her beautiful body that I wanted to ravage. I'd spent the morning burying myself in work, then in Frisbee time with my dog, then in a long swim in my pool. Now I had some of my favorite people to help keep my mind off the woman who'd nabbed center seat in my brain and my heart.

A picture of Sophie in her black cherry dress and white sunglasses, inviting me to the gala, popped into my head then, unbidden.

Tempting and tantalizing, the image of her was like a summons. And I wanted nothing more than to appear before her. Tell her how I felt. Tell her I wanted in her life, not out of it. But I was no good at talking. Despite what my grandma had said, I was no more skilled at opening my heart to a woman this morning than I had been last night.

I desperately needed the diversion of this game. "Colin, grab a cue and join us. You're on Brent's team. Shan, you're on mine."

Shannon arched an eyebrow. "You must really want to win, Ryan. You know I can beat the two of you blindfolded." She did have a knack for the game. Our dad had been a bit of a pool shark and had taught all of us to play at a young age. Maybe Shannon would help me regain my mojo.

Shannon handed Colin the remaining bottle, then she grabbed a stick, leaned over the table, narrowed her eyes, and assessed the best angle for the break shot. She pulled back the cue, snapped it seamlessly, and sent the top of the table into motion, balls scattering, with an orange one landing easily in a corner pocket.

"Nice," Brent said with an appreciative whistle. "Can't even get annoyed, because that was such a perfect shot."

I pointed my bottle at Brent. "Sucking up to the opposing team—I approve only because it involves my sister, and you should always compliment her."

"And I always do," Brent said with a laugh as he held up his drink in an air toast. I lined up the next shot and then proceeded to whack the purple ball neatly across the table, sinking it easily. Shannon held up a hand to high-five me, and we smacked palms. I turned to Colin as Shannon set up another shot.

"Hey, Colin, I heard your firm is one of the sponsors for the big fundraiser for the community center. I knew you were a volunteer, but I had no idea you were putting your money where your mouth is too. Another one of your quiet *give back* projects?"

My brother nodded. "Yup. They do great work, and Elle, the director, is passionate about helping. Some of the kids there have had rough childhoods, so the center is all about giving them a place to hang out, and, man, do they need help refurbishing that place."

I tipped my chin. "Proud of you, bro."

"Hey," Brent cut in, setting down his soda. "That reminds me. I heard from my friend Mindy earlier today. I already told Shan, but I wanted you both to know too. Remember the guy I saw hanging around outside her house a month ago?"

The pool game ceased, and all eyes turned to Brent. After the murder case was reopened, Brent had mentioned spotting a guy in a Buick idling outside Shannon's old condo. He'd snapped a photo at the time, and while the guy in the car hadn't done anything suspicious, he'd spent far too long doing a whole lot of nothing in the car while staring at her building. Turned out Shannon had seen him another time too. Shannon was living with Brent now, so she felt safer. Still, we all wanted to know more about the guy in the Buick, in case he'd been watching Shannon for some reason.

"Mindy talked to her friends on the force. Asked them if the ink on his arms looked familiar." I flashed back to Luke's comments about the Royal Sinners, and the tattoos that bore their mantra, as Brent continued, "The picture I had of him wasn't perfect, but we zoomed in as close as we could, and it looks like one of the tattoos says *Protect*."

My blood chilled. *Protect our own.* "That's the ink of the Royal Sinners," I said, dread laced through my voice.

Shannon moved closer to Brent, visibly shivering, and

he draped an arm around his wife. "Are you serious?" she asked.

I nodded. "We've already got the increased security detail on you, but just be careful, Shan. These guys don't fuck around. Stefano has friends on the outside, and he had a kid at the time he went to prison. I heard the kid's been getting into some trouble. What if this guy watching us is Stefano's son? He looks young enough. We need to be careful," I said firmly, in a tone that brooked no argument, then turned to Colin. "Same goes for you."

"You're getting me a bodyguard?"

"If you want one, I will."

Colin shot me a look that said *hell no*. "Let me see the picture," he said, and Brent pulled it up on his phone and passed it to Colin. But the photo didn't show much of the guy's face.

He stroked his chin and appeared deep in thought.

"What is it, Colin?" Shannon asked.

"This is going to sound strange, but he feels vaguely familiar. Like maybe I've seen this guy shooting hoops at the community center." He tapped the screen and spoke to Brent. "Send me this picture. Let me do a little more digging."

Brent swiped the screen a few times, then said, "Done. And listen, we haven't seen him around in a month, so my thought is maybe he was just trying to keep an eye on Shan before the case got reopened?"

Luke's warning rang in my ears.

Bump into a guy like Stefano on the street and you run the other way.

But I didn't need that man's words about the Royal Sinners to take the threat seriously. My father in the ground, courtesy of a gangland shooter, was all I needed to make sure I did everything I could to keep my family safe.

"We're not taking any chances, because we don't know what's going on. That's the issue. We don't know every-thing that's happening with the investigation. The only one who knows is the damn detective."

We speculated more on the case while finishing the round of pool. When Shannon landed the winning shot, she declared victory for the two of us. Then she raised her cue, tapped me on the shoulder from across the table, and poked me with it. "Now, fess up. What's the story with the woman you had me buy the dress for? I want to know."

"She's pissed at me," I said heavily. I hadn't heard a word from her since last night, so that was probably the end of Miss Peach Pie. A black cloud engulfed me at the prospect of never seeing her again.

"What did you do wrong?" Brent asked as he knocked back some of his soda.

I parked my hands on my hips. "Now, why do you assume it was me who did something wrong?"

Brent nearly spat out his drink. "Dude. You just said you did. You said she's pissed at you."

"It's a long story," I muttered. "I don't even know if she wants to hear from me again."

Shannon hung up her cue, marched over to me, and stared at me, her eyes saying *we're waiting*.

I gritted my teeth, pressing them hard together, locking up my words and shutting off the details in my head.

Old habit.

This was my way.

This was how I dealt.

Jam all the personal, private information into the vise of my mind, then crush it and let the tension live in my bones for years, like a coiled spring. The one time lately I hadn't felt like a taut power line was when I'd given John the initials I'd gotten from my mom. Instead, I'd felt a sense of freedom from the weight of the past.

The memory of that feeling was a soft knock on the door. A gentle reminder that I'd gotten in this predicament with Sophie by keeping my secrets airtight.

Maybe it was time to try a new approach.

"So here's the story," I said, then told them about the only woman I'd ever even started to let into my heart. I kept it short and simple, sticking to the basic facts.

When I was through, Shannon slammed her hands against my chest. "You ass."

I stumbled into the pool table, surprise racing through me.

Brent cracked up. "She doesn't pull any punches. You gotta watch out for Mrs. Nichols," he said.

"Tell me about it," I said, straightening up.

"Why are you here? Seriously? Go," she said, pointing to the door. "Go find her and tell her you weren't using her, and she's the first woman you've ever felt a damn thing for, and you're all sorts of messed up in the head"—she tapped her temple—"but you want to try for her. Or do you want to wait ten years for her to come back into your life?"

"Can't think of a better endorsement for going after the woman you want this very second than our example," he said, gesturing from Shannon to himself. "Go get her now, man. Get her now."

Shannon turned to her husband, and the look in her eyes and the smile on her face said it all. They were in mad love.

I didn't know if that was what I was pursuing with Sophie. It felt more like . . . *possibility.*

And hell, *possibility* seemed worth it. When it came in a package of brains, beauty, and heart, wrapped up in a peach dress, it seemed worth it for sure.

I searched through my mental files, trying to remember where Sophie said she'd be on Saturday. Something about the fundraiser. Doing some work with her ex. Was she at home? At her office? I snapped my fingers when I remembered.

"Fine," I said, then leaned closer to Shannon and whispered, "But can you give me that dress?"

She smiled widely. "Of course. It's in my car."

I turned to the rest of them. "All right. Wish me luck. You gonna stay here and keep Johnny Cash company and eat the sandwiches?"

"We are, and then we're going to spend the day in your pool and wreak havoc," Colin said. "Leave now so we can start this pool party."

39

SOPHIE

The ballroom at The Venetian was perfection.

I had just walked Clyde through a quick rehearsal of his opening remarks, showing him where he would enter the stage and demonstrating how the podium would be set up for his introduction at the fundraiser.

I thanked the operations manager for the quick use of the room and then headed to the elevator with the event's biggest donor. Clyde wagged a finger at me as we stepped into the elevator. "I can't wait till next Saturday."

"It's going to be a great event," I said with a bright smile I hardly felt.

Inside, my mind was a cluttered mess. I still didn't know what to make of Ryan, or whether I wanted to move forward with him. Too bad relationships weren't math problems with precise answers. They were essay questions in a philosophy class, and they came down to judgment.

I wasn't sure what choice I wanted to make, or if there even *was* a choice anymore. For all I knew, Ryan might have closed the gates on that flicker of possibility I'd sensed last night. Shut it off like a switch. I was willing to bet he was good at that. The man had a built-in eject button, and could easily parachute himself to a soft landing far away from me.

"That's not what I meant. I meant that I'm looking forward to meeting your gentleman at the event," Clyde said with a wink, mentioning the man in limbo in my life. "The man who has captured the attention of Las Vegas's most eligible bachelorette."

I cringed, absolutely cringed from head to toe, at that designation. The feminist in me wanted to brandish her claws, yet the shrewd businesswoman in me affixed her best shiny, happy face. "Oh, Clyde, you do shower me with compliments," I said as we reached the ground floor. I attempted to steer him back to the matter at hand, so I could avoid the topic of my date, since I might not have one anymore. "I'm glad everything is in order for the benefit. Thank you again for stopping by on a Saturday morning to have a look-see."

He was undeterred. "Sophie, I want to say, if it doesn't work out with this fellow for whatever reason, you have an open door with me to connect with Taylor."

In the blink of an eye, my wishes went from blurry to crystal clear.

I didn't want an open door with Taylor. I wanted Ryan. I wanted the one and only man I'd felt such passion and lust and desire for.

There it was. My answer. My choice. This relationship *was* a math problem. Two plus two equals four, and four was Ryan Sloan.

Now I needed to figure out what to do with the result of my simple addition.

"You are so very sweet. And now I have an appointment I must rush off to," I said, waving goodbye.

Once out of earshot and eyeshot, I breathed a huge sigh

of relief and headed to the Grand Canal Shops to meet Holden for a cup of coffee and some much-needed retail and talk therapy. Over lattes and quality time with Kenneth Cole, Coach, and Christian Louboutin, I caught him up to speed on my latest news, showing him Ryan's photo from his corporate website.

"I hope it's not over," I admitted.

"So, on a scale of one to ten, how much do you like him?" he asked as I tried on a peep-toe silver stiletto with a strap over the heel.

"One hundred," I said, peering at the red-soled shoe in the mirror of the boutique. "But I don't know where we stand."

He met my reflection in the glass. "Those look amazing. And honestly, it sounds more like you're in a holding pattern."

"I detest holding patterns. I hate uncertainty. Not to mention the whole thing just makes me feel stupid."

"So tell him as much. Tell him what you need. That he needs to be open with you," he said, as I slipped off the shoes and gestured to the counter so I could pay for them.

"And I feel stupid too because Clyde is breathing down my neck. It's like everyone is using me. I'm sorry if that sounds dramatic, but Clyde clearly has his sights set on me because he thinks I'll never try to touch his money. And then I have to wonder if Ryan had his own agenda."

"Did it seem like that?"

As the saleswoman rang me up, I let the reel of my time with Ryan play before my eyes. Date by date. Night by night. Text by text. Moment after moment of intoxicating, inescapable pleasure. Ryan had always seemed focused on me. Only me. My pleasure, never anything else.

I floated back to the diner and his heady words.

If you were mine, I'd never let you want for anything. I'd take care of you and all your needs. Whatever you needed, I'd give you.

A current of longing swirled inside me. Of missing. Of wanting.

"No," I admitted, taking the bag from the employee. "I was his only agenda."

"Then," he said, as he patted my shoulder, "it seems you might want to let him know you're falling for him. Especially since I think he's here right now."

"What?"

He gestured to the entryway of the Louboutin store. "I'm assuming the insanely handsome man in the University of Michigan T-shirt, holding a shopping bag and looking just like the guy in the photo you just showed me, is here to see you?"

40

SOPHIE

"Hi."

"Hi."

I was too stunned to say much more, but the softness in his voice and the vulnerable look in his beautiful dark-blue eyes, settled my nerves.

Ryan turned to Holden standing next to me. "You must be Holden. I've heard a lot about you. Pleasure to meet you," he said, extending a hand. "I'm Ryan."

Holden took it. "Likewise. Nice to meet you too."

"Sophie tells me you're a talented piano player, and that I'll get to hear you next week at the benefit. That is," he said, returning his focus to me, "if Sophie will still have me."

Holden smiled broadly and dropped a quick kiss on my cheek. "I believe that's my cue to go."

I was left in the middle of the Louboutin store with the man I'd kicked out of my house last night. "How did you find me here?"

"Don't forget, I was Army Intelligence," he said with a grin.

"And they taught you how to locate women who are shopping?"

He shook his head. "No. But you told me you were going to be here today, and since you're a classy woman, I picked the classiest shoe store as your possible location." I loved that I was the object of his treasure hunt. "So," he began, rocking lightly back and forth on his feet. "I'm not terribly good at this whole talk-about-feelings-and-stuff thing, as you've probably gathered by now. So I'm just going to be blunt and lay it out."

He took a beat, drawing a breath. My heart raced as I waited for his next words. "I want to try with you. And I want to take you to the benefit, and introduce you to my brothers and sister, and I'm pretty sure Johnny Cash is eager to meet you."

My heart tripped over itself. "I want all that too."

He wrapped an arm around my waist, and I melted, just melted from the simple touch. "I need you to know, I was never using you. I won't lie and tell you I didn't put it together that you were the detective's sister, but I want to be clear that I wasn't trying to hide the fact I'd made the connection—it had to do with struggling to share the truth about my family with someone for the first time. And I won't insult your intelligence by saying I didn't wonder if you knew anything about the case. I *did* wonder," he said, and I nodded, listening intently to his serious tone. "But that literally lasted for a minute, maybe two. And it ended as soon as I set eyes on you at Aria. Because once I saw you again, none of the other things mattered. I wanted you with an intensity I've never felt before. And the more time I spent with you, the greater that desire became." His fingertips traced soft lines on my waist. "I know we haven't seen each other that much in the grand scheme of things, but I already feel something for you, Sophie. Something deep and powerful," he said, and those words weaved through me, humming in my body, buoying my heart and my spirit.

"I feel the same," I whispered. "I barely understand how it's possible that I only met you a little over a week ago."

"I know." He pressed his forehead to mine. "It makes no sense to me either. It was pure, one-hundred-percent lust at first sight, and then it somehow became more. And I can't risk losing you by being so damn stubborn." He pulled back to look me in the eyes again. His dark-blue gaze made my stomach pirouette, and the way he brushed his fingertips along my arm had my skin sizzling.

"You didn't lose me. I promise."

"I know I messed up, and I can't promise I won't mess up again. And I don't really know if I'm able or ready to sit down and tell you every single sordid detail of my life—"

I pressed my hand to his chest, thrilling at the feel of his firm body beneath the light cotton of his T-shirt. "You don't need to tell me everything. You don't have to deliver your entire life story, Ryan. I just want to know more about you. Bit by bit, day by day, as you're ready to share."

He nodded and clasped his hand over mine. "I meant what I said at the diner. I don't ever get beyond three dates, because I don't like to open up. So you need to know you're the only woman I've ever wanted to get closer to. You do something to me that drives me wild and makes it impossible for me to think about anything but you."

I couldn't contain my grin if I tried. "You're pretty much ever-present in my mind too."

"Now, listen, I'd really like to get you naked, but I also want to get to know you. So what would you say if we did something totally Vegas and took a gondola ride and talked?"

"I would love to get to know you better, Ryan Sloan," I

said. He held out his elbow, and I hooked my hand through it, walking with him to the gondolier, excitement ping-ponging through me because we were starting something.

Starting over, and starting anew, and starting fresh.

We were going to make a go of this for real, with stripped down and bare hearts and minds.

And—probably pretty damn soon—bodies too.

But for now, there was a boat, and there was water, and there was a fake skyline that looked like a bright blue summer day, so I settled into his arms as we bobbed along the canals inside The Venetian.

RYAN

Whew.

That was not easy.

That was like . . . scaling a mountain.

Lifting a car.

Leaping over a tall building.

But to have Sophie in my arms again, her lush, ripe body snuggled next to me as we floated down the man-made canal? Yeah. Worth it.

Giving voice to emotional truths was exhausting, but she was happy to listen to me talk about hockey, and I was relieved, so damn relieved, not to have to dig any deeper right now. I knew I'd probably have to later.

"And why do you like hockey?" she asked, resting her head against me. I stroked her hair, and this moment was one of the most surreal of all—living in the present on our own terms.

I shrugged and smiled. "It's just fun."

"Fun is good."

"Were you looking for some deeper reason? Like it was my dad's sport?"

"No. But was it?"

"Nah. He wasn't a sporty guy. He was all about cards and cars and poker and pool. He loved this town because he loved the little bets. He had a regular card game going with a couple of his buddies once a month," I said. My dad was good at cards and had used some of his winnings over the years to pay for night-school classes the last year of his life, always trying to better himself. But while I might be able to share little details of my dad with Sophie, I wasn't ready to delve into the fights my mom and dad had had, over things like money. Letting Sophie into my life didn't mean baring every single little detail—it meant *not* hiding the things that mattered. Like my memories of my father. "He was a good man. He wasn't perfect, but he took care of us, and he taught us manners and respect, and he never missed a chance to go to the park with us."

She slinked out from my hold and turned to face me. "He sounds like a great guy. I'm sure you miss him."

"I do," I said with a nod. "I really do."

I sighed heavily, and Sophie must have decided the hockey talk and this admission were enough for now, because she cupped my cheeks and brushed her lips to mine. It was a soft kiss at first, and she explored my lips as if she were kissing me for the first time. Soon enough she pressed harder, nipping me with her teeth, nibbling and sucking, and making me groan in the middle of the canal, with the stripe-shirted gondolier mere feet from us.

The kiss was a new beginning. A promise of more that we would share. A hint of what we might become.

And it blurred the rest of the world. Because all I knew, felt, and wanted had been reduced to the soft, sweet feel of her lips, the smell of her skin, and the scent of her hair.

Then she picked up speed, veering out of poetic and into ravaging. I'd never let her lead in a kiss before, but I did now, and she sure knew what to do to me. I was turned on well past the point of propriety in a gondola.

I broke the kiss, clasped my hands on her shoulders, and looked her in the eyes. "Spend the rest of the weekend with me. Come to my house. Swim with me. Meet my dog. Play a round of pool. Besides, I have a change of clothes for you if you need one," I said, holding up the bag with the peach dress in it.

She made grabby hands, and I yanked the bag back. "You can have it if you say yes."

Her eyes lit up. She tapped her chin, pretending to think about it. "I feel like you left one very important thing off the to-do list."

I lowered my hand to her ass and squeezed hard. "No, beautiful. That's a given. Fucking you will be the main item on the agenda."

42

RYAN

I opened the sliding glass door to my deck and stood on the threshold, stopping to take in the gorgeous sight before me.

Sophie wore a white bikini and huge black sunglasses as she stretched out on a lounge chair by the pool, reading her iPad under a big yellow umbrella. Her skin was so fair, I doubted she was a sun worshipper. But even so, she looked stunning with the rays casting their glow on her legs.

Late-afternoon shadows fell across my yard, along with a quiet hush. The stillness of the moment—both the silence and her beauty—felt like a dream. But the image was too sharp, too crisp to be anything but real.

My real life. My real chance. A real change.

Okay, some things hadn't changed. I couldn't keep my hands off her.

After a pit stop at her condo, since she'd insisted on picking up clothes, I drove her to my house once I'd ensured my family was already gone. I wanted Sophie to meet them, but I didn't have the patience for a get-to-know-you session when I simply had to have her. We'd christened the hallway the second the door was closed. I took her against the wall, with Johnny Cash hiding his snout under a pillow on the couch as if he couldn't bear to watch. Now, my mutt was sprawled on the cool grass under a tree, back legs sticking out behind him like Superdog.

But the woman.

Oh, the woman.

Sophie was all mine for the next twenty-four hours. No dropping her off at midnight. No final kiss in front of her building. And no bumping into her brother.

I struck all thoughts of her brother from my brain as I walked across the deck, down the wooden steps, and over to the pool area where she was. I had two drinks with me, and when I arrived by her side, she lowered her shades to the bridge of her nose, looking exactly like a glamorous movie star on vacation.

"Are you playing my waiter today?"

"Maybe I'm the pool boy," I said as I handed her a mojito.

She laughed. "I don't have pool-boy fantasies, I assure you."

I sat at the end of her chair with my Macallan on ice. "What fantasies do you have?"

She raised an eyebrow as she took a sip of the drink. "I fantasize about a man who can make a drink like this. This is divine. How did you know I like mojitos by the pool?"

I shrugged, quirking up the corner of my lips. "Lucky guess."

She shot me a skeptical glance as she pushed her sunglasses on top of her head. "I'm not so sure that's just luck. I suspect it's more of your military intelligence training."

"You think they teach us how to identify a woman's drink of choice?"

"No, but I think you have a supremely analytical mind and like to piece clues together, and somehow you decided that a woman like me drinks mojitos."

"And what traits would suggest mojito drinking?" I asked, enjoying the banter as the sun dipped toward the horizon.

"You tell me," she said, crossing her ankles. Her toenails were painted violet. I wasn't a man who cared about polished fingers or toes, but somehow this little detail seemed so very Sophie.

"Gorgeous, confident, smart, fun . . . and likes to enjoy things that taste good."

She made some sort of sexy humming sound in her throat. "You taste good," she said.

My dick leaped to attention, and I was ready again—I was always ready with her. I dropped a hand to her leg, wrapping it around her calf and squeezing, as I tipped my forehead toward the iPad. "What are you reading?"

"A biography of Tommy Lee from Mötley Crüe. I have a thing for rock-star biographies."

"Interesting. Where does that come from?"

She pursed her lips, as if considering the answer. "I think because the lifestyle is so extravagant and extreme. I read them for fun back in college, with a sort of wide-eyed awe, and these people seemed so foreign but so fascinating. They still are—the hours rock stars keep, the crazy things they do, the excess, the conquests, the dangers. It's like a vicarious thrill ride into a world I'd never want to be in but love watching unfold."

"Are you a voyeur?" I asked with narrowed eyes.

"Ha. Hardly. I just like to see the curtain pulled back," she said, taking a quick drink. Then she set her glass on the small table next to her lounge chair. "What do you like to read?"

"Business strategy books to stay sharp. Thrillers to keep the heart rate up. And international news to stay educated. That probably sounds terribly prosaic."

She shook her head. "No. Not at all. I love your reasons too. They tell me more about what matters to you," she said with a sweet smile. "Plus, I think whatever anybody's reading is a good thing. Truth be told, I was actually switching back and forth between reading the Tommy Lee book, and this email exchange with my contact in Rüsselsheim."

My ears pricked. "Your Bugatti?"

A grin stretched across her features, like a very satisfied cat. "I'm going there to check it out in ten days."

I arched an eyebrow. "Are you bringing it back?"

"An import service will. But I want to touch it and feel it and drive it myself before the final sign-off."

An image of Sophie running her hands along the sleek body of a high-end sports car played before my eyes. "What milestone is this one? You said you reward yourself for hitting charity milestones."

"I like numbers, especially the big fat ones with lots of zeroes, so I decided that since I sold my company for a hundred million dollars, when I hit that goal in money raised for others, I'd get this car."

I whistled in admiration. "To say I'm impressed is an understatement. Both with the sale, and also with what you've raised."

"Thank you. Though that's not all from my pocket. I do give a lot to every cause I raise money for, but my bigger job is simply asking others to open their wallets. I'm lucky to know many generous people I can call on," she added, as if that somehow lessened the accomplishment.

I tapped her knee lightly with my fingertips. "And you convinced them to part with their money for a good cause. It's amazing, however you slice it. Why did you decide to go into philanthropy?"

She reached for her glass and took a long drink. "Because I could."

I brushed my fingers along her thigh, loving the simplicity of her answer. She'd chosen to do good because she was in the rare position of being able to. She could have done anything with her time, her money, and her access, and she'd opted to donate the hours in her day to help others. The choice was a deliberate one, and it said so much about her. "Beautiful answer. I love that. I respect that. Did you ever think about starting another company? So many other entrepreneurs launch additional businesses."

"I had no interest in being a serial entrepreneur," she said, shaking her head. "I know I'm lucky to have had the successful run I had with my company—to start it when I did and sell it when I did. And now I'm lucky enough to use all my business skills to help with things that matter more in the world. I've raised money for animal charities, for sick children, for cancer research, for kids in need, for troubled kids, and so on. I'd much rather devote my time to doing that." Then she added, almost apologetically, "Even if it can be just as much work and require just as much management as running my own company."

"I hear you on that. It must be consuming at times. Everyone needing and wanting things," I said, flashing back to the gala and the way the two ladies there practically hunted Sophie down to make their own cases for the children's wing.

"That's true. Which is why it'll be all the more fun to go

for a joyride in my new car," she said with a glint in her eye.

Though I could jet off anywhere in the world with her and hole up in a five-star resort on my dime, she could do all those things for herself too, and then some. I did well for myself, but I wasn't in a position to drop that kind of cash on a car, and she was. Perhaps for the first time, I was keenly aware that while I was successful, Sophie was in another class. It didn't annoy me and didn't make me feel any less of a man. But I wanted to make sure she felt the same way. "There's not much I can give you materially that you can't get on your own," I said matter-of-factly. "Does that bother you?"

She laughed loudly. "Not in the least," she said, then reached for my hand, lacing her fingers through mine. Her smile was gentle and tender. "You don't have to shower me with expensive gifts. You don't have to give me presents at all if you don't want to. I loved the peach tulips and the pinot grigio, and I am in some kind of mad love with the dress you had your sister track down for me. It's beautiful, and it's perfect for me, and I didn't have one like it, and I've been coveting one. So thank you," she said with a squeeze of my hand, then added softly, "Besides, the things I want from you don't cost money."

I tensed for a moment, shoulders tightening and chest burning. I wasn't ready to have a more serious talk about commitment. Letting her in and talking more was all I could handle. "Such as?"

She took her time answering, trailing her fingers along my bare arm. "What I want is for you to take me for a ride in my new car someday."

A groan rumbled through my chest, escaping my lips. My God, I'd struck gold when I met her. She was precious and rare and so fucking giving. "Pretty sure I'm the luckiest guy in the world."

"So that means you'd like to get behind the wheel?"

"There's only one thing I want to do in that car more than drive it," I said in a low voice, raking my eyes over her gorgeous figure.

She tapped her index finger against her lips and peered skyward. "Hmm. You mean you want to see how far back the passenger seat goes?"

"Exactly. That's exactly the kind of test-drive I want to give you in your new car."

She gestured to her iPad. "What if I told you I had pictures of it?"

I made a *show it to me now* gesture with my fingers. "I want to see that car," I said, then ran my palms up and down her calves, my way of imploring her. She murmured softly, a sound that said she was enjoying my touch. I took advantage of it, digging my thumbs into her ankles and working my way up her legs, stopping to kiss her calves along the way.

She reached for her iPad, swiped a finger across the screen, and then brought up the email. "Are you ready to be dazzled by its beauty? Can you handle it?"

"If I can handle how gorgeous you are, this car won't be a problem, because I'm sure it doesn't hold a candle. But show it to me anyway."

"Flattery will get you everywhere." She turned the iPad around and showed me the photo. My heart skipped a beat. The automobile was a thing of beauty. A gorgeous, gleaming emerald-green sports car that stirred up every desire in me to hug the curves on a downhill, to hear the purr of the engine, to stomp on the accelerator in this sleek ride. I actually pressed my fingertips to the screen and stroked the photo.

She tossed her head back and laughed throatily. "Do you want me to wipe the drool from your chin now or later?"

I snapped her iPad case closed and set it down on the table. Reaching behind her, I lowered the lounge chair, then crawled over her, pinning her with my body. "You think I'm just going to let that impudent comment slide?"

The look in her eyes changed as she transformed from that confident, saucy woman to the vulnerable, submissive one. "Are you going to punish me?"

I shook my head. "No. I'm not going to punish you. I'm going to make you work for it."

"How?" she asked, and in that one word, I heard the thrill of anticipation. Her own desire to be led like this was her drug.

I clasped her hands, threading my fingers through hers, watching every move she made—the way her lips parted, how her eyes followed mine, how her chest rose and fell. I stretched her arms over her head, and gently pushed her hands beneath one of the wood slats at the top of the lounge chair.

"Hold on to the chair the whole time," I said, then moved off her to reach for an ice cube from my drink. I held it above her chest, as the first bead of liquid fell from the cube and landed between her lush breasts. Her nipples pebbled through the fabric of her bikini.

I lowered the ice cube closer to her skin. "Are you hot?"

She bit her lip, and answered, "Very."

"I had a feeling you might be." I brushed it through her cleavage, and she shivered, gasping out loud at the first contact with the cold. "Does that make you feel better?"

"Yes," she said on a feathery gasp. I ran the ice under her breasts, down her belly, and to the top of her bikini bottoms, picturing the treasure that lay beneath the white fabric—her wet, hot pussy. My dick throbbed in my swim shorts, and my need to have her intensified.

I glided the ice up and down her sides, and she squirmed, writhing under my touch. She was a live wire. With every touch, she sparked. She ignited, responding to my words, my voice, my hands, and my body. It was intoxicating. It was addictive. I bent my neck to her, licking the shell of her ear with the tip of my tongue. She moaned softly, whispering my name in a barely audible voice.

It sounded like a plea.

My shorts made a tent, pitched high. "Do you want me to touch you?"

"Yes."

"My yard is big. My neighbors aren't around today," I said as I traveled up her body with the ice cube, watching her shiver as it left a wet path across her hot skin. I reached the hollow of her throat, making circles, watching the ice melt some. I leaned in and kissed the water away. Then I pulled back, and said firmly, "Put it between your teeth."

She opened her mouth and waited for me to insert the cube. She held it in place with her teeth as I ran the backs of my fingertips down her arm. "I could untie your bikini straps right now. Take off the top and tie you up with it. Flip you over onto your hands and knees and fuck you from behind on this chair," I said, not looking at her, but instead reaching for my glass and finishing off my drink.

I returned my focus to her, and the look in her eyes was already glassy, on the path to red-hot desire. "Would you like that?"

She nodded.

Starting at her collarbone, I brushed my finger over her chest, then through the valley of those gorgeous tits, on a fast track to her legs. I danced my fingers along the waistband of her bathing suit, taunting her. "Or I could take these off right now and feel how wet you are. Since you're all nice and slippery, right?"

She bucked upward, giving her yes. A drop of liquid drizzled from the cube down her chin. I kissed it away. "Don't let go of the ice," I instructed. "Hold on till it melts between your lips."

I moved my hands down her legs, placing my palms on the insides of her thighs. I spread them apart and stared at her bikini bottom. "Or maybe I'll just torture you by brushing one finger against this wet spot I love so much. Just play with your hot pussy through this bikini until you're moaning, crying, and begging me to take it off."

Her eyes floated closed momentarily, and she lifted her hips.

Desire tore through me, twisting and curling like a wildfire. I was desperate to quench it and bring her to orgasm. But I had to fight that urge and restrain all of my lust for her.

Waiting made everything better.

With her hands stretched above her head, hooked in the slats of the lounge chair, she was bound for me.

43

SOPHIE

Yes. Yes. Yes.

Every single answer was a resounding yes.

I was so wet, so turned on, so slippery, and all I wanted was his touch. I had no idea how long this torture would last. I could bite down on this ice cube now, but that would only prolong the waiting. He'd find a new way to draw out his touch if I defied him.

Lust and desire ricocheted through my body as I gripped the slats above my head and writhed my hips on the lounge chair, baking under the hot sun.

Soon. He had to touch me soon.

Mercifully, he looped his hands around my neck and untied my bikini, then unsnapped the hook at my spine. My first taste of freedom came as he lowered the straps along my arms, taking off my top. His breath stilled as he took in my breasts.

I willed him to lower his mouth to my nipples and suck, bite, and taste. I tried valiantly by arching my back, lifting my breasts closer to him.

He got the message. Oh hell, did he get it. He reached

for my mojito. "Let's see how this tastes," he said as he poured some of the drink down my chest. I drew in a sharp breath, even with the ice cube melting in my mouth. He buried his face between my breasts, lapping up the liquid. I wanted to moan, to cry out, to shout *yes* as the sun shone down on us, illuminating what he was doing to me.

He looked up and ran his finger along the cube in my teeth. "You want this so badly, don't you?" he asked.

I nodded. I didn't even know what he was offering. Whatever it was, I'd take it.

"It doesn't matter what I do, does it? You just want me to make you come?"

Yes. So much yes.

I arched my hips, seeking him out. His eyes roamed over my bikini bottom. I was soaked. Surely he could see the evidence of my desire through the fabric.

He stood up and ran his hands over the thick bulge in his shorts. "You like that, don't you? When I touch myself?"

I breathed a *yes* around the melting cube.

He let go of his dick then and kneeled over me, kissing me, devouring my mouth, taking the last chip of the ice cube into his own mouth.

Then he tugged down my bathing suit bottom, pulled it off, and thrust a finger inside me.

Not a second passed before I started fucking his hand. I was so turned on, so worked up, and so aroused from him. My hands were twisted around the slats, the wood rubbing against my wrists, and I didn't care. I was reduced to only moans and groans and murmurs as he crooked his finger inside me and hit the magic spot no one had ever discovered until Ryan Sloan walked into my life, fulfilling every fantasy.

This commanding, intense, powerful man loved to

tease me and please me, and, oh God, he was doing just that. My belly tightened, an orgasm cresting.

He added another finger, then one more, as his thumb rubbed my clit. My eyes squeezed shut, and I gripped the wood as I writhed into his hand, his fingers deep inside me, and then I went over the edge.

Before the orgasm even subsided, he grasped my hands from the slats, released them, and threaded his fingers through mine, as ripples of pleasure continued to spread through my body like aftershocks. He'd taken off his shorts, and now he wedged himself between my thighs, and told me to wrap my legs around his hips.

I did as instructed, and then he sank into me. He filled me so completely that I moaned loudly, my voice carrying across the heat of the afternoon, floating on the hot air as he buried himself deep. He gripped my fingers hard.

"*Sophie,*" he growled in my ear as he thrust. It vaguely occurred to me that this was one of the first times we'd had sex face to face. It occurred to me, too, that I wanted to try every position with him. I wanted to be taken, I wanted to be owned, and I wanted to be his.

Completely his.

"Oh God," I cried out, because he was doing it again. He was taking me there, and as the hot sunlight rained down on my skin, liquid pleasure flooded my veins.

He let go of one of my hands to palm my breast, squeezing my nipple as he rocked into me. He pinched me, and it hurt so good as I came hard around his cock. In seconds, he followed me, biting my shoulder as he reached his own climax, grunting in gorgeous pleasure, the sound of his deep, sexy moans driving me even higher.

"It's you," he said a minute later as he spooned me, holding me in his arms and kissing my neck. "It's only you."

I knew what he was trying to say. I felt it too, inside my body and deep in my heart.

44

RYAN

"I have a confession to make," I announced, as I set two plates on the kitchen table then opened the cardboard box of pizza.

"Confess." She held out her hand grandly, inviting me to talk—something I was increasingly enjoying doing with her.

I snagged a slice of the cheese pie I'd ordered from Gigi's, my favorite pizza shop, and placed it on Sophie's plate. With the salad tongs, she scooped out some of the Caesar salad for me then for herself too.

I sat down, joining her. "You already know my secret about being completely unable to cook." I held up one finger to make a point—a point of self-defense. "Though I am unbelievably proficient at calling the pizza place."

She nodded approvingly. "Gigi's is the best in Vegas. I absolutely approve of your dinner choice. Cheese pizza, Caesar salad, and chardonnay." She picked up her fork and dug into the salad first. "So, tell me."

I took a bite of the pizza, rolled my eyes in pleasure, and pointed to my chewing mouth to say *wait just a moment*. When I swallowed, I made my confession: "I ate the peach pie you made."

She smiled broadly, then took a drink of her white wine. "I'm so happy to hear that. It's my mother's recipe. It's divine, isn't it?"

"That's exactly what my grandmother said about it. *Divine*."

She tilted her head curiously and asked, "Your grandmother?"

"I took it to her house after you gave it to me. I had some with her."

Sophie's blue eyes seemed to show her processing this information—I was a man who took pie to my grandmother. Maybe I'd made a strange choice to go see her last night, but it had made as much sense to me as anything had then. So I quickly added, "She told me I should never give up a woman who could bake like that."

Sophie raised her wineglass, a toast of sorts to my grandmother. "Smart woman. Sounds like you're close to her?"

"Definitely. She and my granddad pretty much raised us after Mom went to . . ." I let my voice trail off.

Sophie nodded immediately, letting me know she understood. "And that brought you all closer, I imagine."

"It did. I was almost fifteen when we moved in with her and my granddad, my dad's parents. I guess that kind of thing can either rip you apart or bring you closer," I said, more easily than I'd ever expected to be able to voice such words. Perhaps because the deadbolt was undone. The door was open, and the heavy weight of years of closeting secrets had lightened. My heart felt freer than it had in ages, my head lighter. Funny, I'd never known that talking like this, to someone who wasn't in the inner circle, could feel oddly peaceful. "In our case, mostly it brought us closer," I said, and took another bite of pizza, savoring the delicious cheese and tasty crust.

She took a drink, then asked, "Mostly?"

Yes, mostly. Because I knew exactly how my grandmother felt about my mother. The past's hard grip resurfaced, like claws clamping down on my throat, and my newfound voice. The familiar urge to lock up my history kicked in. But I fought back. "I say that because she doesn't know I actually visit my mom still."

"Ah, I understand," Sophie said softly. "I imagine it would be hard for her to accept that's something you want. But it's clearly important to you to see your mom."

My God, it was like morning sunlight streaming in through the blinds. Talking to Sophie was lightness; it was patience and safety. I barely had to explain a thing. She simply understood it all. She got it—and me. But I didn't want Sophie to think I was a liar, after what we'd gone through to get to this place. "It's not that I hide it from my grandma, per se. I think she knows on some level, because she's aware that I go there for Christmas and other times. But I don't tell her about all the visits. I didn't tell her I went earlier in the week, for instance. Or that I'm going again next weekend. Guess it just doesn't seem like something to keep bringing up."

"How often do you visit?"

"I try to see her once or twice a month. Sometimes more, sometimes less." I sighed heavily. "She gets her hours cut now and then because she acts up."

"Acts up?"

I looked away, focusing on the steady breathing of my sleeping dog on the floor by an air conditioning vent, his black-and-white fur fluttering lightly. "She's not . . ." I said, tapping the side of my skull. "She's . . ." I let my voice trail off again. A lump rose in my throat. This was so hard to say. "She's not all there," I said, practically kicking the words past my lips.

Not only was my mother branded a murderer, not only was she the orchestrator of a gang-led shooting, she was also barreling down the path to insanity. I saw the evidence each time I visited her.

Sophie reached for my hand, threaded her fingers through mine, and held on tight. "It all must be so hard," she said softly, and then she quickly moved on. I could kiss her—for the segue, and for knowing one was needed. "Who are you closest to among your siblings? I only have one, obviously, so it's an easy answer for me. But you've got three. That must be a different story."

A small smile returned to my face. I could do this. I'd made it through the harder topic. My brothers and sister were way more manageable. "On the surface, I guess Michael, since we run a business together and we were in the Army together. And we are a great team when it comes to the company. But Michael and I don't always see eye to eye. About my mom," I added.

"How so?"

"He never visits her, and he doesn't like that I do. So we're close, but sometimes that causes problems. Shannon has gone with me a bunch of times to Hawthorne, so in some ways, I'm closer to her. She still talks to our mom and gets her letters. But," I said, stopping to take a drink of my wine, then setting it back down on the table, "that's not what defines us. I mean, it did for a long time in the eyes of strangers. But that's not what our family is all about. We're more than that. We all support each other and love each other and look out for each other. A few years ago, once we were all back in Vegas, the four of us got together and bought our grandparents a house. The one they live in now. It was our way of giving back to them after all they did to help raise us right and make sure we didn't turn out as fucked up as we were," I said with a light scoff. "We were pretty messed up, Sophie."

She shot me a gentle smile that said she understood.

"We kind of wanted it to be a surprise, but it was hard to buy a surprise house, since we wanted them to like it. Colin's the money guy, though, and the idea was his in the first place, so he was able to get it all going. And, back to your question, sometimes it feels like I'm closest to him. He's the youngest, and Michael's kind of taken on a fatherly role. Colin and I feel more like equals. With Michael, sometimes it seems like he still thinks he has to look out for all of us, even though he's only two years older."

Sophie laughed. "Let me tell you, I completely understand that older brothers can be a total pain in the ass," she said with a knowing smile, and I matched her grin. Something was changing between us now that the veil of secrecy had been removed. Her brother had once been the cause of the rift, and now she was able to make a joke about the guy.

After we finished eating and cleaned up, I pointed to the shopping bag with the dress in it in the living room. "I'm thinking now would be a great time for you to show me that peach dress."

"I would love to give you a fashion show."

She retreated to my bedroom, and while she was changing, I turned on some soft music and dimmed the lights in the living room.

"What do you think?"

I turned around to see Sophie twirl for me, then stop and strike a pose. She looked extraordinary in the white pinup dress with a peach pattern and the silver shoes she'd picked up at the Grand Canal shops.

"That you look edible. But I'm not going there just yet. For now, I want to do what we did on our first date," I said, walking over to her and running my fingers through her soft blonde hair. She lifted her chin to look at me, and the look in her eyes melted me as I wrapped my arms around her.

"Dance with me."

"I would love to."

And we swayed together. It was better than the first time. Everything was better with her every time.

"I like talking to you," I said, my lips brushing her hair.

"I like listening to you," she said as we swayed.

"You make it easy."

"It shouldn't have to be hard. *This*," she said, and I knew what she meant by *this*.

"*Us*," I echoed. "And it's not hard. It's incredible."

45
___

SOPHIE

Lick. Lick. Lick.

The next morning, a long tongue slurping across my cheek greeted me. Yawning, I opened my eyes to find a black-and-white border collie kissing my face and wagging his tail.

He whimpered lightly, and I glanced over at a sleeping Ryan. He was flat on his stomach, his face pressed into a pillow, an arm slung over his head.

I turned back to Johnny Cash. "Want to go outside?" I whispered, and he thumped his tail on the floor at the last word.

I slipped out of bed and headed to the sliding glass door. The door was locked with a regular latch and a deadbolt. It took me a few seconds to wiggle them free, but I managed, and then the dog shot out, racing across the grass and lifting his leg on a tree in the far corner of the yard.

Pale-pink fingers of light streaked across the morning sky as the sun rose. Taking a deep breath, savoring the fresh scent of a new day, I soaked up the scene before me.

Waking up at Ryan's house, spending the weekend with him, exploring all that we felt for each other had been a day and night of rapture, of passion, and, most of all, of connection.

Fine, it had *only* been one night, but I knew with both my heart and my analytical mind that Ryan Sloan was changing. He was opening up. He was sharing.

For me.

I practically giggled at the thought as I watched his dog finish his business then tear across the yard and conduct some morning recon with his snout, checking out the fence, perusing the edge of the pool, and sniffing some bushes. I felt bubbly, effervescent even, because I was close to having that elusive *thing* I'd craved for so long. For my whole damn life. The very gem I'd hunted for and thought I'd found in Holden was actually a diamond in the rough with Ryan. Led by lust, hormones, and desire, our relationship was a risk that had paid off. I was thrilled by the glimpses of his heart and soul that he'd offered. I felt special, I felt admired, and I felt madly desired. To have this kind of crazy, kinky, dirty sex with a man I was falling for . . . this was my dream, and I was close, closer than I'd ever been, to having it.

It was almost too good to be true, and for a brief moment, my heart seized up. What if it all fell to pieces? What if this was just a bubble? A weekend of bliss and loveliness that would all go away at midnight?

Ryan's dog raced to my side, and I pushed those thoughts away as we headed back inside. After a quick bathroom trip to freshen my breath, I returned to the kitchen and decided breakfast for my man would be a fine idea. I rolled my eyes at the contents of his fridge—it was pure single guy. Beer. Mustard. A loaf of bread. I scanned the shelves and drawers for bacon, certain I'd find some.

Personally, I couldn't stand it. But what bachelor didn't like bacon?

I found none.

At least he had a carton of eggs and some butter, so I set to work whipping up some scrambled eggs, and as I turned off the stove, a sleepy, sexy Ryan padded out of the bedroom with rumpled hair and a cute yawn.

"Is this a dream? Or are you really waking me up with a homemade breakfast?"

He walked up behind me and wrapped his arms around my waist as I served the eggs. He planted a sweet kiss on my neck, and his breath was minty fresh. "It's real," I said. "If this were a dream, there would surely be bacon. I bet you love bacon."

He shuddered. "Hate it."

I turned and stared at him with one eyebrow raised. "I have never met a man who hates bacon."

"Well, you have now, beautiful. I do not understand the fascination this country has with bacon."

My heart skipped a silly beat. "I have to tell you something, Ryan." Turning my voice intensely serious, I whispered, "I hate bacon too."

He cupped my cheeks and kissed me. A quick morning kiss. "You let my dog out to pee, and you hate bacon. I knew you were my perfect woman."

"Sit and eat or your eggs will get cold."

After the meal, he pulled me onto his lap in his chair, and thanked me for breakfast. "And now I have a question for you. You told me yesterday you don't have pool-boy fantasies," he said, reminding me of my joke at the pool.

I nodded. "That is true. Nor stable-boy fantasies either, I might add."

"Good." He kissed my earlobe. His voice went low and

husky, sending a shiver through me as he asked, "What fantasies do you have?"

That was an easy answer. I pulled back to look him in the eyes. "You."

He grinned wickedly. "You don't have to fantasize about me. You can have me. I want to know what you fantasized about before you met me so I can do it to you."

I widened my eyes and stared at him, then gave the same answer. "You."

He furrowed his brow. "What do you mean?"

"I wanted someone like you. I fantasized about the things we do. The kind of sex we have is the kind of sex I've always wanted to have. Dirty, kinky, rough."

He groaned sexily. "You told me in your car you've never had it like this before. How did you know you wanted it like that?"

"The same way I can code with my eyes closed and one hand behind my back. The same way I can tell which cards are most likely to be played next in a blackjack hand. The same way I know two seconds after I see a dress if I want it. I just know. It's second nature."

"And you just knew you wanted to be tied up? You wanted to be spanked? You wanted to be told what to do?"

I nodded eagerly. "If you're making sure I'm still on board, the answer is yes. I want it this way. But if you want to know why, I think it's because my mind feels so busy all the time. Like mild OCD. I always make sure I've turned off the stove before I leave my home, and I check twice that I've locked the door. I've always felt like I have all sorts of information and facts and details clanging around in my head, back when I was in school and then when I was running the company. And now, even though I love what I do, I feel like I'm juggling a million things. But when you tie me up, I'm living in the moment. And I'm loving the moment. And that's why I fantasized for so long about being on my knees, tied up, or bent over the bed for a man like you. And now, just for you."

He groaned and crushed my lips in a bruising, demanding kiss, giving me exactly what I wanted and erasing anything else in my mind. Just like I asked for. Just like I dreamed about for years. When he broke the kiss, he spoke firmly to me. "I need you to do something right now."

I recognized that tone instantly—he was going to give me an order. "Go to my bedroom. Strip down to nothing. Go into my closet and pick out a tie. Put it around your neck. Then wait for me, bent over the bed, ass raised high in the air, wearing only my tie."

46

RYAN

I found my beautiful woman standing at the end of my bed, my green tie nestled between her breasts, the very tie I'd been wearing the day I met her. The fact that she'd chosen that one made me even harder.

I unknotted the tie from her neck and used it to bind her wrists together tightly, then ran my hand down her spine, watching her back bow as I mapped her body, as if I were an explorer and she was the territory I planned to claim.

When I reached her round and luscious cheeks, I bent down to bite the soft flesh, and soon I was sinking into her as I clasped her ass in my hands.

"Did you fantasize about me fucking you like this?"

"Yes."

I squeezed her ass cheeks roughly as I slammed into her. "You want it harder, right?"

"Please."

I took her savagely, both of us needing more, so I reached down to dip a finger between her slick folds before I returned to her rear, rubbing against her entrance there, gently at first, then insistently as I kept fucking her.

Her high-pitched pants were my permission to slide my finger inside all the way. "And this too? Tell me. Did you fantasize about this too?"

"With you, yes," she whispered, unearthing deeper and darker fantasies that I intended to fulfill, today and beyond. The promise of that was enough to send us both over the edge, and we came together with her shuddering beneath me.

Later, when evening rolled around, I asked her if she'd consider spending the night again. She said yes.

It was all I wanted her to say.

Once upon a time, I'd wanted that yes for the sex. And I *still* wanted that from her, over and over.

But I wanted *more*. I wanted everything else. I wanted the woman, inside and out, body and mind, heart and soul.

For the first time ever, I was falling.

47

RYAN

The game moved too quickly for me to talk to Marshall about anything more than our strategy on the ice. The opposing team demolished us for the first two periods, rattling my teammates with penalty after penalty. The last period wasn't much better, and the game ended with a loss for my team.

I hardly cared today. Marshall had texted me earlier that he had an update, so when the other guys headed to the showers, Marshall pulled me aside. We took off our skates, and then trudged up a few rows, removing our bulky gloves before parking ourselves on the blue plastic seats.

The ice rink was mercifully empty.

"Got some news for you."

"Tell me," I said, and a mix of both desperation and anticipation gripped me. I wanted facts. I prayed Marshall was dealing in that currency.

"Seems that Stefano had a broker," he began, and I furrowed my brow in question. Marshall made a rolling gesture with his hand to explain. "Like, a guy who set up his hits."

The ice in the rink had nothing on me right now. I was chilled to the bone. My body temperature plunged subzero just hearing how this killer operated. "This guy set up murders for hire?"

Marshall nodded. "He brokered them. The Sinners were all about drugs then, and stealing. Fencing stolen goods, some territory battles—the usual gang stuff, to be honest. But sadly there's money in murder too, so the broker started working that angle for Stefano." Marshall shook his head in disgust. I gritted my teeth, trying to tamp down the treacherous ball of rage that reared up inside me. "Sounds like he's one of the guys the detectives are looking for."

"TJ and K," I said in a hiss, the initials slithering out of my mouth. "That has to be them. His friends. His fucking accomplices. Who the hell are they? Do you know their full names?"

"That's the problem. They're slippery. They're smarter than you'd expect a bunch of street thugs to be. The Sinners were quiet for a while, sort of fell apart, but now they're rising up again, and the word is this broker played a role in some serious shit that went down. But we don't have a name yet. Not a real one, at least. The detective would probably sell an arm for a name."

I probably would too.

48

SOPHIE

The week flew by, hurtling toward the benefit in a heady blur of emails and texts, of days and nights, of sex and sleepovers, of dinners and drinks, and time together that I craved more of . . .

Tonight was the next big step. I'd be meeting his brothers and his sister.

And I was ready.

After I gave myself more pep talks than I had ever needed when pitching to investors or proposing media companies use my compression services. And after taking more deep breaths than I'd ever required before walking into a billionaire's office with my head held high and asking him or her to generously support a cause.

I'd handled those situations without batting an eyelash.

But meeting the people who Ryan cared about most was new to me. I had no clue what to expect as I headed into The Chandelier bar in the middle of The Cosmopolitan hotel.

I was decked out in a simple red linen dress with a hip-hugging pencil skirt and a strappy bodice. White piping lined the neck and the hem, giving the dress the retro look I embraced. My earrings matched, and my lipstick was red and neat.

I'd only checked twenty times on the way from my building to the nearby hotel.

As I waited nervously with Ryan, Shannon arrived first with her husband, and immediately wrapped me in a big hug.

After the embrace and hellos, I placed my palms together, as if in prayer, and pleaded, "Will you please tell me everything you have in store for the *Dance All Night* reunion special? I promise I'll be your best friend forever if you do."

Shannon eyed Ryan approvingly and squeezed my shoulder. "I like her. Keep her around."

"The big secret is . . . she's bringing me on the show. I have all the moves," Brent said, adding a gyration of his hips like a stripper.

Shannon rolled her eyes. "You wish."

"Hey! I know you!" I said excitedly, pointing at Brent. He was tall, sturdy, and had sparkling brown eyes. "Your late-night show was the best. And King Schmuck cracked me up on many occasions."

Brent nodded at Shannon. "What she said. I second it. I like you too."

Soon, Michael and Colin joined us, and I understood what Ryan had meant about Michael's intensity. He was like a sheepdog guarding the flock, even in the middle of a chichi Vegas bar. He had that "my eyes are everywhere" watchfulness in his cool blue gaze. His eyes were lighter than Ryan's, but his hair was darker, making for an interesting contrast. Colin was the laid-back one, easygoing, quick with a joke, and even able to hold his own among Brent, the former comedian, as well as two super-protective older brothers. He had an infinity symbol tattoo on his wrist, with four interlocking circles in black ink, nearly the same shade as his hair.

Colin was also a kindred spirit, and as a venture capitalist, he inhabited some of the same worlds I had trafficked in. "I had my eye on your second round of funding for InCode several years ago," he said. "I tried to get in on it, but it was too late."

"Oh no! Shame on me, then," I said, lightly smacking my own hand, admonishing myself.

"Yeah, it's one of my greatest regrets in business. That was a hell of a sale you made."

"Thank you," I said with a wide smile.

"I'm looking at some start-ups that are playing in the same space. I'd love to get your thoughts sometime," he added, taking a drink of what looked to be iced tea.

"I'd be delighted to talk shop. I haven't had the chance to in ages."

"Then we'll make it a date," Colin said with a wink.

"Date?" Ryan asked, arching an eyebrow as he draped an arm around me.

I turned to look at him, and couldn't resist planting a kiss on his cheek. "Just to talk numbers and other geeky things."

Michael whistled under his breath. "And Ryan Sloan gets a kiss in public from the first girl he ever introduces us to," he said, holding up his palm to high-five Shannon, then Colin. "I knew he liked her for real."

Ryan made a *pshaw* sound, then must have decided to say *screw it*, because he grabbed me, dipped me, and kissed me deeply in front of them all. The hooting and hollering intensified. The clapping grew sonic. When he pulled me up, I felt woozy and stunned, and I was sure my lipstick was smeared.

"And we have a winner," Colin declared, smacking his glass lightly on the counter.

Winner. I felt like one tonight.

* * *

"I told you they'd adore you. Every single one of them already texted to tell me how awesome you are. I'm going to keep you around," he said, raining kisses on my cheeks, my shoulders, and my lips as we walked through The Cosmopolitan, his arm wrapped around me.

"You better," I said with a murmur as he ran a finger through my hair.

When the first blast of hot summer night air pelted us, I turned to him. "Where do you want to go now?"

"You're five minutes away. I'm twenty minutes away. I took the initiative and already asked Colin to go let my dog out," he answered with a wry smile.

"Ah, so you're assuming I want you to come over?"

"I'm not assuming anything," he said, gripping my shoulder. "It's a fact. You want me to come over because you want what I'm going to give you."

"What's that?"

He stopped in his tracks there on the Strip. I stopped too. Summer crowds of tourists thronged past us, cameras around their necks.

"My thank-you for being so amazing with my family," he said.

"It was easy. They're wonderful."

"You were nervous, but you did great. I want to show you how much it means to me that you met them."

"You have a gift for me?" I asked, arching an eyebrow.

"I have something I think you'll like."

I could hardly wait.

49

SOPHIE

A glass of white wine later, along with some soft music and Ryan's hands all over my back, shoulders, and neck, and I was wholly relaxed. His touch made me moan softly, as he rubbed the oil on my shoulders, down my spine, and along my arms.

"I want your ass tonight, Sophie."

I looked up, surprised, but immediately warming to his command. "I've been hoping you would," I said, as if it was a naughty admission, and I shivered, goosebumps rising on my skin.

"You beautiful, dirty woman," he said in awe.

"But I've never done it," I said. "I don't want it to hurt."

"I don't want to hurt you either. It doesn't have to hurt. I'll make it good for you, Sophie. We've already got the wine and massage oil," he said with a smile.

"What if I'm too slippery now?"

He laughed softly and leaned in closer to my ear. "I promise I won't let you escape."

I laughed too, and he continued to work his way down my body. He massaged the top of my ass cheeks, and I wriggled as the pressure sent sparks of anticipation through my body, settling between my legs, beating a pulse in my very wet, very hot center. He parted my legs more, widening the space between them and working his fingers lower on my bottom.

I tensed briefly, unsure how this would feel. But then I remembered last weekend at his house when he'd slid a finger inside my ass and I'd wanted to sing hallelujah.

I raised my ass for him.

"Yeah," he said, all slow and sexy. "Like that, gorgeous. Give yourself to me."

I lifted myself higher, then turned my face to the side, watching him as he reached for lube this time. He poured some into his hands then returned to my rear. He slid his fingers between my cheeks and pressed lightly against my entrance. I breathed slowly, letting the air spread through my lungs.

He rubbed his fingertip in circles, and soon I moved in time with his finger, chasing it, circling my hips, inviting him to penetrate me. He slipped the finger past my entrance and waited, letting me adjust, then slid it all the way in. "You're so tight," he murmured.

"How am I going to fit you?" I asked, a fleet of nerves briefly reappearing.

"Lots of lube. And lots of preparation," he said, as he continued to work his finger inside me. I squirmed as he pushed, then he added another finger, and soon I was panting, and my clit was aching, and whatever he was doing to me was turning me on. Wildly.

"Oh God," I said, as a spark zipped through me.

"You like it?"

I nodded. "I do. It's so good," I said, as I rocked my rear back into him. The pressure added to the pleasure. The new sensation of all those fingers inside me sent a wave of heat through my body, settling in my pussy. I rocked back onto his hand, craving being filled in both ways. Barely aware of what my body was urging me to do, I started rubbing my pelvis against the bed, desperate for attention in my sex too.

Within seconds, he looped his free hand around my thigh, hitching my leg up, giving him access to me.

I breathed a sigh of relief, then a long, low purr of pleasure as he stroked my hard clit with one hand, while filling my ass with fingers from the other. The double wave of sensations blasted through my core, like a tornado of lust whirling through me. Some deep and primitive part of me gave myself over to these animalistic impulses, to these basest of carnal wishes.

I whispered his name. It sounded like pure sex on my tongue, even to my own ears.

"I'm ready," I murmured, then I rose on my elbows and knees, lifting my ass for him.

Waiting.

He let his fingers slip out of me, and moved away from me to wash his hands. I inhaled. It was going to happen. I was going to give up a part of myself to him, only him. He was the only man I could ever imagine having me like this.

But he didn't take me that way when he returned.

Instead, he moved next to me, lying on his back. He tapped my leg.

"Straddle me," he said softly.

"What?"

His command didn't compute.

"You're on top," he added.

"But," I said. "Don't you want it from behind?

"Yeah, I want it that way. *Next time.*" He clasped his hands around my hips and guided me on top of him. "And we'll get there. But I want it to feel amazing for you *first.*

And it'll be better for you if you can control it. If you can ride me. If you can set the pace."

I swallowed and took a deep breath, his sweet dirtiness rushing over me. I ran a hand through my hair, trying to calm my overactive heart. How could I be so turned on, so aroused, so ready to do something thoroughly forbidden, and also feel on the cusp of falling deeply?

I had no rational answer. So I listened to my body, and I positioned myself over him. He shook his head and whispered, "Not yet."

I furrowed my brow.

"I told you I'd get you there," he said as he brought his hand between my legs, rubbing my swollen bundle of nerves once again.

"Oh God," I said, closing my eyes.

"Remember the night I met you?" he asked as he stroked my clit, setting off spark after spark inside me.

I nodded on a pant.

"Even then, before you even knew my name, I made you come like this." He circled my clit, sending waves of intense bliss through my body. I shuddered. "I didn't even touch your flesh, Sophie. I made you come through your panties, and it was fucking beautiful," he said in a husky, smoky voice that brought back all my memories of the way he'd owned my body before I knew who he was.

"It felt so good," I said breathily as I opened my eyes. "Just like it does now."

He pinned me with his gaze, holding me captive as he fingered my clit, rubbing up and down in a blur as I rocked into him, wetness spreading to my already slick folds. "Your pussy is like paradise to me. I want you to feel like you're in heaven every time."

"I do, Ryan. I do."

"And this time, beautiful—this time you're going to ride

me," he said softly, slowing the pace on my clit to a lingering, lazy speed, leading me step-by-step to the next event. Moving a hand to my hip, he lowered my center to his hard cock. I gasped in pleasure as he ran the head through my slickness. "Just a little natural assistance," he said with a wink, then reached once again for the bottle of lube. "Do you want to put it on me?" he asked, handing me the bottle.

"Yes. I love touching you. Any chance I get to touch you, I'll take."

I poured some into my palm, then rubbed it over his shaft, from the head to the base and back. I set the bottle down, wiped my hands, and gazed at him. He rubbed himself across my pussy before traveling further. To my ass. He pressed the head against me, and I closed my eyes.

I felt precarious. Wobbly. I breathed shakily.

"Put your hands on my chest, Sophie. You need to hold on to something," he told me, and I lowered myself slightly to anchor my hands on his pecs. "Like you're riding me. Like you're fucking me," he said, as he pushed in, his finger lightly brushing my clit once again. Somehow that contact, that delicious touch on the part of my body that was designed *only* for pleasure was enough to take the edge off. I drew in a sharp breath as he breached me then stilled his moves. "Because you are."

His eyes stayed on me the whole time. His gaze guided me. His reassuring look told me this would not only be okay, but that it would be amazing. "I've got you," he murmured, holding my hips and playing with my clit as I started to slide deeper onto him, the pressure sending sharp jabs through my stomach. This was all so . . . tense and bizarre. But even through all the foreign sensations, I felt the potential for ecstasy.

He guided me down, down, down. His voice was smoky as he whispered one last command: "Fuck me, Sophie."

He closed his eyes and groaned.

That sound, that primal, thrilling noise raced through me, turning all that strange stretching into something else. Into the start of a whole new world of sensations.

"You feel so fucking good," he said. "I've wanted you like this for so long. I've wanted all of you since I first saw you."

And I did—I felt fucking amazing.

I rocked into him, letting him fill me, letting him stretch me to the limits. My skin was hot, and my heart felt feverish as I rode him, my ass gripping his cock as a tidal wave of intensity tore through me.

He opened his eyes and blinked. "Wow. Just wow."

"It's incredible," I said, riding him as if I was fucking him . . . and I was. I was fucking my man in a whole new way. I loved that I could take him deep into a new place inside me. That I could explore the far reaches of my fantasies with him.

"You are perfect," he murmured, his words tripping back to the compliment he gave me after our first time together. "Every single part of you."

That.

That second.

That moment.

That ode to all of me.

It was enough.

I combusted. I was a rocket, and I soared. Every nerve ending fired. Every inch of my skin sizzled. Every cell in my brain buzzed.

"That's why I wanted you on top. I want to touch your pussy and fuck your sweet ass at the same time," he said, taking the reins, thrusting upward as he rubbed. "So I can look at you. All of you."

I gasped as he seized control. I moaned loudly as he set

the pace. I cried out in ecstasy as his fingers worked their delicious magic on my wet, hot, slippery center, coaxing the edge of an orgasm out of me.

Then, sheer and unadulterated pleasure pierced my body. It washed over me like a tsunami. As I thrust harder and faster and deeper, he sent me deliriously into a new type of climax, the kind that could be felt in places only he had touched.

He felt like the only lover I'd ever had.

He was the only lover I wanted to have anymore.

I shuddered, trembling in exquisite pleasure.

"Can I come in you?" he asked in a ragged voice.

"Yes," I shouted. "Please, yes."

He followed me there. Filling me with his heat. Flooding me with his release. Coming inside me. I collapsed onto his chest, a hot, sweaty, satisfied woman.

50

RYAN

I cleaned her up.

With a warm, wet washcloth, I erased the remnants of what we'd done, tenderly taking care of her, as she deserved. After gathering the towels and placing them in her hamper, I carried her into the bathroom, then set her on her feet in the shower. She was so soft and warm, and I savored the chance to wash her hair. I soaped her up, her breasts, her belly, and her bottom. Kneeling down on the floor, I cleaned her legs, then handed her the soap and she finished.

After a quick wash myself, I ran a tub for us. When it was full, I scooped her up and brought her into the marble bath, letting the water soothe her. I wrapped my arms around her and snuggled her close.

"Does it hurt?"

She shook her head. "No, but it might tomorrow."

I kissed her forehead.

"But I'll probably still want to do it again, even if I'm sore," she said, wiggling her eyebrows.

"That's my woman," I said playfully. I tugged her close. "You are my woman. You belong with me."

"I know," she said, resting her face in the crook of my neck. "Do you think everyone at the event will know?"

"That I took your ass tonight?"

She nodded and splashed water on me.

"As long as you walk like normal, only you and I will know I own your body. But everyone will know you're with me. And that it's much more than it was when you first asked me to go with you."

"It's so much more for me too," she said. Then she seemed to think of something. "Am I going to spend the night at your house tomorrow or will you come here again?"

I pulled her closer, loving that she assumed we'd be together. I wanted to be with her. "Stay with me. But I have to leave early on Sunday morning. It's a visiting day."

"Ah," she said. "I'll leave early too and head home, so you can get on the road." She seemed to drift off in thought for a moment, then she asked, "Do you ever take her gifts? Can you give her gifts?"

"Only a few things are allowed. She usually just likes company. She likes seeing me, so I go. Why do you ask?"

She screwed up the corner of her lips as if she was deep in thought. "You said she was a seamstress, right?"

"Yeah. She actually gave me a pattern to hold on to," I said with a light laugh. It was absurd. But it was also very much like my mom. "It has a dog bone design on the back. At the time she went away, she had this dream to start making clothes for dogs."

"Do you have it?"

"I do," I said, dipping my head to look her in the eyes. "Why?"

"I have an idea. Would you like me to make it for her?

As a gift. You could take it to her. I mean, obviously she doesn't have a dog in prison. But she might enjoy seeing the jacket. It might make her happy, right? Just to see it. If that was her dream to make them."

My heart stuttered. It stopped beating for a moment, then it thumped harder against my chest, as if it were trying to fight its way out to get closer to her.

"You'd do that?" I asked, dumbfounded.

"Sure. I can sew. I'm sure I'm not as great at it like she was. I couldn't make a living from it. But I know what I'm doing. I still have a Singer machine. It's not hard to make a doggie coat if there's a pattern."

"And you'd do that for my mom? Who's in prison? For murder?" I asked, and I was sure shock was etched on my features.

She shifted in the water that was now cooling. Some sloshed over the side of the tub. "I don't judge her. It's not my place," she said softly, her blue eyes so honest, so guileless. "She's your mother, and the only thing that really matters to me is that without her, I wouldn't have you in my life. And I want you in my life."

And then my heart managed to break free. It jumped from the steel cage I'd once kept it in and raced to the wet woman in my arms. I belonged to Sophie. I cupped her beautiful face in my hands and memorized this moment. The dark of the night. The stillness in her home. The racing of my heart.

She'd bewitched me, and I didn't ever want to be without the only person, besides my family, who I'd ever loved. "I'm in love with you, Sophie. I'm so in love with you."

She beamed. A smile broke across her face. "Oh, Ryan. I'm madly in love with you. I never stood a chance of not falling in love with you."

I smothered her with kisses in the tub. Then I lifted her out, dried us both off, and led her to the bed. Holding her close, I planted kisses all along her sweet skin, from belly to breasts, elbows to ears. "I'm so in love with you," I said, over and over. It was like a dam breaking inside me, and I couldn't hold back anymore. I'd spent so long keeping all my secrets clutched tight and locked up, and this one truth, this incomparable, all-encompassing fact of my existence now, insisted on being heard tonight.

I couldn't stop telling her as I held her tight. "I'm so in love with you I don't know what to do."

"Just love me," she whispered back, and a tear rolled down her cheek.

"I do. I will," I said, and I kissed the tear away. "Please love me too."

"I do, Ryan. I love you so much."

Then, I made love to her as midnight fell across Sin City. As I moved over her, we were the only two people in the whole wide world.

She'd become my world.

51

SOPHIE

Something wasn't right.

I'd noticed it when I traced the pattern on paper, and now I was seeing it for sure on the muslin fabric.

I studied the cloth in front of me, trying to figure out where I'd gone wrong. The little doggie neck-to-tail measurement simply didn't line up. Was it a shorter jacket perhaps? Mid-back? But as I peered at the printout of the pattern again, I reconfirmed that the coat was supposed to cover up the belly and back, as a coat should do.

Bright morning sun streamed in through my living room window. It was an early morning for a notorious late sleeper, but my day was packed, especially since I needed to squeeze in this sewing project before I began my final prep for the benefit tonight. Ryan had departed at the crack of dawn to take care of his dog, and I'd dusted off my sewing machine, setting up on the table by the window, ready to tackle this gift.

He'd emailed me a photo he'd taken of the printed pattern, and I'd grabbed some fabric I had on hand from a few years ago when I'd made a mod retro skirt.

Grabbing a new section of fabric, I followed the measurement once again.

Whoa. That was definitely wrong. Wrong size. Wrong shape. Wrong everything.

Had it been that long since I had sewn? No, it was only two years ago when I'd made that skirt. This pattern didn't seem so complex as to throw me off like this, even with a dog bone design on the back.

Staring at the pattern again as if it would reveal its secrets, I spotted something odd in the first row of instructions, then my brain turned it around. A light switch flicked on.

"Ah!" I said, tasting victory.

I'd just reverse a few of these steps to make the pattern work. Easy enough. Grabbing my pencil, I jotted down the correct order of the steps.

I blinked.

I peered more closely at the numbers in the first row. They lined up precisely with the reverse letters of the alphabet.

I counted off in my head, quickly transposing the numbers into letters, my analytical mind easily sliding into coding mode.

James Street.

A hotbed of crime once upon a time.

Studying the numbers more closely, they clicked into place, sliding like puzzle pieces.

This pattern wasn't a dog jacket.

The measurement was wrong because the first row spelled out a street name, then what appeared to be two addresses on James Street. My mind raced back to a few weeks ago when John had let slip a small detail from the case. *Today was like a goddamn puzzle. You know the math problems you can't solve? This had to do with addresses. Fucking addresses from years ago.*

Oh God.

I dropped the paper as if it were on fire. I scrabbled back in my chair, standing up then backing away from it as if it could curse me.

Could it be? Did that pattern hold the clues to what my brother was looking for in the case? Was this dog jacket pattern from Ryan's mother something else? Something more? Something that revealed . . .

Breathe in.

Breathe out.

I inhaled sharply, remembering what my brother had told me the very first day, before either of us realized my Ryan was *his* Ryan.

Something that would help me find the other guys I think were involved.

John was looking for accomplices. He'd thought Ryan was hiding something. But if this pattern unfolded into a code, as I reasoned it would, then Ryan wasn't hiding anything at all. He couldn't possibly know there were addresses buried inside his mother's "prized" dog jacket pattern.

Only a seamstress would know this pattern wasn't a pattern. Only a man or woman who attempted to make this jacket would be able to tell it wasn't for a dog.

Pacing in circles in my living room, I tried to settle my galloping heart. I worked to calm my overactive brain. I didn't want to jump to conclusions. I needed to check and double-check. That was what I'd done in school. That was always my strategy.

I headed to my desk, flipped open my laptop, and started plugging in the two addresses on Google Maps. They showed up near each other in the same neighborhood—a dangerous section of town years ago that had since been gentrified. I wanted to know who lived there. Property records weren't hard to find—everything was online these days in realtor databases. I plugged the addresses into a realtor search. But the records revealed only when the homes were last sold—a few years ago. Nothing showed the owners' names now, or from when this pattern was made, nearly two decades ago.

But I'd spent a lifetime solving problems. Cracking codes. Creating my own damn codes.

Grabbing the pattern again, I started writing out notes, trying to figure out the rest of the rows of instructions and what they meant. But only that first line translated neatly. The code seemed to shift in each row. Something was missing from the next line. I peered more closely, and it seemed a letter had been turned into a symbol. On the next one, a number was simply missing, like a dropped stitch. I'd have to deal with those later.

For now, I zeroed in on the first row of instructions, puzzling over how to find out who these addresses belonged to. I could easily call John and hand him this information in its current form. Or I could tell Ryan what I'd discovered. But I'd never been one to turn in my homework half done. This code was only partially cracked, and my job was to break it wide open. Whatever I had in my hands—whether it was a cold, hard clue or a dead end—I was determined to figure it out.

I tapped my fingers against my temple, as if I could coax out the way to find the names of the inhabitants. Then in seconds, I had it, because I had friends everywhere in this city, including in the county records office—my friend Jenna's aunt worked there.

Ringing Jenna, even though it was early on a Saturday

morning, I gave her only the barest details, adding that discretion was key.

"I'll see what she can do," Jenna said, and five hellishly long minutes later, she called back to say her aunt would be home shortly from a hike and would log into her work computer to check the records for those addresses. "Give me an hour."

"I can't thank you enough," I said, then tried valiantly to keep myself occupied.

But fifteen minutes of checking and double-checking that my shoes, jewelry, lingerie, and evening dress were ready for tonight did nothing to calm my mind.

A deep obsession kicked in, telling me to *do something*.

To understand.

To look.

To see.

I tried to shove all those urges away, and simply exist in this state of waiting. Maybe some tea would help. Maybe I should bake something. Maybe another long shower would keep my focus off of waiting for Jenna's call.

But something insistent was knocking around in my skull, telling me not to sit still.

My mind was a pinball machine, whirring and whizzing with crazy silver flippers, sending dozens of balls in new directions. I weighed my options. I could stay here and wait. Or I could conduct some recon on my own.

Twenty minutes later, I drove along James Street, my sunglasses on, as if that would hide me from the kids playing in driveways, the men and women walking dogs, the average, every-day feel of this suburban stretch of street that had been riddled with crime years ago. Following the path of the addresses in my hand, I drove past the two homes from the pattern.

Two clean, neat, modern, standard-order suburban family abodes.

They gave away no clues as to why on earth Dora hid these addresses in a pattern many years ago. I gritted my teeth, wishing I truly understood what I'd uncovered.

My phone rang.

I nearly jumped out of the driver's seat, then settled myself when I saw Jenna's name.

Swiping the screen, I turned my phone on speaker, then pulled over near a park and cut the engine.

"Hey, girl," Jenna said. "I've got what you're looking for."

"Tell me," I said breathlessly.

"So, eighteen years ago, one was owned by a family named Stefano," Jenna said, and I cringed, squeezing my eyes shut at that name—the name I knew belonged to the shooter. "The second was a rental. Owned by a guy named Carlos Nelson at the time. But he didn't live there. He rented it to his two cousins, TJ Nelson and Kenny Nelson."

"TJ and Kenny Nelson," I repeated, as if I could decode the names by saying them out loud.

But they meant nothing to me.

Of course they meant nothing to me. I wasn't investigating a crime. I wasn't the detective. I wasn't the victim's family.

I was, however, the woman stuck between the two.

After I said goodbye to Jenna, I didn't move. I stayed behind the wheel of my parked car, staring ahead at the swing set, the world around me fading as I realized that I had the names of the two men John could be looking for in the murder of Ryan's father nearly twenty years ago.

Ryan had no idea he'd been holding on to evidence all these years. He'd thought his mother had given him a memento, a symbol of her hopes and dreams, for safekeeping. Instead, she'd asked him to hide something that was clearly evidence, and managed to do it without anyone being the wiser.

My insides roiled. My head pounded with frustration and so much aching sadness. But underneath that storm of emotions was another one, rising up. *Excitement.* I had something in my hands that might help solve the murder.

The trouble was, I was stuck, and I understood precisely why I'd been so consumed with the need to keep myself busy for the last hour.

I didn't know who to tell first.

My head told me John. My heart said I should call the man who'd given me the clue he didn't even know he had.

I tossed my phone in the back seat and headed home.

52

RYAN

She wasn't herself. Hadn't been all night. I wanted to figure out why, and to make it better if I could.

"Is it that guy?"

Sophie knit her brows and shot me a confused look. "What do you mean?"

"Is that why you're so tense tonight?"

I squeezed her shoulder, then traveled to her neck, gently massaging. "The guy who wanted to set you up with his grandson. The reason you invited me in the first place," I reminded her, as I tried to work the knots of tension from her neck and shoulders. "Is he why you're so tense?"

"No." She shook her head quickly. Then she nodded just as vigorously. "I mean, yes. That must be it. Or it's just that I want this whole event to go well."

"It's going great," I reassured her as we stood at the edge of the ballroom, watching the guests mingling and chatting, enjoying hors d'oeuvres that fancy waiters and waitresses offered on trays as they circled. The huge ballroom glittered under the glow of boat-sized chandeliers. A four-piece orchestra played soft classical music from the stage as guests filtered in. "Or do you want me to make you feel better? Sneak into the fancy bathroom for a quickie?" I suggested in a low voice.

She seized up and spun around. "No. I can't do that," she said sharply.

I held up my hands in surrender. "Hey. Don't bite. I've just never seen you so nervous. I want to help. I know this event is important to you."

She breathed erratically, then waved her hand in front of her face as if she felt faint. "I know. I'm sorry. I'm just . . ."

But she didn't finish her sentence.

I eyed her up and down as if I could somehow figure out what was wrong with my normally polished, poised, and outgoing Sophie. She handled crowds with aplomb. She was unflappable, so it was odd to see her off her game.

On the surface, she was as impeccable as always. She looked extraordinary tonight in a violet dress that hugged her curves, a teardrop necklace that nestled between her breasts, and sheer black stockings I'd peeked at earlier when I'd tugged up her skirt in the town car on the ride over to see how far up they went—all the way to the lace tops at her thighs. Her blonde hair was twisted high on her head, with loose curls framing her face.

I parked my hands on her shoulders. "Breathe, beautiful. Everything here is perfect, including you," I said, then turned her around to let her soak in the room and all the guests—the glitterati of the city mingling and talking. Many of my clients were here, from casino owners to my new White Box clients. I recognized plenty of familiar faces too, from the mayor, to a popular magician, to a big-time high roller. Even my brother Colin was here, though he was busy chatting with a pretty brunette at the bar. Sophie's brother, John, was somewhere among the guests. I had said a quick hello earlier, and it hadn't been as uncomfortable as I'd expected it to be. Maybe John *didn't* hate me.

Sophie bit her lip, then words seemed to tumble out, laced with guilt. "I just feel bad because I couldn't make the pattern," she said, fiddling with a bracelet on her wrist.

I made a scoffing sound. "That's what's upsetting you?"

"I tried," she said apologetically. "It was too complicated."

"Don't worry about it. It's sweet that you even offered."

"I did try. I tried so hard." Her voice sounded as if it was about to break. Then suddenly she plastered on a huge smile as an older man with gray hair strode up to us.

"Clyde Graser," he said to me, holding out a hand, and I spent the next few minutes chatting with the man who was in some way responsible for this incredible woman and me growing even closer. If Clyde hadn't pressured Sophie, she might not have asked me to the event tonight. And knowing we had this date had pushed us even faster into each other's arms.

But then, I also believed Sophie and I were an inevitability. Funny, because I'd never been one to put any stock in fate and love. But I did now, and if this man in front of me had played a role in driving me closer to the woman I loved, then he deserved my gratitude, even if his motives were ulterior.

"I can't thank you enough for all you've done for the community center. It means so much to so many people," I told him.

Then Sophie remarked that it was nearly time to bring Clyde onstage with the director of the center, so I said goodbye to the two of them.

I turned around to look for Colin, but my younger brother was still quite busy with the brunette.

53

COLIN

Sure, there were other people here. Quite possibly I should talk to them. Maybe even interact with my brother. But Elle hadn't slipped away from me yet, so I remained at the bar with her, club soda in my hand, a glass of water in hers, talking about one of our favorite topics — tattoos.

"Did you get the new ink you were talking about?" she asked.

"I did. I'm close to the ten percent mark now," I said, not looking away from her, because how could I? I hadn't seen her dressed to the nines before, and she was jaw-droppingly stunning in her evening finery. But then, she was hot-as-sin in the jeans, short-sleeve blouses, and the little flat shoes she wore on the days I saw her at the community center, so I wasn't surprised. This dress though —I was sure it had been painted onto her lush figure.

I wanted to tear it off.

Trouble was—we were friends.

We'd only been friends for the last year.

I had to wonder if that could change, and if it could change tonight.

She laughed. "No way are you that covered in tattoos," she said, calling me on my fib. She was right, but I had plenty across my body, and she was an admitted tattoo junkie. The back of her neck boasted a line of sparrows I wanted to kiss.

"Fine. Maybe not yet. But close," I said.

She raised her chin, peering over my shoulder, then at my ear, like she was hunting for the new art. "Are you going to show it to me? Or are you hiding it behind your shirt again?"

Chuckling, I raised an eyebrow and shot her a dirty look, then moved my hands to my belt buckle as if I were going to take off my pants.

"Colin!" she hissed under her breath, her eyes widening. She waved her hands frantically as if to stop me.

"What?" I said, deadpan. "It's on my hip."

Her eyes fluttered closed momentarily. Maybe she was picturing my hip. A man could hope.

"So that's a no?" I asked, lowering my voice to a whisper.

She seemed to collect herself, wagging a finger. "We're supposed to be dancing. And hanging out. Not undressing."

"Ah, my bad. I didn't realize half undressing was not on the to-do list for the benefit," I said, giving an exaggerated *oops* shrug.

It was met by an eye roll. Deservedly so. "That is definitely not on the agenda tonight. Especially since Sophie is going to introduce me and then I'm going to introduce Clyde, so no more talk of undressing. Or ink on your hip. Talk about something else. Like potato chips."

"I hear there's a new avocado flavor."

Her eyes twinkled. "Yes, perfect topic."

But truth be told, there was something else I needed to

discuss. My tone dropped to serious. "Actually, I've been meaning to show you a picture my brother-in-law gave me of a guy he's seen around. See if you know him. I think he's one of the guys from the center who plays hoops," I said, reaching into my back pocket for my phone. I came up empty. "Ah, shit. I left it in my car."

"Send it to me later, okay?"

"I will," I said, then added, "Along with a picture of my new ink?"

Her lips curved into a grin. "Maybe."

I held tight to that *maybe*, and to all its possibilities.

54

RYAN

"Be an artist. Be an athlete. Be a leader," Clyde said, his voice booming into the mic and across the ballroom. "The local community center has a mission to provide all these services to young men and women in our fine city, whether it's shooting basketballs, learning photography, or even getting a healthy meal for dinner. The center has cooking, parties, poetry, volunteer services, and thanks to our fearless director, Elle Mariano, we have wonderful support and counseling for young people today. I couldn't be more delighted to be a key supporter of this very fine center and its services. And I am thrilled that so many other local companies have opened their wallets and checkbooks to get on board with us." Clyde then rattled off the names of other supporters, from Colin's firm to the newest ones like White Box. When he was through, the crowd clapped and cheered, including Charlie and Curtis, who I had been enjoying a drink with.

"Glad to hear you guys are on that list. Impressive to see you get behind the local community," I said to the two men.

"Thank you. We were glad to help," Charlie said in a gentlemanly and gracious tone. "As a younger man, I was a bit of a troublemaker. Now that I'm older, I try to stay out of trouble."

"We were all troublemakers one way or the other, weren't we?"

"Indeed we were. We try to do better as we grow older and wiser," he said, like a sage advisor, dispensing wisdom gleaned over the years. "By the way, your security team is doing a spectacular job already with my clubs. I couldn't be more thrilled to be working with you to help keep my business safe and secure."

I flashed a smile. Nothing delighted me more in business than a satisfied client and a job well done. "I'm thrilled. Anything you need, you let me know," I said, then we turned to the stage.

After sharing the details of the fundraising goal—an announcement met with robust applause—Clyde passed the speaking baton to Sophie's brother. John walked to the podium, then gave a short speech about the importance of keeping the streets safe, finishing with a call to support the community center. "Places like this can make a big difference. I believe if we give young people a chance early on to be involved in something other than gangs, crime, and the trouble they can get into on the streets, we'll have a safe community and a better Las Vegas."

I soaked in the atmosphere in the ballroom, and the sense that maybe there were enough people who cared about change. Who cared about this city. Who wanted the best for this town we all called home.

I was filled with pride, too, over Sophie's work, bringing such a motley crew together all in the name of such an important cause. I only hoped seeing the support from the crowd would lift that knot of tension she'd been carrying all night. Even as she introduced the orchestra and asked the guests to find their seats to enjoy some Beethoven, I could tell she wasn't herself.

I doubted anyone else could, but it was in the small details, from the way she cleared her throat before she spoke to how she briefly fiddled with her hair onstage. Sophie was not a fiddler. Or a throat-clearer.

All the more reason for me to tie her up to a chair tonight, or maybe blindfold her for the first time. Yeah, I liked the image of that. I suspected that was just what she needed to clear her mind and rid her body of all that stress.

I excused myself from my clients, found my way to my seat, and waited for Sophie to join me.

When she did, I brushed my lips to her neck, then whispered something dirty in her ear about what I wanted to do to her later. She shivered slightly.

Slightly.

That was all.

Something was wrong with my Sophie.

55

SOPHIE

I wanted to vomit.

I wanted to hurl.

To crawl under the covers, pull them over my head, and pretend I'd never offered to make that damn jacket.

I should have baked a pie instead. Made a homemade card with construction paper. Knit a scarf.

That damn dog jacket was tormenting me. Its secrets hounded me. I repeated the names—TJ Nelson, Kenny Nelson—over and over in my head all day.

Then the other names.

John. Ryan. Ryan. John.

Like a pendulum, I swung back and forth, seesawing between the two men. I couldn't last much longer in this state of suspended secrecy. I hardly knew how Ryan had ever managed to keep so much locked inside his head. It was painful. It hurt my skull to have this knowledge I needed to share sealed up in my mind.

My stomach clenched. Evil butterflies swarmed my belly, the nightmarish, haunting kind.

As the orchestra swelled during the gorgeous piece of

music, I clutched my belly. When Holden joined in on the piano, I dropped my head to my knees. Ryan rubbed my back and whispered, "Are you okay?"

I shook my head. I clasped my hand over my mouth, then whispered, "I need to go to the ladies' room."

I took off.

In the bathroom, I washed my hands over and over, as if that would somehow give me the answer. When I pushed open the door to leave the restroom, I found Ryan waiting in the hallway. The sounds of Beethoven playing from the ballroom could still be faintly heard.

"You're worrying me. Are you pregnant?"

I laughed. Deeply and maniacally. Oh, but it would be easier in some ways if I were.

But as I met his gaze, the pendulum stopped swinging. I had my answer. It came in his presence here, his pursuit of me tonight, his clear and real concern for me. It came in the facts too. It was his mother's pattern; it was his family's story.

"I lied to you," I blurted out.

He furrowed his brow. "About what?"

I grabbed the lapels of his jacket and pulled him to the end of the cavernous hallway, standing against the gold-trimmed, scalloped wall as I confessed. "I lied to you about the pattern. I *did* make it this morning. But it's not a pattern, Ryan. It's a code. A hidden code of addresses. And those addresses match names of people who lived there years ago. Do the names TJ and Kenny Nelson mean anything to you?"

He froze. His face turned white. His lips parted, but no sound came out. Then, he managed words, and they sounded dry and cold as he whispered barrenly, "What did you just say?"

I repeated the names.

"*TJ and K*," he hissed, his eyes full of fire. He stepped back, his hands shooting behind him to grab the wall. As if he needed to hold on to something. "How do you know those names?"

I quickly explained what happened that morning—reversing the steps, then calling Jenna, then finding the addresses from years ago. "I don't know what it means," I said, my voice rising with desperation. Maybe it was nothing after all. Maybe everyone would have a good laugh at my half-baked code-cracking. "I might be overreacting. Maybe I'm just going crazy. It's possibly nothing at all. But is there a chance that it means something? Is there a chance that these are the two names that John has been looking for?"

56

RYAN

I might be shocked to my bones, but I was dead sure of one thing.

There was no way I was keeping this to myself.

"Let's go get John."

* * *

Treasure Island glittered across the Strip.

The glass of the window cooled my forehead as I stared at the hotel across the street from the room at The Venetian. Sophie had rented this suite for the event. The orchestra members had used it as a green room before going onstage, and now for me it was a waiting chamber.

The gold-colored hotel shone brightly back at me. I could still remember when my father had taken me to see the towering structure. To my young eyes, Treasure Island had seemed majestic, a true giant among its neighbors, and I'd gazed skyward with that childlike sense of awe, my father's arm around me as we explored. My memories of my dad were here in this city, and through it all, this was my home, and always would be.

And through it all, too, I'd been a fucking mule, carrying secret names and addresses in a goddamn dog jacket pattern.

I'd held on to that pattern all through high school, college, the Army, and beyond. Stowed it safely away because I'd thought it meant something to my mom.

Something real. Something about hope, the future, and another chance.

It was supposed to be her redemption.

What was it really though? Was it her own notes she'd never had a chance to toss out? Names of users? Names of dealers she owed money to? Or worse? And if so, had I simply been in the right place at the right time when she was arrested and she'd thrust it into my hands, whispering for me to keep it safe for her?

She knew I'd do what she asked.

I was her favorite.

I was the only one she could ask.

Latent rage roiled inside me, rising and twisting through my veins. I breathed out heavily, an angry plume, like a dragon. The lights on Treasure Island flickered, and I snapped my gaze away, staring at my black leather shoes as my emotions shape-shifted again.

Now, I was flooded with shame—so much shame at having been deceived.

Because, dammit. She could have asked me to throw the fucking thing out instead. Lord knows I would have. I would have crumpled it up on the way to school the next day and chucked it in a trash can. At least then I wouldn't have carried it around like some sad sack year after year. I wouldn't have held on to the patternless pattern like a fool, running my fingertips over it as if it were a symbol of her freedom someday.

When now it seemed more like a glaring piece of evidence.

A lie now exposed.

What else had she told me that was a lie?

I wanted to know so badly my bones vibrated with coiled tension. I wanted to know who those men were. I wanted to know what role they played in my father's death.

The tension in me spiked, and I pressed my fingertips to the dark window.

When the door creaked open, I turned around, straightening my spine and lifting my chin, ready to stop guarding the secrets my mother had asked me to keep. John and Sophie walked into the suite.

"Sophie said you had some new details," John began, cutting to the chase as he motioned for me to take a seat on the couch. Sophie sat next to me, and John opted for a chair.

"Thanks for taking the time out of your night," I said, then drew in a deep breath, letting it fuel me, letting it feed me as I proceeded to tell John about the pattern that was never a pattern. I traded off with Sophie, and she weighed in too, explaining her role in the discovery and then sharing the names.

TJ Nelson and Kenny Nelson.

Marshall's words rang in my ears. *The detective would probably give a right arm for those names.*

57

JOHN

Yes.

This was everything.

My eyes surely flickered with wild hope. This was what I wanted.

Names.

I'd been hunting these names for the last few months. Ever since Bianca tipped us off.

These had to be the guys we wanted. The guys she'd said had called her. The names she didn't know either.

My fists tightened with anticipation.

"Are those the guys you're looking for?" Ryan asked, his expression taut. "Because you asked me when I first met you who she was associating with at the time. You said you had new evidence and were trying to determine the validity of it. Is this the corroboration you needed?"

I'd kept my lips shut the first time we'd talked, holding all the cards, telling him little.

He hadn't needed to know. Hell, he didn't need to know when I was still trying to assemble the clues.

But as he swallowed roughly, I could tell he was hoping

the information exchange would flow both ways tonight. And truth be told, I owed him one. "I can't say for sure, but this is as close as we've come, and it lines up with my leads," I said, giving him something. He released a deep breath, clearly relieved this wasn't a fool's errand after all. "I know it hasn't been easy for you, but I really appreciate you sharing this—"

"I did nothing." He pointed to my sister. "She figured it out."

I cracked a smile. No surprise she'd done the hard work. My brilliant sister. "I like to say she's my code breaker," I said lightly.

Sophie waved us off. "Hardly. There's more to it, but the other rows are going to take more time to figure out."

"I might need you as a consultant on this case, then," I said to her.

Her expression was earnest, helpful. Exactly how I knew her to be. "You know I'll do whatever I can, and whatever you need," she said.

"This is a good start, and I appreciate it." I turned to Ryan, scratched my jaw, and gave him some details. "I want to let you know we've been looking for Stefano's accomplices, so I'll share what I'm able to." I leaned forward, elbows on my thighs, eager as I spoke, sharing what I could —there were others involved, and we wanted those others behind bars too. "We believe that Jerry Stefano did not act alone the night of the murder. We believe he had help. We believe he had both a broker who arranged his hits, and a getaway driver who, of course, drove him away from the scene of the crime that night. At the time he was questioned, Jerry repeatedly claimed that after Dora Prince hired him, he acted alone in the crime. He steadfastly stuck to that statement for eighteen years and still remains wedded to it. But we have reason to believe he never gave up the names of his accomplices as a sort of exchange. In return for his silence, these two men made a pact to look out for Mr. Stefano's child, who was born shortly before he was incarcerated."

He seemed to take in the information quickly, absorbing it.

"Wow. That's a lot," he said, rubbing a hand across his jaw, taking his time as he asked the next question. "Do you think my mother protected their names too, in some sort of exchange?"

That was the question. The biggest one of all. What was the exchange? What was Dora Prince protecting the Nelsons for? That was what I need to know.

"I don't have the answer to that. But this is the biggest break we've had so far in potentially finding the other men who we believe were involved in the murder of your father," I said.

Something seemed to change in Ryan when I said those last words.

Cruel words.

But words that were surely a part of him now.

Except, as I read his face, I swore he was hearing them in a new way.

And my senses went on high alert. I rubbed my thumb against my forefinger, a habit, one I indulged in when I had a feeling a witness was about to serve up the goods.

58

RYAN

Even though I had heard those words countless times over the last eighteen years—*murder of your father*—they took on a deeper meaning then.

They echoed in my bones and resonated in my blood.

For so long, I'd protected the rest of my mother's story. Kept it locked up in case the truth would ever set her free. For nearly two decades, I tried to make sense of my mother's urging me to stay quiet about the drugs, and if her warning had something to do with the other men involved rather than with her quest to prove her innocence.

But this was no longer about her. This was about finding everyone who was responsible for my father's death.

Every single one.

And to do that, I had to speak the whole truth.

Everything I'd kept locked behind bars in my head.

"There's more I have to tell you," I said, steady and even. Strong too. I looked to Sophie, who'd been by my side the whole time, like a partner, like a rock, like my foundation. She had given me strength to speak the truth to her, and to speak now for my family. Her blue eyes were full of honesty, full of love. She'd said a few minutes ago *I lied*, but that was nothing compared to what I had done my whole life.

The lies of omission.

The lies of protection.

I shucked them off. Shed them all. Everything was coming undone.

Scrubbing a hand across my chin, I unraveled another secret. "I found my mother doing cocaine when I was thirteen. She told me she was quitting. She said she met her lover, Luke Carlton, in Narcotics Anonymous. She also told me Jerry Stefano was her dealer." John arched an eyebrow, tilting his head at that bit of information. I explained more. "She always claimed she'd been framed for the murder because she owed him money. That's why she was taking on more work for the gymnastics team," I said, serving it all up, giving everything to the one man who might be able to exact justice. A sense of freedom rushed through me as I answered each and every question John asked.

When I was done, Sophie excused herself to the restroom.

John thanked me profusely. "I know it's not easy to share all that. But I'm grateful, and this will help. I assure you."

"Find those fuckers," I said, looking him in the eyes.

"That's my goal."

"Are you going to talk to my mom about all of this?"

John nodded. "I will, but she usually doesn't say much."

I scoffed. "Tell me about it."

"And I'll have to coordinate with her attorney, so it'll be a few days."

"I'll be seeing her tomorrow. I'll keep you posted."

"Appreciate that." John extended a hand. "By the way, it's no secret that I wasn't thrilled when I found out you were dating my sister. But she's incredibly happy. And all I ask is that you keep it that way."

"That's my goal," I said, and it was number one on my to-do list.

59

SOPHIE

I understood everything now. Why he visited his mom so much. The way the secrets had twisted over the years, like a string running through a labyrinth. Ryan had kept them all inside his head, locked up tight, clutching like a lifeline the wish of his one living parent.

My place wasn't to judge the guilt or innocence of Dora Prince. The state of Nevada had already done that. But my role, the self-appointed role I embraced, was to be there for my man.

"I'm proud of you for speaking all those hard and terrible truths," I said as the town car driver took us to Ryan's house after the event, and the intense visit with my brother ended.

"I barely know what to think anymore," he muttered, staring out the window as the streetlights and cars in his neighborhood streaked by.

I dropped a hand to his shoulder. "You were brave to tell him."

"Hardly," he said, mocking himself as he turned to look

at me. "If I were brave, I would have said something years ago."

I stared at him levelly and shook my head. "You didn't know what you were dealing with. You still don't entirely know. That's why it's brave. You took a chance."

Once we were inside his house, I grabbed his shoulders then cupped his cheeks. "You said something now. That's all that matters."

He swayed closer to me, his eyes floating closed, his hold on gravity seeming precarious.

"Come with me," I whispered.

I took his hand and led him to the couch, holding him close. Johnny Cash leaped on the cushion and curled up at our feet. Running my hands through Ryan's hair, I let him rest his head in the crook of my neck, sensing what he needed right now was a safe landing. I wanted to be that for him. I wanted to be everything he needed.

"I just . . . Soph . . . if she . . . I don't know." His words beat out a staccato rhythm of what was said and unsaid.

"I know." I ran my fingers through his hair. "I know."

He sighed heavily, then pressed his lips to my chest. It wasn't sexual; it wasn't the start of something dirty. It was a gesture of the familiar, of comfort, and I was glad he found it in me.

"For so long, she's said one thing to me. She said she was set up. She said she was framed." His voice was low and sad.

My heart ached. It cried for him—heavy, mournful tears for what he had borne all those years. "So you go see her and you ask her. You tell her you need to know for your own peace of mind."

He shook his head. "She won't tell me. Talking to her is like pulling teeth."

I brushed a kiss on his forehead. "Then you find the

answer in yourself," I said, and wrapped my arms around him. He held me tight.

We stayed like that, curled together, him in his tux, me in my dress, nestled snug on the couch, a ball of fur by our feet. We talked more, whispered confessions and admissions, hopes and wishes.

"There were days when everything felt so out of control. So beyond anything I could ever manage," he said softly, and for a moment, I understood that there was something more to his quest for control in the bedroom. With the way his life had spiraled, I suspected some part of his mind needed the solidity of that kind of dominance—sexual dominance—just like I needed submission to let go. I kept that notion to myself, though, not because it was a secret, but because it wasn't my goal to psychoanalyze him. Whether that was his reason, or whether he simply liked it that way, I was happy to be on the receiving end.

"It was hard to manage because you carried so much. The weight of so many secrets. The pressure of so many things you should never have been asked to keep to yourself. Forget guilt or innocence or who was framed or not framed. You were fourteen. You deserved to be fourteen, not a secret keeper," I said fiercely.

Then, when the conversation seemed to unwind, and sensing it was time to move on to something lighter, I sat up, straightened my hair, patted him on the leg, and said, "How about you teach me how to play pool finally? I believe that was one of the promises you made when I stayed here last weekend, and pretty much the only one you failed to deliver on."

A sliver of a smile crept across his face. "I failed to deliver on something, did I?"

I nodded. "I'm wretched at pool. Show me how to play."

He stood up and offered me his hand. "Why do I have

the feeling that after one game you're going to be a pool shark?"

"If that's the case, maybe for this first round, we should just play strip pool?" I ran a hand between my breasts as if to demonstrate the possibilities.

A groan escaped his throat, and he looped his arms around my waist. He brushed his lips against my neck. I closed my eyes and smiled, and we were right back there. Our flirty, dirty, and naughty side was never far away. All was not perfect. All was not completely right in the universe. There were so many questions left unanswered. But we had moved through something difficult together tonight, and each obstacle we faced made us stronger.

We grabbed beers and headed into the den to the pool table. He took a cue down from the wall and handed it to me, then grabbed one for himself.

"Have you played before?"

I nodded. "A few times. All badly. I barely understand how it works. There are stripes, solids, and an eight ball, and we hit them in the pockets, right?"

He laughed. "Something like that," he said, taking a sip of his pale ale and setting it down on the table. He removed his tux jacket and his tie, and tossed them on a chair in the corner of the room.

"Wait. You're already taking off your clothes?"

"Consider it my handicap," he said, then racked the balls.

He explained the basics to me, and I quickly processed them, since rules and games made fast sense to me. My challenge lay in the execution. I wasn't known for my coordination.

Still, I was determined, so I pulled back the stick, stared at the ball, aimed squarely, and missed it by a mile. I laughed and brought my free hand to my mouth. "Oops."

Then I removed an earring, tossing it on his pile on the chair.

"Want me to show you how it's done?"

"I do," I said, and he moved to my side of the table, behind me, then pressed his hand on top of mine, his chest along my back. As he positioned the cue just so, I felt him grow harder. I wriggled my rear as he shot the ball.

And missed too.

"Hey. Take off your shirt," I said playfully.

"That wasn't my shot! I was helping you set up."

"Fine. Help me again," I said in a flirty tone, and he lined himself behind me once more. I couldn't resist. Screw pool. I dropped the stick, shoved all the balls randomly around the table, then turned around in his arms and laced my hands around his neck. I moved my lips to his ears. "You win. Strip me."

He wasted no time, unzipping my dress in a flurry and leaving it a silky puddle on the floor. I backed up to the table and perched on it. "Show me where you'd touch me to land the shot."

He gripped the back of my head, and whispered roughly in my ear, "Everywhere. Every-fucking-where on your perfect body." And then he proceeded to do just that, teaching me pool in a whole new way.

60

SOPHIE

He was too cute to resist.

The way he wagged his tail and dazzled me with his puppy-dog eyes melted me.

"Fine, you win," I cooed, kneeling to scratch Johnny Cash's soft white chin. He lifted his snout for me, letting me rub him. When I rose, I reached for his leash from a hook by the front door.

I spun around, hunting for a key, and found an envelope with my name on it by the door. "Aha," I said, like a treasure hunter who'd found the *X* marking the spot. Inside was a key and a short letter. Ryan had had to leave early, much too early, this morning for his drive to Hawthorne, and had insisted I stay and sleep in. I'd leave first thing tomorrow for Germany to pick up my long-awaited Bugatti, and we'd be a bit like ships passing in the night, so I loved that he'd left me my first real note from him. I unfolded the sheet of lined white paper.

By now, Johnny Cash is probably trying to convince you to take him for a walk. Please don't feel that you have to give in, even if he bats those big brown eyes. He is a well-trained boy, and he will be fine inside the house during the day. Just take the key, and lock the door behind you.

Oh, I suppose this would be a good time to let you know that this is your key. I have nothing to hide from you, and my house is your house. If you feel like going for a swim, the fence is high enough that the neighbors won't see you if you swim naked. If you do that, though, it would be great if you could send me a photo, as I think a shot of you in my favorite outfit would do wonders for me.

Also, I want to see you before you leave, but I don't know when I'll be back. I promise to call when I'm done, and then I'll come see you, no matter how late it is. Because I can't stay away from you, Sophie. I swear, I can't.

I'll be thinking of you. I'm always thinking of you.

Always . . .

I grinned wildly as my heart beat like a hummingbird's wings. I tucked the note inside my clutch purse from last night. Smoothing a hand over the pink cotton of my sundress, I was grateful that I'd left this outfit behind last weekend, because it was far easier to walk a dog in this little number than in my violet evening dress. I had no change of shoes, though, so I'd be walking him in my Louboutins.

I shrugged happily. So be it.

I lowered my shades over my eyes, opened the door,

then locked up behind me. Johnny Cash trotted happily by my side for the next twenty minutes as I click-clacked around Ryan's neighborhood, soaking in the wide lawns, the gorgeous houses, and the palm trees that were ever present in our desert town. My skin heated up from the hot morning rays, and my shoulders started to bake. The dog panted heavily, his tongue lolling out of his mouth. When I returned to Ryan's block, I spotted a young man walking up the steps to his house. The guy was wearing jeans and a red T-shirt. He knocked on Ryan's door, then shifted back and forth on his feet.

He glanced around, scanning the porch, tapping his feet as he waited.

Odd. I tugged the dog closer to me.

As I neared the house, the guy was fidgeting, his right hand rubbing up and down his left arm, which was covered in tattoos. He sighed in frustration, then muttered something under his breath. His jaw was unshaven.

I narrowed my eyes.

Was he a neighbor? A deliveryman? He didn't have a box or package with him. The pool guy? No supplies in his hand.

He turned and walked down the porch steps, heading to the sidewalk.

I flashed back to last night, to those names, to the details my brother had shared. Gangs, brokers, getaway drivers. My pulse jumped. Was he one of those guys?

Oh God. My skin prickled with fear.

Wait.

My logical brain took over, and I talked myself down. The people John was looking for were older—much older than this guy who barely looked old enough to drink.

Still . . .

His eyes were on his car, and I followed his gaze to a tan Buick parked in front of Ryan's home.

Recognition kicked in. I remembered who he was. I'd seen him, and his car, at the community center.

I breathed more easily now.

I reached the walkway to Ryan's house at the same moment the young man arrived at the sidewalk. I straightened my spine as a flurry of nerves skated over my skin. I was grateful to have the dog by my side. The collie's ears pricked up, and he went on canine alert.

But I wasn't entirely sure that I needed protection.

Something about his brown eyes seemed almost . . . hopeful. He kept running his palm up and down his arm. A nervous gesture perhaps?

He stopped short when he saw me. Classic deer in the headlights.

"Good morning. Were you looking for someone?" I asked, opting for directness.

"I'm looking for Ryan Sloan. Is he here?"

"You just knocked on his door," I said, pointing to the house. "It seems he's not in. But would you like me to pass on a message to him?"

He shook his head. "No. I'll stop by another time."

He turned toward his car, gripping the handle.

"Wait. I've seen you at the community center. Playing basketball," I said, trying to figure out who he was. "Why are you looking for Ryan?"

"I need to talk to him." He opened the door and got into his Buick.

"What's your name?"

But he didn't give me his name. He yanked the door shut and took off.

Johnny Cash and I waited until the guy's car disappeared around the corner. My heartbeat slowed down, and

I patted the dog on the head, glad I'd had a companion. I had no idea what to make of that young man. Why on earth would he need to talk to Ryan? Then it hit me. He might not be TJ or Kenny Nelson, but could he be related to one of those men? A son perhaps?

A chill shimmied through me.

When Ryan returned from Hawthorne, I'd tell him he'd had an unnamed visitor. For now, he had more important matters on his mind. Once inside his home, I locked the door, then checked again to confirm it was closed, then checked once more. I peered out the living room window, making sure the guy hadn't circled by again. The street was quiet. I called a cab and headed home.

Today was not the best day to go skinny-dipping.

61

RYAN

Surprise her.

That was my strategy. It was a tactic I'd relied on in the military from time to time, and my mother needed to be treated like the enemy today with a sneak attack.

She was always most vulnerable when she didn't expect something. As I turned into the parking lot, showing my ID at the gate, my stomach churned. I hated manipulating her like this, but I'd spent the drive fortifying myself, talking back to my fears, and kicking them aside.

Today I was on a mission, and my one and only goal was finding the facts.

Once inside the visiting room, after a hug and a hello, I launched into one of her favorite topics: the soap opera *General Hospital.*

Her green eyes lit up. Yup, that did it. Like a fisherman casting a rod, I'd dropped the lure in the water. She was the fish taking the bait.

She chattered on about the show, and because I had listened to a soap opera podcast on the five-hour drive, I was up to speed on which long-lost twin had reappeared, who had been kidnapped and sequestered away in a mansion, and who was pregnant with a secret baby.

Soon she was laughing, and I'd done it—I'd lulled her into a false sense of security. Tension curled through me, but this was the only chance I had to shock her into revealing the truth. I reached into my pocket to remove the pattern subtly. Under the table I unfolded it. Then I laid it on the wood surface, jammed my finger against the center of the paper, and interrupted her.

"Who are TJ and Kenny Nelson, and why are their names hidden in a code inside your prized dog jacket pattern?"

62

———

DORA

Shock.

It radiated through my brittle bones.

It swelled in my chest.

Those names.

God, those names.

All those names haunted me.

Was he truly saying them?

Names I only muttered at night when I couldn't sleep.

My jaw dropped, my eyes widened, fumbling over my words. "What did you just say?"

Ryan was resolute, his eyes like bullets. "Mom, I know what this is. Don't lie to me now. Please, God, after all I've done for you, don't lie to me now." He sounded so desperate. My sweet baby was so desperate. "Who are they, and what role did they play in my father's death?"

"I don't know." I dropped my gaze to my hands, twisting my fingers together.

"You do, Mom. You do. You gave me this pattern; you asked me to keep it safe. I did that." Exasperation seeped into his voice now. "I believed it was some kind of sign of hope for your future," he said, brandishing the paper, faded and wrinkled from age, the thing I'd asked him to protect. "I kept it safe for you. I was even going to have a friend make the damn jacket for you as a gift, to cheer you up. But when she did, she figured out it wasn't a pattern. It has addresses in it, and those addresses correspond to names, and one of those names is the man doing life for murder, and two of the others might be the broker and the getaway driver in the crime."

I blinked, willing my face to remain stony.

My son pressed on. "Those other two names match the initials you told me last time I was here, when I asked you who Stefano's friends were who were looking out for his son. You asked me if they were TJ and K." He leaned back in his chair, stretching his arms out wide in a waiting stance. "The initials all line up. Talk to me, Mom."

But talk?

How could I?

That's what I wasn't supposed to do.

I pursed my lips and squeezed my eyes shut. Sucking in all my own secrets and holding them in with my breath.

63

RYAN

I huffed through my nostrils. *Enough.* This was fucking enough. I wanted to slam my fist into the wood. To knock the damn table over on its side. To throw things. But I wasn't that kind of a man. I didn't do that on the ice, and I didn't do it here. Violence begot more violence. Fear spawned more fear. I had to rely on my head and my heart.

"Don't you dare shut down on me again," I seethed, the words curling out of my mouth like hot smoke. "Don't you try that routine with me. I have a right to know what I've been carrying around for you. It's not a secret anymore. The pattern was made. The names are revealed." I thumped my fingertip against the table. *"Jerry. TJ. Kenny.* They were in *your* pattern, Mom. *Yours."* I pointed at her for emphasis. "I want to know why the addresses, and therefore the names, of those men were hidden in there. Because for eighteen years, you tricked me into thinking this was special to you. I kept it safe. Because I fucking love you, Mom."

My throat hitched, and wild tears threatened to rain from my eyes. I stopped speaking, pressed my thumb and forefinger over the bridge of my nose, and pinched, keeping them at bay. "I love you, and I love Dad. I came to see you all the time, even when I was in college and when I had leave from the Army. I'm the one. I came here. I saw you. And I have been a messed-up son of a bitch most of my life because of this. Please, I'm begging you. Tell me something."

My mother parted her lips and bit nervously on her thumbnail. Her eyes welled up. "Ry," she whispered, like a fearful creature. "They told me not to say a word about anything. That's why I gave it to you. To get rid of it. To hide it."

I knit my brow. "Who? Who told you not to say a word?"

"Those men."

But that didn't add up. "Why didn't you just tell me to throw it out?"

64

DORA

I glanced from side to side then under the table, checking for spies, for bugs. You never knew who was listening. Leaning across, I lowered my volume, whispering the truth. The truth was messy. The truth was I messed up. "I thought I'd gotten rid of that stuff already," I admitted. I thought I'd gotten rid of all of it. "But then the cops came, and I still had it, and I couldn't have you throwing out something the cops might think was evidence." My lips quivered as I remembered those times, remembered how I'd tried then to protect him. "I didn't want to put that on you, or make you responsible for that. I had you keep it, knowing no one would ever look inside my sewing pattern."

His face pinched. "You played me for a fool."

Tears welled, and I nodded, shamed by what he'd said. I had. I'd tricked him but only because I loved him, and all my other babies.

"Why? Why did you have it in the first place? Why did you put their addresses in there?" he asked, pressing on like a cross-examiner.

I twisted a strand of my hair back and forth, tight against my skull. A hard reminder to keep most everything inside. *Most.* "They were just my notes. That was all. They were notes about who I was meeting, and I was taking on so much extra sewing work to pay off my debt, so I wrote things down on my patterns."

He huffed, his voice intense. "But this wasn't *on* a pattern. It was *in* a pattern. It was part of the pattern."

"I know," I said through gritted teeth. "But I didn't want anyone to know I was meeting them." I dropped my forehead in my hands and hissed, "About the drugs. And I told you why. I wanted to try to stay quiet about the drugs in case I ever got out, and I fought so hard to have my conviction overturned."

Ryan heaved a sigh. "You put their addresses in a pattern because you were meeting them about drugs, Mom? C'mon. Why would you do that?"

My jaw was set hard, because I had my reasons. Dear God, I had them. "I told you. I wanted to keep you all safe from them. I had to protect my babies. I had to."

He stabbed his finger against the table, pushing, pushing. "So you put the info about Stefano's accomplices in a pattern to fucking protect us? You told me not to say anything about the drugs because you were trying to get out of here, but then you hid their addresses in a pattern. Something doesn't add up."

I flinched at his assessment, but didn't answer, then brushed something off my shoulder. Lint. Were they doing my clothes wrong too? All I had to wear was orange—the least they could do was wash it without getting lint on it.

"Or was there something else going on? Did they have something else on you?" Ryan asked, and my sweet boy sounded like he was grasping at straws. Like his life was at stake if he didn't know why I had to shield all those names so much.

I covered my eyes, giving him the truth. "I was scared. That's why I hid the info. That's why I didn't want anyone to know the addresses and who I was meeting."

He kept pushing, kept going, insistent, so insistent. "Why? What did they have on you? Why were you so afraid of them? What did you have to hide? What was so important about those names that you asked me to hide this pattern? Because if it was that goddamn important, it sounds like it was more than drugs. It sounds like you gave me your own notes for planning a murder. Is that what it was? Was this your goddamn blueprint?"

"No!" I raised my voice—the same tone I'd admonished my kids with when they were younger. "That is the truth. I put their addresses in there because I needed to remember them. That's all."

"Were you meeting them to plan the murder of my father?"

"I told you, I didn't do it," I said in a ferocious whisper. Facts were facts. I needed him to remember what was true. "I told you I didn't kill him. Are you ever going to believe me?"

He scrubbed a hand over his chin. "I know you didn't pull the trigger, Mom. Everyone knows that. But you've told me other things that have turned out not to be true. So I want to know this—were TJ and Kenny Nelson working with Stefano? Were they his accomplices?"

Don't say a word.

"Were you? Were you working with these men?"
Keep it inside.

I gripped the edge of the table, pleading. "I didn't do it. I told you I didn't do it."

"Were you involved?" he continued, a dog with a bone,

unwilling to relent, unable to let go. "Like the cops say you were. Like the state of Nevada says you were."

In his eyes I saw his desperation. I sensed it. And I felt it in my heart. Everything I'd done, I'd done for my children. And I wondered if this, this I could do for him.

As dangerous as it was, as risky as it was, perhaps I had to give this to my son.

Perhaps I could save him from his own wild torture.

"I didn't do it," I said. But that wasn't entirely true.

65

RYAN

Wear her down. Just fucking wear her down. "Did you hire Jerry Stefano to kill my father? Did you? Did you hire him and plan it with those three guys? Did you go to their houses and plan the crime down to every last detail with the broker and the shooter and the goddamn getaway driver? Did you kill him for his life insurance money, like they put you in Stella McLaren for?" I asked, my voice rising with each question.

I ran my hands through my hair, tugging hard on it because I was at the end of my rope, but I couldn't let go. "Don't you understand what this has done to me? I don't trust people. I don't believe people. I don't get close to people. Because of this. Because of what happened," I said, trying a new approach. Go for the heart. Try to pierce that damn organ in her, or whatever's left of it. "But, Mom, I finally met someone. Okay? I finally met a woman and, my God, I am in love with her, and it's the best thing that ever happened to me." I softened momentarily as I thought of my sweet, sexy Sophie. I'd come so far with her, she'd shown me so much, and she'd opened up so many possibilities in my life and helped me feel wonderful, amazing, incredible things. I hated the prospect of slingshotting back to who I was before—closed off, shut down, and obsessed.

"I need some clarity for once. I need it so I can have a normal life with the woman I love. Don't you want that for me? Don't you want me to be happy? Because I do, Mom. I want it so damn badly that I'm here, asking you to just tell me the truth."

I waited. Seconds passed, spooling into minutes as my mother sat like a statue. Finally, she broke her frozen stance, uncrossing her arms and jerking her head away.

I threw up my hands. This was a lost cause. I was getting nowhere. Sophie was right. I'd have to find the answers myself, because I wasn't getting them from my mother. I pushed back my chair and stood up to leave. I bent my head to my mom and kissed her forehead. "I love you, Mom, but I need to go," I whispered.

She grabbed my wrists, her bony fingers circling them. Her hands were papery and rough. "Do you love her?" she asked.

"Yes. So much."

She exhaled. Deeply. It sounded like relief. "I'm happy for you, baby."

"Me too."

"All I want is for you to be happy. That's all I've ever wanted." She gripped my hands tighter. "They told me they'd hurt you all." Her voice was just a thread. "They told me they'd come after my babies if I said a word."

I blinked. Holy shit. She was talking. I leaned closer, resting my chin on her head. "Said a word about what, Mom?" I asked, anticipation weaving a dangerous path through my blood.

"I tried to stop it."

"Did you start it?"

A nod. I felt the barest hint of a nod of her head against mine. Holy shit. "I'm telling you this now because I love you. Because you said you need this to be happy. And all I've ever wanted is for my babies to be happy. But they made me go through with it, Ry. And that's why I did it. I did it for all of you," she said, and then the words rained down. "Please don't stop seeing me; please don't stop coming. I went through with it because I had no choice. They told me they'd hurt you if I didn't go through with it."

Like a wrecking ball to my gut, her admission walloped me. I stumbled and gripped the wall behind me. My head was swimming. It was a roiling sea. Eighteen fucking years were compressed into this moment. Her words echoed across the vast cavern of time, clanging through the days, the months, and the pages on the calendar, stabbing me with a million cuts. My own omissions. My own secrets. Most of all, my foolish hope that my mother wasn't a murderer.

"You had him murdered?" The question tasted like dirt.

"I had to keep you safe."

"Why did he have to die to keep us safe? He didn't have to die." But even as the words came out of my mouth, I knew there was no point to them. The decision had been made eighteen years ago—whether for drugs, for money, for her lover, or from fear. I might not ever know *why* she did it. All I knew for sure was that she did.

"I love you and your sister and your brothers so much, and I do, I still do. I swear, I love you so much. I love you, baby. I love you, Ryan." She began weeping, a deep, dark keening sound like a bruised, battered thing heaving itself onto the shore, defeated.

Like me.

I'd traveled here hoping for an answer, but never expecting to get one.

Instead, I'd received her confession.

66

RYAN

My legs were lead. My head was concrete. My heart had mutinied. It was somewhere lost in time.

I made a beeline for the exit, pushing past Clara and the other correctional officers, putting blinders on to avoid the rest of the visiting families. The second I left the facility, the door falling shut behind me, I crumpled on the hot stone steps. I didn't care one lick that you could fry an egg on them.

Let me burn. Let me feel. Let the pain erase the foolishness, the shame, the utter shock.

I dropped my forehead into my hands, replaying my mother's last words. Wishing I could go back and redo them, erase them, rewrite them.

Make them make sense.

Not that this—my life visiting a women's correctional center each month—would ever make much sense. I shut my eyes, but all I saw was the blood in the driveway. All I heard were the screams when she found the body.

Were those fake too? Had she practiced them? Did she

go to some abandoned house somewhere to rehearse her reaction to finding her husband shot dead?

My stomach seized, and I coughed—a dry, hacking bark.

Then, I flinched.

A hand was on my back, rubbing the space between my shoulder blades. I lifted my head to see Clara. "Rough visit?" she asked gently, kneeling next to me.

"Yeah," I muttered.

She nodded sagely. As if she'd seen it all. "That happens sometimes. Can I get you a Coke from the vending machine? Or a Diet Coke?"

I shook my head, then realized my throat was parched. "Coke would actually be great."

Two minutes later, she returned with two cold sodas. With a weary sigh, she settled in next to me on the steps, handed me a can, and cracked open hers, taking a hearty gulp. I did the same, narrowing my focus to the coldness of the beverage and the bubbles in the drink. "She did it," I said heavily as I turned the can around in my hand.

Clara patted my knee. "They all did it, Ryan. That's why they're here."

"Fuck," I muttered. "I really thought . . ."

"Of course you did. You love her. She's your mother. If you listen to the ladies in there," she said, pointing her thumb at the concrete building, "there's not a guilty one among 'em." Clara shook her head in amusement, her curly brown hair bouncing with her. "Amazing, isn't it? A whole facility full of the innocent? *Judge made a mistake. Someone else did it. Framed, I was framed,*" she said, rattling off the stories the inmates no doubt told.

The last one seared into me like a cattle brand.

"That one. That was hers," I said. *Framed.*

Sure, there were details I didn't know, like twisty rat tails coiled together, which would likely take years to unravel. I didn't know why those men made her go through with the murder, or what their motivation was. I didn't know precisely who played what role. I didn't know how far back in time the planning went, or where the other two men were.

But I knew this much—my mother was involved in my father's murder.

My eighteen-year obsession had an answer.

"You'll still come see her, right?" Clara asked.

I shrugged. "I don't know. I mean, what's the point?"

Clara answered in a plain, simple voice. "That's what we do for family."

"But she did it," I pointed out. The specifics didn't need to be outlined. The who, what, when, where, and why could be sorted out by others.

"Right," she said slowly. "But that's not why you come see her. You don't come see her because she's innocent of a crime. You come because you're a good man. Because you have compassion. Because even the criminals of this world need someone who cares about them. Maybe she's in for life and she'll never have a chance to be redeemed on the outside. But maybe the fact that you come here helps her to be a better person in this place. Maybe she finds her redemption behind bars, because of you."

"Do they? Find redemption?"

Clara shrugged. "Some do. Some don't. You still gotta come to work every day, right?" she said, then drained more of her soda.

I did the same, then rose. "Better hit the road."

She nodded. "I'll be looking for you around these parts."

I managed a half-hearted smile of acknowledgment. I didn't know if I'd ever be in these parts again. I didn't know where the ground was, where the sky ended, or how to find my way back home after hearing her confession.

The only thing I knew for sure was how to avoid the speed traps, so I turned on an app to do just that when I got in my truck.

A little more than four hours later, I'd dodged a speeding ticket, but hadn't been able to stop playing the cruel song on repeat in my head—*they made me do it, they made me do it, they made me do it.*

Did she set the wheels in motion, then try to cancel? But they forced her? How would that even work?

Gripping the wheel tighter, I cursed up a storm. I'd been such a fool. For so damn long, I'd clung to a big *what-if.* That possibility had tied me up, tethered me, and obsessed me.

Today, I was cut loose. Left adrift and unmoored.

Glancing at the green sign on the highway, I registered that I was five miles from my house. I wanted to see my dog, but I also didn't want to be alone. The closer the truck wheels came to the exit, the less I wanted to be by myself.

I needed company. I needed someone.

Though I desperately wanted to see Sophie, I didn't want to see her like this. Not when my head was messier than it had ever been, and not when my heart was twisted into tattered strands.

The time I'd spent with Sophie over the last few weeks was like shedding a skin, molting my old self, leaving it behind.

But now?

Hell, I didn't know if I was coming or going. If I was the guy I'd been before or the man I'd become with Sophie.

Limbo. This was the utter hell of limbo. I was stuck in it like quicksand, and I didn't want to drag her down with me.

I needed the three people in my life who'd known me before, during, and after.

As I turned on my blinker to exit the highway, I called Shannon and gave her the rundown, and she told me she'd gather the crew.

Then my phone rang, and it was Sophie.

67

SOPHIE

Passport? Check.

Luggage packed? Done.

Flight checked into? Good to go.

After zipping my suitcase, I left a small toiletry kit on top of it, which I would tuck inside tomorrow morning. Then I called the car service that would take me to the airport at the crack of dawn, to confirm that everything was set for my pickup.

When I hung up, I scrolled across my home screen in case it revealed a missed call from Ryan. It had been ten hours since he'd left, and I was eager to know how his day had gone. The more time passed, the more nervous I became about what had happened in Hawthorne. But I wasn't a teenager debating whether to call a boy I liked. I was a grown woman dating a man, so I dialed his number as I walked into my kitchen to grab a glass of water.

"Hey," he said, his voice hollow.

I had never heard him sound so dead. "Hey to you. So how did it go?"

He sighed heavily. "Let me pull over."

The sound of the car engine stopping greeted my ears as I turned on the tap. Then he told me his mother had confessed. I gripped the counter and set down the water glass. Words sputtered out. "Oh my God, Ryan. I can't believe she told you that. How? Why? How are you doing?"

"I don't know. I honestly don't know how I'm doing. It's like my world is upside down. Because I believed in the possibility of her maybe being innocent for the longest time, and now it's been twisted and turned inside out. I don't know what to do now, or what to think about anything," he said in that same monotone.

My heart ached for him, and I wanted to comfort him and hold him close. I wanted to be the one he leaned on. "Do you want me to delay my trip so that we can spend time together? So I can be there with you as you deal with this? I can easily push my flight back a few days if you need me."

If you need me.

Oh God, I desperately wanted him to need me. My pulse raced with longing for his yes.

"No," he said quickly. "I can't let you do that."

"I don't mind. I want to be here for you," I said, trying to comfort him.

"It's okay. I need to go see my sister and brothers now anyway."

"Of course," I said, and I understood logically why he'd want to go see them. I just wished my stupid heart didn't hurt the tiniest bit that he hadn't needed me. "Go. See them," I said in my cheeriest voice. He didn't need to detect my worry right now. He had enough on his plate.

"I should probably call your brother too. I guess I'll see you . . ." he said, but his voice trailed off.

I picked up the thread, crossing my fingers. "Do you still want to come by later? Or do you want me to come over?" I asked, ready to kick myself for sounding like a lovesick teenager.

"Soph," he said, his voice heavy. "I'm not in a good place right now. I think I just need to give John the news, then be with Shan, Michael, and Colin. Everything—the visit, the pattern, the stuff she said—it's hitting me hard and fucking with my head again. Let me deal with this, and then I'll see you."

I gulped. "Of course, of course. This is a huge thing, and you need to talk to them."

"When do you get back from your trip?"

"End of next week."

"I'll see you then. We'll do something special. Finally ride the roller-coaster at New York–New York together. Okay?" But he didn't sound as if he was looking forward to our reunion. He sounded as if he didn't care.

"Sure," I said, nodding several times, trying to convince myself that he still cared.

"Yeah. I just . . . right now . . ."

"You need to take a step back," I said, filling in the gap.

"Not from you. Just from . . ."

"Feeling so much?"

"Maybe. I don't know. I just need to see them right now."

"You go. Drive safely. I love you."

"I love you," he said, but he didn't sound as if he believed it, and the deadness in his tone made me want to cry.

When he hung up, I let the tears fall, even though they felt selfish, even though they felt like weakness. The tears fell for myself, and for him too. For all he was dealing with. For this new bombshell dropped in his lap. His family couldn't catch a damn break, and I hated that the tragedy in his past was tearing new fissures in his present.

A little later, after I'd dabbed my cheeks and dried my eyes, I let the reel of the last few weeks play, trying to understand the man. He'd been private and circumspect at first. When pushed, he'd become more open and vulnerable. But what if the talking was more the exception than the norm?

Had he returned to the man he was before?

Three dates and out. Over and done. Protect your heart. Don't get close to anybody but your family.

Even then, family could stab you in the back. He'd learned the hard way.

Call me overdramatic. Call me a conclusion-leaper. Or call me a cool analyst of the situation.

That very morning, Ryan had left me a note saying he would come see me tonight. *Because I can't stay away from you, Sophie. I swear, I can't.*

I could live without seeing him tonight. I wasn't seventeen. But what worried me was the complete 180-degree shift he'd made in ten hours. He'd left his house determined to find his way back to me that night, no matter what. But when everything changed, so did his desire for me. His family story had prevented him from getting close to me in the first place. His family background wasn't going away. It was only becoming more complicated, with more players, more names, and more threads.

More time.

More space.

More chances to retreat.

Hunting for information, I sank down on a kitchen stool and called my brother. "I know you can't give me any details on the case, and I'm not asking for them, but I need to know—is this going to end anytime soon?"

John exhaled loudly. "Sophie, you know I don't have an answer. Even if this were an open-and-shut case, I wouldn't have the answer. These things can go on forever. Oddly enough, this case was something of a rarity in the first place when his mother was arrested and tried in a matter of months. Most cases go on for a long time, especially when they're reopened and involve gangs and crimes committed over the years."

Years.

That word clung heavily to the air, like thick smog.

What would that be like? Every time there was a new wrinkle, would Ryan retreat? Would I always be the one who had to step closer to him? To offer the shoulder to lean on?

I'd offered it tonight, and he hadn't taken it.

Would he ever want it or need it? And would I be satisfied if he always turned elsewhere for comfort? Compared to him, I'd had an easy life. As he reeled over his mother's guilt, here I was jetting off to Frankfurt to check out my new car. But that was all the more reason why I wanted to be the supportive one—because I *could.* I could be there to hold his hand when he needed me. But he didn't seem to want that.

To keep myself busy, I called Holden and met him for a drink at The Mirage.

"I have news," he said, his eyes lighting up after he'd ordered his white wine.

"Do tell," I said, glad to focus on something else.

He leaned in to whisper. "I met someone."

I clapped twice. "Tell me everything. What's he like?"

Holden wiggled his eyebrows. "Actually, he's a she."

"A she?" I blinked.

He laughed. "I'm seeing a woman."

"You are?"

"Indeed I am." The answer seemed so strange, even though this had always been a possibility. Somehow it had been easier to think of him with men than with women.

"What's she like, then?"

"Oh, she's lovely. Natalie is very sweet and friendly." As he waxed on about the new woman in his life, I tried to ignore the strange new sting in my heart from this conversation. Seeing Holden through the lens of a preference for men had been far more manageable for my ego, it turned out. Now, my confidence was suffering another blow, unexpectedly, with this realization that I hadn't been the right woman for Holden either.

But there was more to this hollow ache in my heart. A new worry took root—the fear that Holden would slip away from me too, as he cozied up to Natalie. Because I couldn't help but wonder how this new lady would feel about him being so friendly with his ex-wife, and if this most predictable relationship in my life was about to become unpredictable too.

I loathed instability.

68

RYAN

Colin arrived first, with two six-packs. I side-eyed the beers. "Corona?"

My younger brother shrugged. "That's not what you drink?"

I shook my head, grabbed the beers, and shut the door. "Haven't had a Corona since I was in college."

Colin shrugged. "What do I know about beer?"

"Nothing. As you fucking should. I'm all out of that near-beer shit. Want a soda?"

"Always," Colin said, and we headed for the kitchen. I handed him a can of Diet Coke, then opened a Corona and took a long swallow. It tasted like spring break.

"Guess you don't hate it that much," Colin said pointedly.

"Guess I needed a drink after my day."

"So what's the deal? Shan said Mom confessed to you?" Colin made a *keep rolling* motion with his hand. "What the hell?"

"Yup," I said, taking another drink, then setting the

bottle on the counter and telling him everything that went down in the visiting room.

Colin scoffed. "*Made her do it.* See? Even now, she holds on to the notion that she somehow isn't to blame."

I shrugged. "Yeah, well. That's not what this is really about. That's not why I feel like I'm pretty much having the second-worst day of my life."

Colin yanked me in for a hug. "Yeah, I know," he said softly. "I know, man. You wanted to believe her. You wanted to hold on to the possibility. You wanted that hope that maybe she hadn't done it."

"Can you blame me? Wouldn't you want that too?"

"Sure," Colin said with a nod as he broke the hug, stopping to pet my dog, who'd wandered into the kitchen. "Of course it would be really fucking fantastic if she didn't do it, Ry. It would be, like, the greatest thing in the world if our mother didn't have our father killed, right?"

Though there was a touch of sarcasm in Colin's remark, there was also the bare truth. It *would* be the greatest thing.

"But you see, I came to peace long ago with the fact that she did," Colin continued. "Maybe details are still coming to light. Maybe the detective is looking for accomplices. And maybe he'll find them and they can join Jerry fucking Stefano in the big house where they all belong. The fact is, our mother was into some fucked-up shit, from associating with the likes of Stefano, to the ass she was cheating with. She was a messed-up, desperate woman who wanted money, and wanted out so badly she killed for it."

Colin dropped the volume on his voice and draped an arm over my shoulder. "This shit happens. Just look at the New York prison escapees and how that woman was going to have one of them kill her husband. It's awful, and it seems shocking from a distance, but up close, when it happens to you, you can't believe it. You wish it didn't happen." Colin tapped his chest with his free hand. "I wish that too. But it did. This is our story. This isn't the news. This isn't the papers. This isn't someone else's tragedy. It happened to us, and deep down somewhere inside you"— Colin moved his hand to my chest, tapping my breastbone, close to my heart—"you know it's true."

I swallowed hard. I scrubbed my hand over my jaw, trying to process the whole damn day, but making no sense of the way the floor beneath me was tilting and cracking. "What do you mean, I know it's true?"

Colin squeezed my shoulder. "You think this confession changes your whole life. You think it changes everything you've believed about Mom. But it doesn't. Deep down, you knew she was involved. Deep down, you knew she was responsible. But you hoped, because you're human. Because you wanted to believe in redemption, in basic goodness, in good overcoming evil. You held on to that tiny kernel of hope," Colin said, cupping his palms together as if he were holding a precious seed. "You held it, and you wanted it to become something. You wanted to believe that maybe things were different. It's okay to have hope. It's okay to cling to it. We all wanted that too. Desperately. The rest of us just let go of it sooner. Now it's your turn. Let it go," he said, and opened his hands.

I watched the cool, empty air in my kitchen, imagining a dandelion seed falling in the breeze, the wind blowing it away. Was Colin right? Had I truly known in my gut, in my heart, all along? Had some part of me known she was responsible, but some other part clung to the idea that she might be innocent simply because hope felt good?

Was that why I held on to the pattern? Why I went to see her every month? Why I nursed the possibility of innocence like a gardener tending to the first buds of spring?

Because hope was a precious thing, it was a gift, and when so many things had gone wrong, I'd needed an anchor?

Hope was my anchor.

Hope that the past could be rewritten.

But the past didn't have to be redone. It was still playing out in the present, unfurling new wrinkles every day, and I'd have to roll with them, to dodge, dart, and avoid the punches.

My true anchor was right here with me. My brother. And my other brother, Michael, who'd just arrived, along with my sister, Shannon. They were my foundation. They were the ones who'd helped me make it through the years.

Today had floored me. But tonight had taught me that I'd been clinging to something I was ready to say goodbye to. "Anyone want to go for a late-night swim?" I asked.

"Hell yeah," Michael said.

69

MICHAEL

A few hours later, Ryan and I were buzzed, Shannon was tipsy, and Colin was hyper on caffeine. We'd also lost track of who was winning the water volleyball match, but who cared?

This was a momentous night.

One I'd hoped would happen for nearly two decades.

My brother had turned a corner.

Finally.

After all these years, Ryan had *moved.*

He'd let go of that tenacious grip, that desperate hope he'd held on to. The wish he'd clung to.

And *accepted.*

The truth.

And the truth that mattered most was this one—we were still here, still together. This was our family, and the four of us were unbreakable.

The clock was closing in on two in the morning, and we were having a blast in the turquoise water, lit up from the lights in the pool. We'd talked some, and we'd cried some, and we'd laughed some more. Through it all, we were together, just as the four of us had always been.

Colin hit the ball to me, and I slammed the volleyball out of the water, sending it careening across the dark grass.

"Does that mean the game's over?" Colin asked, curious.

"For now," I said.

It was time for something else. An acknowledgment. Of where we were. Of how far we'd come.

I swam to the shallow end, and they followed.

"Let's drink a toast," I said when I reached the steps and grabbed my beer.

"You've been drinking all night," Colin said, hopping out of the water to snag a towel and dry his hair.

"No need to stop now," Ryan chimed in as he reached for his bottle and rested his arm on the edge of the pool. "Besides, Col, you brought us the beer. Your fault."

Colin pushed a hand through his damp hair, then tossed his towel on a lounge chair. "I'm sure you had plenty in your fridge. I was just trying to be nice to my sad sack of a brother."

I raised my Corona. "Never let the nondrinker pick beer again, please. Can that just be a rule?"

Colin rolled his eyes and dipped his foot in the water to splash me.

I cleared my throat, tone turning serious as I zeroed in on what I wanted to say, what I wanted them to focus on. "Listen. We've spent enough time talking about her. She had Ryan in her clutches for far too long. Tonight, he's letting go of all that stuff, so let's drink a toast to the man we all love and miss." My eyes started to water, and my throat hitched as I pictured my father. He deserved to be here now. But at least we could honor his memory. "To Dad. I still remember the little things, like how he didn't freak out when I was learning to drive. He was strong and steady, and he bought me a donut the first time I nailed a three-point turn. Said he was proud of me for that small accomplishment. He was always saying that about the things we did, and always ready to celebrate with a donut," I said, taking a moment to collect myself. "They were just donuts, but they were, in some ways, so much more. He celebrated us. He celebrated life. That was who he was."

"That was Dad," Shannon said softly.

The water lolled gently in the pool. Somewhere in the yard, crickets chirped.

My sister took her turn. "I remember when he taught me to play pool. He was patient and determined. He told me he wanted his only girl to be able to beat all his sons, and he coached me until I was able to."

"And she does. She schools us all," I said, with a tip of the cap to Shannon.

Colin raised his can. "In middle school, I went to a school dance, and when he picked me up, he spotted a hickey on my neck. He was cracking up, and I tried to deny it by making up some ridiculous story that the girl had scratched me accidentally during the dance. He went along with it, even though he said, 'Someday you might like it.'"

"And now you do, right?" I asked.

"Oh yeah. I love hickeys," Colin deadpanned.

Ryan set his bottle down on the pool's edge, the clink signaling a shift. "I remember when he went to work that night," he began, his eyes seeming to mist over at the memory. "He told me he was taking some kids to prom, and that someday I'd be the guy taking a girl to prom, and that I should be nice to the driver, because girls like that, and because it was the right thing to do. And then he told me he loved me. That was the last thing he said to me. That he loved me."

Shannon clasped her hand over her mouth, and a huge sob fell from her throat. She threw her arms around Ryan, and then grabbed all of us, yanking us hard into another group hug.

"I remember love," she whispered in a broken voice. "Most of all, I remember love."

"Me too," I said, doing everything I could to keep my voice steady. But then, I didn't need to.

"I remember love," I echoed, but it wasn't only a memory. It was the way we were, here and now. Because of him. Living with love.

70

—————

RYAN

Later, after we cleaned up and headed inside, I nudged Colin with my elbow. "Hey, what was the deal with that woman at the benefit last night? Is there something going on with you two?"

Colin shrugged as we gathered bottles into a paper shopping bag for recycling. "She's just a friend."

"But you want more?"

"Absolutely."

"Go for it then."

"It's complicated."

I stopped, holding a bottle. Had I really just told my brother to go for it?

And what was I doing?

Sophie and I weren't just friends. We were in love. And there was nothing complicated about our feelings.

Sophie was always clear, always present, always giving. She put her heart on the line every day, every night. Every second.

My loving, giving, supportive, beautiful, amazing Sophie.

Who was leaving the country for more than a week come morning.

I'd told her twenty-four hours ago that I *had* to see her tonight, no matter what. That I couldn't stay away from her. And instead, I'd done the opposite. I'd stayed away from her. I'd told her I was fucked-up again, and hell, I felt that way.

But that wasn't fair to her.

Especially when she was always fair. Always open. Always honest.

As I carried the bag of bottles to my recycling bin in the garage, I muttered a string of curse words. I'd been sending her mixed messages. Telling her I had to see her, then telling her I couldn't handle seeing her. Saying I desperately needed her, then not taking the time to properly say goodbye before she left the country for a trip.

Fine, there was no rule that said we had to see each other every day.

But this wasn't about managing a lover's travel schedule. This was about how I talked to her, how I cared for her, how I tended to her needs. She was so even-keeled, so reliable, so fucking wonderful, and I'd taken advantage of that. I hadn't been attentive to the woman I loved. Understandable, some might say, given the way my day had gone.

But it wasn't acceptable to me.

Sophie had given me something I thought I'd never have. I had never trusted in love. I'd always believed love could be gunned down. Then she came into my life and turned everything I believed about myself upside down.

That was the real change in me.

Not my mother's confession, but Sophie's love.

Falling in love with Sophie Winston was the most magical, wonderful, intense experience of my life. When everything around me wobbled, Sophie was the constant.

I shut the top of the recycling bin and glanced at my truck. My buzz had worn off. I needed to see her. To tell her she rocked my world, then tell her again and again and again. The only problem was, it was four thirty in the morning, and I was pretty damn sure her flight left in a few hours.

But so be it.

I'd simply have to drive over there now and see her before she got on that plane. Kiss her hard before she left. As I walked back into my house, my mind latched onto something she'd told me by my pool last weekend.

The things I want from you don't cost money.

I turned to Colin, dropped a hand on his shoulder, and said, "Little brother, I need a big favor."

I explained to Colin what I needed, and my brother said yes. Then added, "Hell yes."

Because that was what family did for each other.

I slid open my phone screen and dialed Sophie's number. It went straight to voicemail. Maybe she'd turned her phone off? No idea. I sent her a text.

Then I saw she'd sent me one.

71

SOPHIE

Fifteen minutes earlier

I was late.

I was always late.

I was pissed at myself too for being so damn late.

Rolling my suitcase behind me like it was a new Olympic event, I ran out of my building at an ungodly hour in the morning, my sandals flapping against the marble-tiled lobby, my phone stuffed into my purse. The car had been waiting for me in the building driveway for a few minutes.

"I'm so sorry I'm late," I told the driver as I slid into the back seat, the night still cloaking the sky.

"Nothing to apologize for, ma'am. I will get you to the airport on time," he said, shutting the door.

I turned on my phone, tapping my foot as I waited for it to boot up. I needed to send Ryan a note.

Because I'd made a decision.

I'd spent a restless night thinking about whether or not

to reach out. I'd tossed and turned, debating whether to give him the space he seemed to need, or to reassure him of how I felt. But then I'd recalled the advice my mother always gave me: *Always talk. Always be honest. Never go to bed angry. Make time for kisses and meals, dance under the stars, and dream together.*

Though I was flying across the ocean, the advice about not going to bed angry still seemed to apply, as well as talking, being honest, and making time for each other. I wanted him to know I was here for him. The reality was, he had a more complicated life than me, and if that was what I was signing up for, he was worth it.

Love was a choice, one that sometimes came with rampant uncertainty.

I might never have stability with him. I might always experience moments, and even days, of pure unsteadiness. But what we shared was worth the risk, the anxiety, and the utter unpredictability of his family life. I'd confronted risk head-on as a businesswoman, and surely I could weather the ups and downs in a relationship.

For so long, I'd been seeking what my parents had, that perfect kind of love, with passion, support, and security. But I might not ever have security with Ryan Sloan, and I was going to have to buckle up and enjoy the highs and lows, the thrills and drops of loving that man.

Before my phone even downloaded any new messages, I tapped out a text.

Sophie: I'll be thinking of you the whole time I'm gone, and I'll be looking forward to our roller-coaster ride when I return. Every second of it.

There. Done. Said.

It was enough, and I was choosing to believe in the two of us rather than listen to my own fears.

I closed my eyes, took a few breaths and tried to calm my nerves as we drove.

I was about to tuck my phone into my purse when my phone downloaded the rest of my messages, including one from him, just as the car pulled to the curb at the airport.

The time on my phone screamed at me. I was really late.

Oh God.

Nerves swamped me. I was dying to read his note, but I needed to get inside. *Now.*

Jamming my phone into my purse, I raced to baggage check-in, then on to the TSA PreCheck, making it through security without having to slip off my shoes.

Safely on the other side, I took out my phone.

Opened the message.

And burst into a wild, wicked, happy grin.

Ryan: I meant it when I said I can't stay away from you.

I spun around, hunting for him, half expecting to see him. He wasn't there, of course. But that was okay. He'd sent this beautiful note. He'd reached out.

These words were all I needed before I left the country —the reassurance that we were fine. After rushing to my gate, I showed my boarding pass to the agent and headed onto the plane, taking my seat in first class in the second row.

From the cool comfort of my cushy gray leather seat, I

started a reply. I stopped typing when I spotted someone standing by my row. My skin prickled with awareness, just like it had at Aria. Before I even confirmed with my eyes, my body *knew.*

My gaze roamed up the jeans, the trim waist, the pullover shirt, the day-old stubble, the soft lips, the nose, the navy-blue eyes, the golden-brown hair.

The face of the man I adored. My heart danced in mad circles, like a wild bird.

"You're here," I said, stating the obvious.

He gestured to the seat next to me. "This may be presumptuous of me, but is this seat taken?"

I patted it. "Would you like this seat?"

He looked at his watch. "For the next twelve hours, yes."

"It's yours."

He sat down and didn't say a word. He placed a hand on my cheek, pulled me gently to him, and breathed my name as if it were his oxygen. *"Sophie."*

The way he said it sounded like a poem, like a love song. He swept his lips over mine. I shivered. I shuddered. I soared.

"Hi," he said when he broke the kiss.

"Hi." I was on cloud nine. I was floating high above the earth, and I didn't want to come down.

"Do you want company for your trip?"

"I want your company."

"Good, because I took the liberty of buying a ticket."

"I can see that. But is this really your seat?"

"Mine's one row up. When the person who has this seat shows, I'll convince him or her to swap." He looked me square in the eyes as he ran a finger over my cheek. "You once told me the things you want from me don't cost money. Well, the ticket cost money, but that's beside the point. The point is you told me you wanted to go for a ride together in your new car. And I'd like to go with you."

I arched an eyebrow. "You're joining me because of the car?"

He shook his head. "I'm here for the woman," he said, his voice so sexy, so certain, so full of passion.

My eyes fluttered closed momentarily, and happiness rushed through all the highways inside my body, infusing my heart and soul with joy. When I opened my eyes, I asked, "Are you taking off work for the whole time?"

He nodded. "I told Michael to run the shop without me."

"Where's your dog?"

"Colin has him."

"When did you plan this?"

He looked at his watch. "About two hours ago."

I shook my head in amazement. "And you bought a ticket, and took care of all that, and figured out what flight I was on in two hours?"

"There was only one flight to Frankfurt at seven in the morning, so I took a chance. Oh, and don't forget, I showered too," he said with a grin.

"I like when you take chances for me."

"I've spent eighteen years living with uncertainty. There are only a few things in my life that I know for sure right now. I love my brothers and my sister and my grandparents and my dog." He stopped to take a beat and hold my gaze. "And I love you. I'm not going to sit around and wait and wonder and question it. I'm just going to feel it. I don't want to stop taking chances with you, Sophie," he said, brushing his lips over mine once more. He tasted so good. I wanted the kiss to turn into so much more.

But not right here. Not as the flight attendants began their announcements.

Pressing a hand to his chest, I asked, "So that's it? You're mine for the next week and a half? All mine in Europe? You, me, and my emerald-green Bugatti?"

"Yeah," he said with a casual shrug. "If you'll have me for that long."

"I want you all to myself," I said, dancing my fingers up his chest. "I'm greedy like that."

"Be greedy with me. I want your greed," he said, then fingered a lock of my hair, turning more serious. "Sometimes I retreat when things get crazy, but I want to keep coming back to you. I know I'm just figuring this relationship stuff out, and I'm sure I'm not an easy man to be with, but I'll do everything I can for you." He kissed my cheek, murmuring my name. "Sophie Winston." Then another time. Softer. Barely audible. "*Sophie Sloan.*"

I wrenched back and widened my eyes. "What did you just say?"

72

RYAN

What *had* I just said?

"Um . . ." I started. "Your name?"

She shook her head and pointed to herself. "My name is Winston. Not Sloan."

I shrugged, trying to cover up my unexpected gaffe. "It was a slipup." Then I thought, *Fuck it.* I was on a plane with her, headed to Europe. I might as well tell her the truth. "I was trying it on for size."

Her lips quirked up. "You were? How did it sound?"

"Hot. Sexy. Perfect. Beautiful. Like you," I said, keeping my gaze pinned on my gorgeous woman. "Did you like how it sounded?"

Her eyes sparkled. "I think I did."

"Someday," I said, threading my hands in her hair and pressing my forehead to hers. "Someday, I want to make you Sophie Sloan. Someday soon. Is that too much? Have I said too much?"

"Oh God, Ryan. You're crazy. You're here on a plane with me, and I have never been happier in my life. All I've ever wanted is a love like this, and you're here. With me. Don't you get it? You're all my fantasies come true."

I kissed her nose. "Look what you've done to me. You're everything I never knew I wanted, and now I can't live without you. Hell, I couldn't even let you leave the country without me."

* * *

The dress, the woman, the car.

Any one of them would be amazing. Together, they were a triumvirate of beauty.

I snapped a photo because I wanted to look at this image again and again—Sophie Winston wearing a sapphire-blue pinup dress and ruby-red lips as she stretched out her lush body on the shining emerald-green hood of her sleek, stylish million-dollar car. We were parked on the side of a road somewhere outside of Rüsselsheim. Trees canopied us from the hillside.

"You like how she drives?"

"I love how she drives," I said, putting my phone away and wedging myself between her legs. "I love everything about her."

"And me too?" she asked with a wink.

"Yes, you too," I said, laughing. "Now let's put this vehicle to the true test."

It would be the first time in her Bugatti, but I was certain it wouldn't be the last. That it would be the start of a countless number of times.

I tugged her up off the hood, and we slid inside the car. God, this car should be classified a sacred space. Everything from the leather seats to the gleaming dashboard to the gorgeous hum of the engine was a dream. But better, because it was real. Sitting in the passenger seat, I lowered it with her in my lap and kissed the hell out of her, sealing my mouth to hers. She ran her hands through my hair and sighed sexily as I kissed her harder. Soon we were swallowing each other's moans and groans, and she was rocking her hips into me.

I broke the kiss, hiked up her skirt, and tugged her panties to the side, giving me access.

"Take me, Ryan," she whispered.

I unzipped my jeans, pinned her wrists behind her back, and gave her what she wanted.

It was what I wanted too. Her. And me. Together.

Like this.

Like bliss.

Like everlasting love.

Later that evening, we'd be together in other ways. Eating dinner at a café. Making love in our hotel after the lights fell in the town and only stars winked in the sky. Then the next day too, cruising along the autobahn in a sleek new car, living life to the fullest, loving without limits.

EPILOGUE

Ryan

Johnny Cash bounded across Colin's front lawn and into my outstretched arms on the sidewalk when I returned. "Hey, buddy," I said, kneeling down to say hi to my pooch at last. My heart hammered as I reunited with my four-legged friend.

The border collie licked my face and whimpered as he thumped his tail. I wrapped my arms around his furry neck, bursting with happiness. I hadn't seen Johnny Cash in nearly two weeks, and even though the time with Sophie had been the best days of my life, I did miss my canine friend.

Colin walked down the steps from his house and joined the reunion on the sidewalk. "Looks like someone missed you."

I stood up and gave my brother a quick hug, glad to see him too. "Thanks for watching him. I really appreciate it."

"He's easy. Welcome back. How was it?"

I briefly considered the question. I could answer it with patent honesty and say *out of this world, amazing, incredible, fantastic,* or *a dream come true.* Instead, I answered with another truth. "I'm going to ask her to marry me next week."

Colin's dark eyes lit up. "Guess you had a great time." He extended a hand and then clapped me on the back.

"Yeah, we did," I said, still grinning over what I had planned for Sophie.

His smile seemed to grow wider, like mine. "Congratulations in advance. Couldn't be happier for you. It all happened so quickly."

"It did. The whole thing happened so damn fast. But I guess when you're certain of something, you have to go for it."

Colin knocked fists with me. "Couldn't agree more. How did you decide?"

As I petted a happy Johnny Cash, I told Colin the story of how I'd said her name on the plane, illustrating with my hand over my mouth, as if the words were spilling out of their own volition.

My brother cracked up. "Awesome. So you just let it slip on the plane that you wanted her to be Mrs. Sloan?"

"I hadn't even thought that far. It just came out, and then I realized I wanted that. She's the best thing that's ever happened to me."

His gaze turned serious. "She is, and don't ever forget it."

"I won't," I said, then walked to my car, and opened the front door to let my dog jump in. A nearby engine rattled, then stopped quickly. I turned in the direction of the car.

The hair on my neck rose. The Buick. Parking outside Colin's house. What the hell? "He's back. Looks like he knows where we all live," I hissed. "Sophie told me he stopped by my house right before we went to Germany."

I straightened my spine, kept my eyes on the guy, and waited, arms crossed, feet planted wide. The guy walked around the back of his car, then stopped short when he saw us.

"Hey," he said softly, a little shy, then he spoke again, louder, more confident. "Hi."

I lifted my chin. My eyes were narrowed. Colin had said something on the phone to me earlier this week about this guy. "What's the deal? My fiancée told me you stopped by my house the other week. Just man up and tell us what this is about."

The guy walked closer, taking big steps toward us. He stopped a few feet away. He was younger than I expected, maybe even a teenager. He had a tough-guy edge with the boots, jeans, the tattoos that snaked up his arms, and a stubbled jaw, but his eyes were young.

And something in them looked eerily familiar. Like I recognized them. My blood froze, and all the hair on my arms stood on end.

EPILOGUE

Marcus

I'd like to say the last few weeks had prepared me for this.

But I wasn't sure anything could.

I wasn't sure I'd ever be ready.

That didn't matter.

Some things you just had to do.

I had to do this.

No, I *wanted* to do this.

It was as necessary as breathing.

Ryan stared at me, waiting for my answer, waiting for me to answer him: *Tell us what this is about.*

Drawing a steadying breath, I tried to shed all my nerves, but before I could speak Colin cut in with a shocked "Marcus?" His jaw fell open as he said my name.

Because I wasn't a stranger.

I wasn't a stalker.

And Colin knew me.

He just didn't know who I was to him. To them.

"You know this kid?" Ryan asked his brother.

Colin nodded, unable to speak, eyes wide as he stared at me.

The surprise was only going to deepen, like a canyon. The surprise he felt now would be nothing compared to what was coming in just a few seconds.

Could I do this?

Yes. Yes I could.

I cleared my throat and cut in. It was now or never. If I didn't get the words out in the next ten seconds they might never come. "I want to talk to both of you," I said, voice as steady as could be, as I forced an evenness into it that I damn well didn't feel. I looked to Ryan, to Colin, and kept going. "We all have something in common."

"What are you talking about? And why are you here?" Ryan asked, fists clenched, like a fighter poised. But he didn't need to worry about me.

I wasn't on that side of their story.

I was on another side.

Ryan looked to Colin, searching for answers "Who is he?"

But Colin was still speechless.

I was not.

I spoke the words I'd practiced in the mirror for months. They were all my truths, and they were their truths now too.

"My name is Marcus. I was born seventeen years ago at the Stella McLaren Federal Women's Correctional Center. My mother is Dora Prince. I'm your brother."

THE END

. . .

Want to know what happens next to the Sloan family now that they've learned they have a new brother? Find out in Colin's love story, told in MY SINFUL LONGING, FREE IN KU!

BE A LOVELY

Want to be the first to know of sales, new releases, special deals and giveaways? Sign up for my newsletter today!

Want to be part of a fun, feel-good place to talk about books and romance, and get sneak peeks of covers and advance copies of my books? Be a Lovely!

I've written more than 100 books! **All of these titles below are FREE in Kindle Unlimited!**

The Love and Hockey Series

The Boyfriend Goal

A roommates-to-lovers, teammate's little sister hockey romance!

The Romance Line

An enemies-to-lovers, player and the publicist, forbidden romance!

The Proposal Play

A brother's best friend/marriage of convenience romance!

The Girlfriend Zone

A coach's daughter romance!

The Overtime Kiss!

A single dad/nanny romance!

The Flirting Game!

A neighbors to lovers, fake dating romance!

Hockey Ever After

Just Breaking the Rules!

A brother's best friend/workplace/one who got away romance!

Just Playing for Keeps!

A grumpy sunshine, fake dating romance!

Holiday Romances

Merry Little Kissmas

Fake dating my brother's best friend at Christmas!

<u>My Favorite Holidate</u>

Fake dating the billionaire boss at Christmas!

Darling Springs

It Seemed Like a Good Idea!

An only one-bed-in-the-room, forbidden, small town bodyguard romance!

I've Got a Crush On You!

A grumpy sunshine, workplace romance where the boss has a secret identity!

The My Hockey Romance Series

Hockey, spice, shenanigans and cute dogs in this series of standalones! Because when you get screwed over, make it a double or even a triple!

Karma is two hockey boyfriends and sometimes three!

Double Pucked

A sexy, outrageous MFM hockey romantic comedy!

Puck Yes

A fake marriage, spicy MFM hockey rom com!

Thoroughly Pucked!

A brother's best friends +runaway bride, spicy MFM hockey rom com!

Well and Truly Pucked

A friends-to-lovers forced proximity why-choose hockey rom com!

The Virgin Society Series

Meet the Virgin Society – great friends who'd do anything for each other. Indulge in these forbidden, emotionally-charged, and wildly sexy age-gap romances!

The RSVP

The Tryst

The Tease

The Dating Games Series

A fun, sexy romantic comedy series about friends in the city and their dating mishaps!

The Virgin Next Door

Two A Day

The Good Guy Challenge

How To Date Series (New and ongoing)

Friends who are like family. Chances to learn how to date again. Standalone romantic comedies full of love, sex and meet-cute shenanigans.

My So-Called Love Life

Plays Well With Others

The Almost Romantic

The Accidental Dating Experiment

A romantic comedy adventure standalone

A Real Good Bad Thing

Boyfriend Material

Four fabulous heroines. Four outrageous proposals. Four chances at love in this sexy rom-com series!

Asking For a Friend

Sex and Other Shiny Objects

One Night Stand-In

Overnight Service

Big Rock Series

My #1 New York Times Bestselling sexy as sin, irreverent, male-POV romantic comedy!

Big Rock

Mister O

Well Hung

Full Package

Joy Ride

Hard Wood

Happy Endings Series

Romance starts with a bang in this series of standalones following a group of friends seeking and avoiding love!

Come Again

Shut Up and Kiss Me

Kismet

My Single-Versary

Ballers And Babes

Sexy sports romance standalones guaranteed to make you hot!

Most Valuable Playboy

Most Likely to Score

A Wild Card Kiss

Rules of Love Series

Athlete, virgins and weddings!

The Virgin Rule Book

The Virgin Game Plan

The Virgin Replay

The Virgin Scorecard

The Extravagant Series

Bodyguards, billionaires and hoteliers in this sexy, high-stakes
series of standalones!

One Night Only

One Exquisite Touch

My One-Week Husband

The Guys Who Got Away Series

Friends in New York City and California fall in love in this fun
and hot rom-com series!

Birthday Suit

Dear Sexy Ex-Boyfriend

The What If Guy

Thanks for Last Night

The Dream Guy Next Door

Always Satisfied Series

A group of friends in New York City find love and laughter in
this series of sexy standalones!

Satisfaction Guaranteed

Never Have I Ever

Instant Gratification

PS It's Always Been You

The Gift Series

An after dark series of standalones! Explore your fantasies!

The Engagement Gift

The Virgin Gift

The Decadent Gift

The Heartbreakers Series

Three brothers. Three rockers. Three standalone sexy romantic comedies.

Once Upon a Real Good Time

Once Upon a Sure Thing

Once Upon a Wild Fling

Sinful Men

A high-stakes, high-octane, sexy-as-sin romantic suspense series!

My Sinful Nights

My Sinful Desire

My Sinful Longing

My Sinful Love

My Sinful Temptation

From Paris With Love

Swoony, sweeping romances set in Paris!

Wanderlust

Part-Time Lover

One Love Series

A group of friends in New York falls in love one by one in this sexy rom-com series!

The Sexy One

The Hot One

The Knocked Up Plan

Come As You Are

Lucky In Love Series

A small town romance full of heat and blue collar heroes and sexy heroines!

Best Laid Plans

The Feel Good Factor

Nobody Does It Better

Unzipped

No Regrets

An angsty, sexy, emotional, new adult trilogy about one young couple fighting to break free of their pasts!

The Start of Us

The Thrill of It

Every Second With You

The Caught Up in Love Series

A group of friends finds love!

The Pretending Plot

The Dating Proposal

The Second Chance Plan

The Private Rehearsal

Seductive Nights Series

A high heat series full of danger and spice!

Night After Night

After This Night

One More Night

A Wildly Seductive Night

Joy Delivered Duet

A high-heat, wickedly sexy series of standalones that will set your sheets on fire!

Nights With Him

Forbidden Nights

Unbreak My Heart

A standalone second chance emotional roller coaster of a
romance

The Muse

A magical realism romance set in Paris

**Good Love Series of sexy rom-coms co-written with Lili
Valente!**

I also write MM romance under the name L. Blakely!

Hopelessly Bromantic Duet (MM)

Roomies to lovers to enemies to fake boyfriends

Hopelessly Bromantic

Here Comes My Man

Men of Summer Series (MM)

Two baseball players on the same team fall in love in a forbidden
romance spanning five epic years

Scoring With Him

Winning With Him

All In With Him

MM Standalone Novels

A Guy Walks Into My Bar

The Bromance Zone

One Time Only

The Best Men (Co-written with Sarina Bowen)

Winner Takes All Series (MM)

A series of emotionally-charged and irresistibly sexy standalone MM sports romances!

The Boyfriend Comeback

Turn Me On

A Very Filthy Game

Limited Edition Husband

Manhandled

If you want a personalized recommendation, email me at laurenblakelybooks@gmail.com!

CONTACT

I love hearing from readers! You can find me on Twitter at LaurenBlakely3, Instagram at LaurenBlakelyBooks, Facebook at LaurenBlakelyBooks, or online at LaurenBlakely.com. You can also email me at laurenblakelybooks@gmail.com